Richard Savage

The Flying Halcyon

A mystery of the Pacific Ocean

Richard Savage

The Flying Halcyon
A mystery of the Pacific Ocean

ISBN/EAN: 9783337319373

Printed in Europe, USA, Canada, Australia, Japan

Cover: Foto ©Andreas Hilbeck / pixelio.de

More available books at **www.hansebooks.com**

THE FLYING HALCYON

By the Author of "MY OFFICIAL WIFE."

In Crown 8vo, fancy boards.

THE LITTLE LADY OF LAGUNITAS. A Franco-Californian Romance.

PRINCE SCHAMYL'S WOOING. A Story of the Caucasus—Russo-Turkish War.

THE MASKED VENUS. A Story of Many Lands.

DELILAH OF HARLEM. A Story of the New York City of To-Day.

FOR LIFE AND LOVE. A Story of the Rio Grande.

THE ANARCHIST. A Story of To-Day.

THE PRINCESS OF ALASKA. A Tale of Two Countries.

THE FLYING HALCYON.

THE PASSING SHOW.

MY OFFICIAL WIFE.

THE

FLYING HALCYON

A MYSTERY OF THE PACIFIC OCEAN

BY

RICHARD HENRY SAVAGE

AUTHOR OF "MY OFFICIAL WIFE"

NEW VERSION

COPYRIGHT

LONDON
GEORGE ROUTLEDGE AND SONS, LIMITED
BROADWAY, LUDGATE HILL
MANCHESTER AND NEW YORK

LONDON:
BRADBURY, AGNEW, & CO. LD., PRINTERS, WHITEFRIARS.

CONTENTS.

6 *CONTENTS.*

THE FLYING HALCYON

CHAPTER I.

" THE LASS THAT LOVED A SAILOR."

"So you really leave to-morrow, Harry?" said Basil
Goodloe, as he passed the cigar box to his guest.

"There are my orders, old fellow!" replied Lieutenant-
Commander Henry Wainwright, U. S. Navy, tossing a
formidable looking official document over to his host. The
two young men were seated in a cosy private dining-room
of the Hotel Athenée, at Paris, under the shadows of the
great Opera House. "I received my promotion, on examination a fortnight ago, and the Admiral told me when I was
detached, that I owed my first command to your going on
leave. It must be a very serious private business matter,
which makes you forego your first ship."

"It is, Harry," said Goodloe, his brow clouding. "The
Secretary very handsomely tendered me the 'Ranger,' and
I looked forward most happily to a change from the eternal
'touching my cap,' of the last fourteen years. It would
have been a pride to me to fly my own flag in the Gulf of
California, even on a surveying cruiser, armed with nothing

heavier than a saluting battery. It cannot be helped! I
am glad you are next on the list, though."

The speaker turned his eyes very kindly on his academy
chum. In the morning of life, with everything bright
before them, no two handsomer lads had ever donned the
middy's jacket and sported the gold foul anchor than the
young men now slowly reaching, at thirty-four, the coveted
rank of Lieutenant-Commander.

"You certainly will not resign?" queried Wainwright,
gazing at Goodloe, who was staring moodily out of the
window. "Promotion is certainly very slow, but you were
born for the Navy. I do not wish to gain a file on you!"

"The truth is that I hardly know what to do now,
Harry," cried Goodloe. "I always thought that a man
should be the sole master of his own destinies, but life as
we live it is not the old story-book version. I am not free
to choose. I do not wish to leave the Service, and yet I
cannot throw the responsibility of my decision on any
friendly adviser; if I could, it would be you, old fellow!"

Goodloe smoked away in silence, until his alarmed classmate said hesitatingly: "See here, Basil, it's not about
money, is it? I should be insulted if you did not let me
know, if you are in trouble."

It was true that the millionaire Pennsylvania coal baron,
who fondly cherished his son, Harry, as the future head of
the Navy, stinted him in no reasonable use of the great
wealth, buttressed on his "black diamond" hills.

Goodloe laughed. "No! Thanks, old boy: it's not
money. I wish it was only a financial crisis. I'm used to
that now. I could seek the sailor's heaven, 'blue water,'

always a sure preventive of pecuniary harassing. Creditors can't swim very far."

The Pennsylvanian thereat grew very serious. "You have not rushed into any love entanglement? Is it about a woman?" Wainwright, in his inner heart, prayed that "the sweet little cherub that sits up aloft" had mercifully guarded Basil Goodloe from the wiles of the fair charmers who wave their rounded white arms from the classic shores of the Mediterranean, enslaving Uncle Sam's gallant officers in all the desperate dangers of that "fancy station."

"Yes, it is a woman," slowly said Goodloe, gazing frankly at his friend.

"You haven't married her?" cried the merciless inquisitor, with visions of Russian princesses, Italian countesses, and fascinating French "aristocrats."

"Not yet," said Goodloe. "And the trouble is, I am afraid that I never shall. She's the sweetest woman on earth; the very sweetest!"

Harry Wainwright sprang from his chair in evident relief. "Oh, come now, Basil, it's not as bad yet as I feared! It may all be arranged. This sort of thing blows over easily, you know!" The speaker glanced at himself with an air of complacency, for the jaunty Wainwright was the "star" lady-killer of the "Wachusett," and had gained a sad renown, from the Pillars of Hercules to Constantinople. "I've been in that kind of trouble, often, myself!"

Goodloe burst out laughing. "You will crack on too much sail, youngster! You always capsize your barque of love! But I am serious. Now, did you ever meet me, in your piratical expeditions, in search of the great goddess 'She?'"

"Never! I admit!" said Wainwright; "and that's why, Basil, I was afraid you had commenced your love making by marriage. You sturdy old chaps often do that sort of foolish thing, you know. I am pretty well posted now. When the action begins to be serious, I quietly sheer off; great safety in lots of sea-room, you know!"

"Yes, you do sail away, you young rascal," said Goodloe, grimly. "But, you see, I don't want to sheer off."

"Well, then, tell me all about it!" said the eager Wainwright. "I'm not in for anything to-night. I am settled for the future. The Secretary's orders are for me to join at once. My vessel is already lying at Mare Island. I don't think that I ever would have had her, but that I'm popularly supposed to know every rock in the Gulf, since I ornamented the old 'Pensacola,' as watch officer down there. Ah! You would have been just the man to command!"

"Perhaps so!" said Goodloe, doubtfully. "I cannot tell you all my story, Harry, but still I will give you enough to set your mind at ease. I know but too well how I feel. I am only puzzled what to do."

Basil Goodloe was the very ideal of a sailor. His clustering dark hair, frank eyes, well-knit form and a winning personal manner, made him a universal favourite at mess. His professional activity and his marked talents led him to be soon detached as a fleet staff officer to the most exacting of our admirals. A great honour! His sudden application for a year's leave of absence, however, greatly astonished the gruff old Boanerges, who said : "Not fool enough to resign, Goodloe ? Don't do it, Sir. Stick to the Navy. All our men go to the dogs in civil life, Sir." Neither had the grim chief nor any of his ward-room chums yet fathomed the mystery of Basil Goodloe's suddenly leaving the choicest berth at Villefranche, to locate in Paris, with no apparent purpose in life. But the arrival of his long delayed promotion was a fair excuse for Basil Goodloe's presumed future visit on leave to his long unvisited Maryland home.

" I wish that I could go with you, Harry," he began, "and show you the dear old place on the ' Eastern Shore.' I am proud of its memories,—its dreamy comfort. Its unsullied hospitality of a hundred years, is my dearest heritage, but I must stay here."

Watch the woman, I suppose," snapped out Wainwright, determined to bear him away, if possible.

" Well, I see I will have to tell you something after all, you young torment," replied Goodloe, with an easy mastery over his Annapolis chum, whom he ranked just one file on the list, and ten minutes in graduation. " You know that I am the last of my family, and have spent more time over the nautical almanac than in gazing into those deceitful living stars, women's bright eyes. I have never before sought my fate in life, but have waited for it to come to me. I supposed that I might settle down finally into a club man, a diner out, a story teller, or a mere service encyclopedia, like old Holmes, Dillingham, Preston, or any of those steady old binnacle lamps of the service. But I have found out lately that there is a world of difference, Henry, between a woman and the woman ! "

"Is this surely the woman, not a woman?" said that experienced lovemaker, Wainwright, as he chose a fresh cigar. "Barometer sometimes at fault, you know! Glass falls suddenly, no rule, no explanation! See peculiar cases in 'Bowditch'!" continued the tease.

"Hang Bowditch! This is serious. I am sure of myself. I am not so sure of her," said Goodloe, doubtfully. "And the only way I can be free to act is to stay here, near her."

"Ah! Yes! I see," said Wainwright. "Sort of blockade, prevent the other fellows running in and cutting her out, under your very guns."

"Exactly so!" remarked the anxious would-be lover. "You see, my boy, she has a mother, and that has to be considered."

"Oh! Decidedly!" remarked Wainwright, with an involuntary grimace. "Future mother-in-law. Can't be too careful in choosing them. Very important party in such cases. And her father?"

"Dead!" sententiously remarked Goodloe.

"That's good," said Wainwright, musingly. "If he left her property and all that."

"Oh! There's plenty of property," said Goodloe. "That's one of the troubles. You see, they don't know exactly where it is. And I might have to leave the Navy to help them find it."

"Now, by Jove, Goodloe! My dear old dad has fixed me, so I'm free of that. But, by Heaven, sir, if I were you, I'd see a surgeon, and take something for the nerves—settle the mind, and all that. If they don't know where their property is, you will never find it."

"That's just what I fear, Harry," said Goodloe, in a despondent tone. "I may not be able to help them!"

"I propose one sensible thing to you, Basil!" cried Wainwright, energetically. "Go out to-night with me, and cable to the Secretary of the Navy, and ask him to revoke your leave of absence. Come on, and take the American steamer with me. You can get your proper command at once, and, if you apply, I will serve under you. By Jove! I will not see you sacrificed to a mere chimera. Marriage must have a solid basis. Another basis than mere love!" concluded the Admirable Crichton of the Mediterranean fleet.

"What's the other basis?" said Goodloe, wearily. "Cash, stocks, bonds, lands," retorted Wainwright, "real property, not castles in Spain!"

"These are not castles in Spain, they are mines in Mexico," slowly said Goodloe.

"That settles it. Next to a dairy farm at the North Pole, a Mexican mine is a 'fleeting show.' Now, Basil, I do hope that you are not going to become the romantic sacrifice of a ten days' passion," earnestly said his junior.

"It is a singular entanglement, and, strange to say, neither Anita Delmar nor myself can do much at present to clear up the mystery."

"Well, her name is certain, at any rate," answered Wainwright. "Is she an American?"

"No. Her father was a French mining engineer and savant; and her mother a Louisville beauty," replied Goodloe, with pride. "He died some years ago, leaving all his vast Mexican interests in the charge of a resident partner of high rank. The ladies are both here in Paris."

"And so you personally know very little about them?" said Wainwright, with a tinge of sarcasm.

"Much more than they do of me," answered Goodloe, hotly. "We, perhaps, value the uniform too highly. My rank, a few old swords and charts, and my visiting card, are all my tangible possessions here. I, at least, know their bankers, home status, and place in the polite world."

"But 'Graystone Manor!'" persisted Wainwright. "I doubt if either of the ladies even knows that beautiful Maryland has an 'eastern shore,'" said Goodloe. "No, Wainwright, it is not a case of property—it is my whole future life. It is the impossibility of any home life, the ability to guide or guard them while in the Service, which makes me hesitate. I must wait for future events."

"Listen! Three months ago, I was going ashore on a stormy afternoon in our steam launch at Villefranche. It was a rough 'mistral' day, and I watched idly a French man-of-war's boat struggling along under a great leg-of-mutton sail. I could see that the boat was overloaded, and also clumsily handled. These Gauls are poor sailors save their Channel fishermen. I had my hands full with our own troubles, until my boat middy sang out: 'By Jove! They'll go over surely! And there are women on board, too!' As he spoke, a hail of distress reached us, for the half-swamped boat was quickly filling. Little Seymour bore down on them, and we pulled our throttle wide open. He was busy with the tiller, and I managed to be the first to spring over and grasp a drowning girl. Old Mike Bowen, our quartermaster, soon reached a second woman, and in a minute our men were also hauling in the screaming French-men, who clung to the life-lines of their overturned boat. One poor fellow, however, was dragged under by the sail and drowned. I covered the exhausted girl with my boat cloak, and we finally reached the shore safely.

" A great crowd had gathered. The accident was visible from the shore. Of course, I was something of a hero. Next day I called at their villa, and found the frightened ladies able to receive me. This bit of very ordinary sailor work obtained for me the ' Cross of the Legion,' which, I am told by the Legation people, will be sent to me later, and the undying thanks of Mrs. Pauline Delmar. She is the mother of the sweet girl I shall marry,—that is, if I ever am a Benedick." He sighed, and resumed : " Her dead husband's brother, Capitaine Delmar, of the ' Insurgente,' at once called to thank me, and from this courtly old French officer I learned that Delmar died in Mexico, after using his École Polytechnique knowledge to great advantage in mining over there. At the time of the French invasion, the late Mr. Delmar turned over his share of the rich mines in the Yaqui County to his partner, Governor Pesquiera, of Sonora. Now, after troubled years, the inevitable Mexican Revolution crops up. Governor Pesquiera received the property in 'sixty-five,—he dies in 'seventy-seven, two years later than Achille Delmar, and now, in 'eighty-one, Mrs. Pauline Delmar (woman-like) is utterly ignorant of every detail of her affairs. Up to the present she has enjoyed a royal income. But there is great trouble now in Mexico,—and General Mateo Pesquiera (the old

Governor's son) is a stranger to both of the ladies. Their whole fortune is imperilled; it may be even lost to them.

"Jose Marquez, a family enemy, has been lately appointed Governor of Sonora, and the widow is now desirous of re-visiting Mexico to gain the needful knowledge of her properties and secure her estates. It is vital to their interests to do so; yet all the bankers here warn the ladies that they may be exposed to all of civil war's grim vicissi-tudes at Guaymas."

"Are you assured that you know all the story?" ques-tioned Wainwright, now very serious.

"Not by any means," said Goodloe, as he finished his Burgundy. "You may understand," he smiled, "that Anita Delmar and myself have had other topics than silver mines to discuss. A three months' acquaintance, limited by the ceremonies of formal society, is a brief span of life. But I am assured of Anita's love! I have not dared to formally demand her hand as yet. She is only eighteen. Her mother is in the most serious pre-occupation as to the future, and they need a son and husband to guard these great interests, now imperilled. Mrs. Delmar left Mexico when Anita was a mere girl. The mines lie in the hostile Yaqui country, and the dangerous climate of the coast near Guaymas caused the thoughtful father to send his wife and daughter to Paris, where Anita has been carefully educated at the 'Sacred Heart.'

"Even kindly old Captain Delmar knows little or nothing of his sister-in-law's affairs. The busy mine owner, struck down by the insidious coast fever, died suddenly, and all his papers and personal affairs are yet in the hands of

Mateo Pesquiera. You surely know of the character of Mexican revolts. Don Mateo may soon be a fugitive, or fall a victim of bloody vengeance,—who can tell?

" Now, I feel, Wainwright, that I should in honour cast my lot in with these people. It is my duty to give them my assistance. I love my profession. I never dared before to resign and turn myself adrift. I fear, even now, to intrude upon Mrs. Delmar's confidence. I am not so sure that I would be a worthy guardian. But I have taken, so far, a middle course. I gave up my first command, which was the realization of my most ardent wishes. I then took this year's leave to give me freedom of movement. I shall abide the wishes of the ladies, and if I should be asked to aid them, I can look forward with pleasure to your being in the Gulf of California with your vessel. Mateo Pesquiera has the most splendid rancho in Sonora, near Ures; his hospitality at Guaymas is well known, and he may possibly weather the storm and hold his position safely, after all. They fear most this Jose Marquez's dangerous personal resentment. You know what 'prestamos' (the forced loans), prison, and trumped-up Mexican trials mean there. Any rich man in Mexico lives in constant danger by his mere social prominence. And a friendly hatred always hangs over this man, Pesquiera, who has a lovely daughter with him. His wife and only son were lost in a shipwreck some years ago. I must either give up my profession finally, or lose Anita! It tears my heart, Harry, to think of doffing the blue and gold. It would simply break it to lose Anita Delmar! I cannot tell even you, dear friend, more. The man who lifts the veil of a woman's first love to any con-

fidante is a traitor to affection! I must wait for coming
events here.   I am sorry I cannot take you to them
to-night. Your orders are imperative. But I'll write you
at San Francisco, and, whether my wooing is fortunate or
not, you must befriend them for my sake, if you go to
Guaymas. You cannot see that darling girl now, but here
is her picture, Harry!"

Basil Goodloe's voice was very tender, as he placed the
miniature in his friend's hand. "Would you be willing to
give up a sea life for that woman's love?"

Harry Wainwright gazed upon the girl's pictured face,
and remarked with a quick decision: "I'd give up the
command of the North Atlantic Squadron to hear that
woman once tell me that she loved me!"

Goodloe smiled. "Then you find her face fair, Harry?"

The jaunty officer sighed in reply: "If the heart and
mind only match her beauty, then she is a pearl among
women!"

"She is tender and true, Harry!" fondly said the lover,
"and as bright a mind, as gentle in mien as any child that
the gentle 'Ladies of the Sacred Heart' have ever nurtured
in their tranquil retreat!"

"I am afraid our Navy must lose the star of its lieutenant-
commanders," mused Harry. "Let me look at her sweet
face once again."

It was indeed a picture of Life's royal springtime. The
promise of a matchless summer lingered there on the dainty
brows, and unwaked love shone in the wistful brown eyes
of the face dreaming in the ivory. Her clustered silken
hair shaded a serious, delicate, proud face, with no shadow

lines of the world's fitful life to mar its bright frank beauty.

"See here, Basil! I have an idea. You should not follow the advice of a man who is as much at sea as yourself. I am still in the service. Now, I shall see Phil May at San Francisco. You know it's two years now since he gave up the sword for the pen. He is at present confidential manager of Battles & Co., the great San Francisco stockbrokers. I have had frequent letters from him. He resigned while serving on the Pacific station. I heard some quaint story that a woman's bright eyes led him to resign and seek his fortune in the stony alleys of Pine Street there. He has had a practical experience of both lives. He has gone out of our hearty companionship into civil life. I will keep your secret, but I will write and ask him to write you at once of his later experiences. He is a man among men. You know that! Besides, should you come out to the Pacific, he has served three years on that station, and sailed on the 'Thetis' as executive officer, and also knows every inch of the Gulf.

"His perfect familiarity with Mexican customs, laws, and their wary officials, would be most valuable. Take his advice. Let me hear from you often. I'll do all that I can for your fairy princess and her mother. But you must be guided by both honour and discretion in your course here. You know, Basil," he said, warmly grasping his friend's hand, "we are a queer lot of fellows—the children of the flag— but our hearts are true and warm. If we ever lose you, there will always be a place at 'mess' for you, blow high, blow low!"

"You're a good fellow, Harry," said Goodloe, in a broken voice. "I'll think over your advice. Do as you propose. I'll keep Phil May posted, and if I come out there, will telegraph him."

"That's right!" said Wainwright, as a sharp knock broke up the confidential chat.

Two letters were presented to Goodloe, which he eagerly perused.

"Sailing orders," thought Harry Wainwright, as he rose.

"See here, my boy, I'll go out with you," hastily said the host. "There's my first call to duty here! Plan as we may, stern events always quickly face us and bury our hopes and fears under their dark shadows. The most careful plots and schemes fall then wide of their purpose."

"What's up, Basil?" said the now sympathetic Wainwright.

"Mrs. Pauline Delmar writes, 'I wish to see you at once, if you can kindly aid me with your promised advice and counsel,'" replied Goodloe, "And Anita," he lovingly lingered on the name, "says,

'Come instantly! We must quickly go on now to Mexico. A messenger has arrived here with the most urgent letters. You are now our only hope! We leave Paris at once.'

"So, I shall probably follow you over the sea immediately!" cried Goodloe, briskly, as he darted away for his cap and cloak.

"You decide to go, then, with the ladies?" queried Harry Wainwright.

"I will assuredly give them every moment of my year's

leave of absence, should they need it," resolutely replied
Goodloe ; " and, if Anita Delmar will consent, she shall have
all the rest of my life."

" Ah ! Decidedly ! Your mind is then made up ? " Harry
replied, as the friends descended the stairway. Their silent
adieu was the warm heart embrace of brothers.

And thinking of the beautiful brown eyes smiling from
the picture which was now resting on a fond lover's heart,
Wainwright, glancing at his watch to note the nearing train
time, said to himself :

" I would not mind being in Basil Goodloe's shoes
myself, even if the Navy lost a good officer—if—if—she is as
good as she is fair ; and—that mysterious mine has a local
Mexican habitation and a geographical name ! "

So while Harry Wainwright hied away to take his first
independent command, under the beloved stars and stripes,
Basil Goodloe bent his steps to the presence of the woman
he loved.

It was a blind path, indeed ! He was led by blind Dan
Cupid toward the mysterious shores of the pearl-strewn
Gulf of California, fenced from the Pacific by the almost
unknown Lower California, and still bordered by tribes of
defiant and primitive Indians.

But, devoted in heart, with a sailor's singleness of purpose,
Basil Goodloe saw only Anita Delmar's tender eyes shining
on him always in that dim future, twin lamps of love !

CHAPTER II.

BASIL GOODLOE's heart was beating excitedly as he eyed the gay throngs pouring over the Place de l'Opera in Lutetia's chief stronghold of pleasure.

The coupè soon traversed the brilliant "Vanity Fair," and reached Madame Delmar's beautiful home on the Boulevard Haussmann. Though he was going into the beloved presence, the officer thought, with a growing envy, of his departing friend's new rank.

He could picture in his mind the trim cruiser " Ranger," every bluejacket at his station, sweeping out under the star flag, past the sea gates of our Pacific world. On that same snowy quarter-deck it was his legal place to stand and order the national ensign dipped in return for the salutation of the great castellated fort, with its grim cliff battery, showing the huge steel cannon behind their innocent looking grassy mounds. The rows of gleaming guns, the long lines of bronzed seamen, with their springy sub-officers, the rise of the dainty craft in the long green swell, and the fresh embraces of a salt wind sweeping from far Japan, all thronged in his mind.

"Well, I am glad, even as it is, that my mantle falls on Harry," he said, dismissing the cherished picture. " The present holds me now—the future—whither will it lead me ? "

The obsequious concierge threw open both the doors at the sight of the " blue and gold " naval undress uniform, for Madame la Capitaine Delmar was a frequent guest of the fair widow, and many young French naval officers thronged Mrs. Delmar's parlours, not alone to pay their respects to a powerful Capitaine's wife, but also to steal glimpses of " La Belle Mexicaine," her lovely niece.

And the ardent Gallic mind had slyly magnified Mademoiselle Anita Delmar's " dot " till it towered over them as solid, even if as distant, as the pyramids.

Ushered within the grand salon, Goodloe found Pauline Delmar there, awaiting him with impatience. And by her side the " one woman in the world " awaited her lover. While bending over the stately mother's hand in chivalric salutation, Basil Goodloe stole a glance at Anita's expressive eyes. They were filled with entreaty and repressed tenderness.

" I have asked Madame Delmar to entertain our messenger, Senor Andreas Vargas, for half an hour, while we tell you all the strange story of our Mexican partner. You can then converse guardedly with him," said the widow, as she welcomed her visitor. " I am so grateful for your coming. I should have telegraphed at once for Captain Delmar, but the fleet is now ' in grand manœuvres,' and he cannot leave his division. You are so good to come to us ! "

Basil, exchanging a few words with Miss Anita, said earnestly, as he gazed at her mother : " Pray, command me in any way in which I can be of use to you, Mrs. Delmar."

" Then, my friend, I will read you first, Mateo Pesquiera's letter ! " said the mother. " After that, I will give you the grave news which the helpless Pesquiera dared not pen ! Though there is no Mexican Legation here, yet, their national spies abound in Paris, and we may be watched even now. I learn to-night for the first time, that the stake of this impending contest may be millions ! "

As Mrs. Delmar rose and sought the desired letter in her cabinet, Basil Goodloe could well imagine the matchless beauty, which, at the culmination of the slavery days' glory, made Pauline Woodford, the star of Louisville's famed queens of beauty. The years of her motherhood had given but regal touches of ripeness to her stately form, and her own dark beauty was to-day the heritage of the glowing heiress of the dead scientist.

" I will read you the General's letter, Commander," said the widow, while Basil stole sly glances at his eagerly curious divinity.

"GUAYMAS, *March* 15, 1881.

" My DEAR MADAME,

" This letter will be handed to you by Senor Andrès Vargas, my foster brother. His father, Colonel Vargas, was Governor Pesquiera's chief military commander, and was killed in battle with the implacable Yaquis. It was from him that my father gained the first clue to those treasure stores which for years your husband and himself concealed from others' knowledge. Andrès would be the first destined victim to Marquez's swift vengeance, if he remained in his power, as the tyrant would try to force r om him what I alone know. My doom, if any sudden trouble comes, would be at first only prison, his would be instant death! He will deliver to you the valuable deposit which I wrote of last year. I enclose a sealed list and description of it. Half of the proceeds I wish to be deposited in the bank of France in Dolores' name, with you as her trustee. The other half is naturally yours. Senor Vargas knows not the location of the mine, neither one other important secret business matter which is for you and your daughter alone. I have provided for the safety of that by the deposit of a sealed letter to your address, with the Archbishop of San Francisco, to be delivered only in the case of my death. The beloved Archbishop Alemany was always a dear and tried friend of my lamented father. I have sent to him the pictures of yourself and your daughter which you sent last year. If you can do so, you should come on at once to San Francisco. Beware of the sly Mexican Consul there! You will know when you arrive there of all current events in Sonora. If my enemy Marquez overthrows me, it will only be by intrigues at the city of Mexico. I dare not fly, for that would be to imperil all our fortunes. With the greatest prudence, I may pass safely through a term of temporary confinement, and if forced to save myself at the last, I can treat with him. I can not hope to conquer him. If I should die, your letters with the Bishop will then tell you all. If I am alive, and merely confined, you should at once try and reach me in any way you can, for, through you alone, could I hope to effect a reasonable adjustment, or, with my jailer, effect my final escape.

"You can use the entire deposit of funds I have made

at the Bank of France in my behalf and to effect my escape. Hear Andrès, and then decide for yourself. He should not be allowed to come back, for even at San Francisco he would not be safe. He is too well known there, as he was educated at Santa Clara College, in California. The wily Marquez has bankers, business agents, and many spies in San Francisco, who would thwart his every effort. You are personally unknown to them, also your child. I would also suggest a change of name. I fear to advise you to come to Guaymas, but the fortune which you might lose by my death is a grave inducement to take the risk. You however need a friend, brave, loyal, wise, and he must be a stranger at Guaymas! Andrès will notify you of every past movement here. We have also arranged ciphers for future telegrams. If I am seized, personally, it will be to be only carefully guarded at present and watched. I shall not try an armed revolution. The Central Government is far too strong, and your fortune would be sunk forever in my own ruin. Hear him, and then act for yourself. I am actuated by no personal fear. Be wise, and above all, beware whom you trust. Silence and discretion!

" Loyally and devotedly, dear Madame,

Your partner,

" MATEO PESQUIERA."

"That is the whole letter!" said Pauline Delmar, " and the verbal message is still stranger in its purport. Before I weary you with it, I will tell you that Senor Vargas arrived here this afternoon, and secretly received, before coming to me, a cipher cable dispatch from the only true Mexican friend now left us, the Bishop of Guaymas. It read :—

" Mateo is now closely imprisoned at the Castle in Ures. No immediate danger. Marquez in full power. He has been regularly appointed Governor. Help needed."

"Now, Commander !" said the widow, " I am in search of that one friend who will be brave, loyal, and wise ! I will unfold all my heart secrets to you. I know that I can trust your honour. But I fear you can do but little. You are tied down to your profession. I dare not trust to any stranger. I also doubt all hirelings. I have, alas ! neither brother nor son ! Death cruelly robbed me of my dear husband. The sad Civil War swept away all the men of the Woodford race in the bloody border feuds of dark Kentucky. I am helpless and alone in the world !"

There were unshed tears lurking in the beautiful widow's wistful eyes as she murmured, " I only feel now what I lost in Achille's death ! "

Basil Goodloe instantly forgot all the prudent counsels of that astute young sea lawyer, Harry Wainwright, who was now joyously speeding towards Calais, with a hastily caught up outfit of bad French novels, worse Cognac and the most execrable cigars. A truly Parisian outfit !

Goodloe's eyes met the pleading glances of the excited Anita, who was now leaning forward with the glowing roses on her fair checks blushing their very brightest crimson.

"Mrs. Delmar ! I can not pledge myself to be wise or brave beyond other men, but I can at least be true in this your hour of need," the young Commander slowly said.

" I have just received my year's leave of absence, and I
will at once escort you to San Francisco, if you desire, and
as I have two tried friends there, men of my own class, I
may be able to help you to rescue your partner.   I apprehend
from his letter that he wishes to finally save his own fortune
by making terms, and to secure you also in all your rights,
thus giving to your daughter her hidden heritage.   Tell me
all the hidden details of the message ! "

Mrs. Delmar rose and clasped Goodloe's hands in joy.
" Dear friend ! my heart grows light when I hear you speak
thus !   But can I accept your counsels, your proffered
heart service ?   You have a home, devoted friends, and
you have been years away !   How can I ever repay you ? "

There was a semblance of a blush on the gallant Goodloe's sea-browned cheeks, as he said simply, " My beautiful
old ' Graystone ' is sadly lonely now.   My parents are not
divided in death, for they sleep quietly side by side in the
lonely churchyard of the Manor !   And I was an only
child !   So I am free to go on this quest with you, for the
hearthstone at the Hall has been cold these many years.
My noble father died when I was away on the China
station, and my home coming was only to see my dear
mother's eyes close in resignation, when she followed him
two years later.   It is a dear old home, but the night winds
there are now fraught only with memories and sighs ! "
Goodloe saw a gleam of answering sympathy in the lonely
widow's kindly eyes.

" I shall then tell you all !   You can think all this strange
story over to-night, and by to-morrow, give us calmly your
final decision !   But, while I insist that I shall be your

banker, and give you carte blanche in what you decide to do for us, what future recompense can I hope to give you?"

"Let the future decide that! When I have established the slightest claim on your kindness, it will be time for such thoughts!" said Goodloe, gravely. "We must not lead the high fates! Let us now labour only to secure your vast interests and rescue Senor Pesquiera from his victorious political foe!"

It was not strange that Mrs. Pauline Delmar, in her many harassing anxieties, failed to see the glad light quickly springing into Anita's eyes. To the sweet girl, the man whose strong arm saved her from the green cruel depths of the ocean, was peerless in his might among men! And so Basil Goodloe became a knight to bounden fealty sworn!

"I shall send Senor Vargas for safety down to Toulon, where he can join Captain Delmar as his personal guest on the 'Insurgente,' after we have deliberated," thoughtfully said Mrs. Delmar, "and Madame Delmar can offer him a quiet home later, after we go away. He can obtain the captain's advice and views and can move freely everywhere, save to appear openly at the city of Mexico or in San Francisco, as an agent of Mateo Pesquiera. As for my dead husband's imperilled associate, he shall be aided, if human devotion can help him!"

The spirited daughter of Kentucky spoke with flashing eyes, for beauty and courage were the twin heritages of her own gallant race.

Seated at a table with maps and memoranda ready, the

three allies carefully followed the story which had been told by Vargas.

"It seems that my husband acquired a wonderful influence in his early travels among the Yaqui Indians, before our marriage. That mystic tribe, which is one of the lingering offshoots of the Aztecs have never yielded to the sway of Mexicans. Their wild territory in Sonora is practically still unexplored, and it covers the whole valley of the great Yaqui river, which flows into the Gulf of California, only twenty miles from Guaymas. The mountain ranges and fastnesses around them are veritable treasure houses, and this strange, unconquered people still defiantly hold the modern Mexicans at arm's length. They yet remember the bloody incursions of the followers of murderous Cortez, who came in with the cross of fire and the bloody sword. From 1735 to 1841, the whole Mexican military power has fiercely waged a futile war against this gallant native people. They are as brave as the Aracaunians, as true woodsmen as the Circassian mountaineers, and as noble in the defence of their native land. The old Aztec secrets, guarded by their tribal love, are still carefully handed down through families of haughty chiefs. Their unknown land has never been mapped out, they are proof against all modern progress, powder, and commercial wiles, and are still sternly resentful towards the blood-stained hands held out by 'Christian' officials. Their skill in partisan warfare is only equalled by their dauntless courage and their unmatched wiles.

"With traditional arts and a semi-civilization of their own, with a rude knowledge of mining and farming, they live gloomily in the shadows of a mystic past. Pesquiera, the great Governor, alone, of all the Mexican intruders, ever guided even an orderly retreat from their dark groves, and Achille Delmar was the only white man of his time who was able to be passed on in safety from Yaqui village to village. His gentle nature, his skill in medicine and amateur surgery, his knowledge of our practical scientific marvels, and his perfect trust in them, made him beloved by the high-souled copper-hued chiefs of the strange old race.

" In gratitude, to him alone was given the priceless secret of the existence of a wonderful deposit of the richest gold ore, not far from the sea port of Guaymas! Its very existence was long successfully concealed, for their hoary grandfathers had told the young princes of the Yaques or the accursed lust of the Spanish race for their useless gold ! To Achille Delmar alone was ever intrusted this precious local secret, and he, only, obtained the one right recognized by the whole nation, to bear away the yellow treasure in peace.

" With a commendable sagacity, my husband never imparted his compact to any one but his friend Governor Pesquiera, and even with him, he made the solemn pact that the Yaquis should never be harried by army incursions as long as they held their mountain lines on north and south, as a peaceful dividing line. The Indians, with an unsullied tribal honor, at once ceased all reprisals, and the Mexican Government has, ever since then, been glad to accept this tacit truce. To Pesquiera's son and my husband's heirs the secret of the gold caverns has alone descended ! The tribes have carefully hidden the entrances to the mines in their own mysterious ways ! "

"It is a strange story, this record of a quaint friendship!" remarked Goodloe, as Mrs. Delmar paused.

"Strange, indeed!" rejoined the beautiful widow. "The Yaquis are the last unconquered descendants of the old Aztecas. They have held the beautiful lake country and mountains, between the Metape, Yaqui and Mayo Rivers, since their ancestors, the old classic Mexicans, separated in 1160 from the main body of the strange northern migration.

"They worship to-day the same awful god whose wooden image was set up at Culiacan in the twelfth century, when the five other tribes pushed eastward to the valley of Mexico!

"From what distant northern country they came, whether from Asia, in their three thousand mile march, . . . no one to-day knows but the union of the Aztecas and Toltecans who were pushed down a thousand years before them, gave to tropical Mexico a new dominant race. The old stone temple builders never reached further north than Yucatan. Their primal route has never been traced.

"Now, Colonel Vargas alone accompanied my husband in his mysterious secret dealings with the mystic guardians of our strangely acquired fortune. It was like rubbing Aladdin's magical lamp! Governor Pesquiera, always sagacious and watchful, concealed this source of secret income during his life, to prevent local envy or forced contributions to the greedy national authorities at the City of Mexico. Achille," she sighed, "as he grew older, promised to impart to me the details of the whole weighty secret. But I only know, alas! that the product was in rudely smelted gold bars, and that the two partners gradually changed these at Guaymas for silver eagle dollars, which were then at a great premium for the Chinese and East Indian trade. In this prudent way, a part of the treasure was used, and all the remaining gold bullion was gradually sent out to Europe by the foreign trading firms.

"After the great Governor's death, my dear husband, wrote me that his son Mateo was the only living sharer of the precious secret. Busied here, in Paris, with Anita's education, I can only recall his brief references to secret meetings with the chiefs; to the annual supplies quietly furnished to the tribes through Governor Pesquiera; and to his own necessary solitary visits to the trackless wilds of the Yaqui fastnesses to smelt out roughly the selected ores quietly gathered in the silent hills by these friendly gnomes."

"But can any one else now carry on this strange intercourse for you?" doubtfully queried Goodloe. The relation sounded like a fairy tale! This mysterious, tacit partnership of a modern French savant with the stern unyielding red men of the Yaqui caves.

"The gravest part of all is to come now!" said Pauline Delmar, "Mateo has always hidden or kept concealed a vast hoard of silver dollars which he quietly assembled for regular final export on our joint account. This is temporarily safe, he sends word—for it has finally been successfully removed from the mainland to one of the wild lonely Islands of the Gulf. My letters with the Archbishop will give me a clue to effect its safe removal at a later day, even should the worst come! But the great prize for which Jose Marquez struggles is another secret hoard of the rough gold bars of the Yaquis! Sly, old General Pesquiera forced

D

my husband, who was entirely in his power, to allow a large
sum in gold to remain always hidden in Guaymas to ensure
Pesquiera's future comfort in Europe, should he be driven
out by any sudden tumult or local conspiracy. He
furnished troops—and gave a safe conduct to the
simple goods needed by the Yaqui chiefs. He also kept all
official hostile movements away from the secretly agreed on
neutral line. In return for this help, without which, Achille
could not have carried on this friendly intercourse, he
forced my husband to let his own half of this reserved gold
hoard lie in his hands, as a guarantee of no injurious
foreign scheming, and of Achille's personal silence. It was
held as a bond of mutual confidence. Often, poor Achille
has told me, 'My Anita's "dot" will be that of a royal
princess! It is safe in the hands of myself and Pesquiera,
as a joint secret deposit of equal shares.' Alas! Death
has now sealed both their lips. The friends died loyal and
true to their weird allies, faithful to each other, and the
secret of the hidden deposit is locked up now in Mateo
Pesquiera's bosom.

"He says that the wild tumult raised by Marquez follows
a coolly plotted conspiracy at the City of Mexico. Even
as guarded as the friends were in their movements, their
heavy money handling at last aroused the jealousy of the
local foreign merchants, and also the bitter popular hatred
of Pesquiera, who was on all sides openly accused of
officially robbing the taxes. To invest all these finds there
safely was impossible! Land, horses, and cattle are
worth almost nothing in the undeveloped State of Sonora.
They could not both of them leave Mexico and abandon

the priceless 'Golden Fleece' they were quietly sharing
every year! Hiding some of their profits and keeping the
rest of the silver treasured up, ready to buttress up
Pesquiera's personal power, they tried also to secure, as
another means of concealing their wealth, the whole pearl
product or the Gulf.

" Here is the rich burden which has made loyal Andrès
Vargas sleepless since it was entrusted to him!" Mrs.
Delmar then rose and led the astonished naval officer to a
desk from whence she took out a carefully made wooden
casket. Opening it, she extracted several packages of
folded papers, where, in folds of fleecy cotton, laid a mass
of suberb pearls of graded sizes, some fit to shine in an
Empress crown, and all worthy to rise and fall on the
peerless bosom of beauty. "They are all duly listed, and
marked, and the package has been carefully valued!" said
the widow. "It shall be your care, my friend, to deliver
them to my banker to-morrow, and to order their realization
forthwith in the markets of London, Paris, and Amsterdam.
I have to-night my faithful guardians here, two of Captain
Delmar's most trusty old sailor veterans," concluded the
speaker, noting Goodloe's apprehensive glances. It was a
great risk to take! For Paris, polite Paris, has its dangers
to friend and foe!

" What is your present plan of action?" said Basil, then
most adroitly seating himself beside pretty Anita, whose
girlish mind was at that particular moment wistfully
calculating the exact number of these lovely blue-white
pearls which would be needed to encircle her own neck
three times!

" Of course, my friend," said Mrs. Delmar, " Mateo Pesquiera ardently wishes his liberty and the preservation of his strange birthright. He hopes that I will now be able to smuggle in, unobserved by Marquez, some resolute stranger who will manage to reach his guarded prison chamber. I shall at once go on to San Francisco so as to be able to act promptly should the worst befall. But a policy of firmness, a waiting patience, and, perhaps, the judicious use of my money at the City of Mexico, may bring about his enlargement. He trusts moreover to the Yaquis, who still sacrifice to their grim idols of a thousand years, the palpitating hearts of war prisoners, as a barrier to keep the Mexicans away from the mines for years ! If our stern enemy, Marquez, should die, the storm would soon blow over. Mateo dares not trust his able enemy with any semi-confidence. Jose Marquez would coolly shoot him, under due forms of law, and then enjoy alone the whole inheritance !

" Moreover, Mateo's sweet child, Dolores, is now in the convent at Guaymas, under the care of the good Sisters, and secretly guarded by the dreaded power of Mother Church, wielded by calm Bishop Dominguez. The first practical labour now before us is the removal of the secret hoard of coined Mexican dollars, now hidden on the Gulf islands ; the next, will be to ensure the safety of Dolores, who will be properly cared for by the Archbishop of San Francisco ; and lastly, if we reach poor Pesquiera, to try and use the treasure already removed to bring about Marquez's downfall. Last, and most important, the strictest secret watch must be kept over the hidden golden ingots, and if no favourable scheme succeeds to liberate our friend, at once, to effect the skilful bearing off of the bars, and to adroitly bargain from a safe shore for the release of Mateo. This would be only our last resort, for his assisted flight might be construed by the National Government as a confession of crime, and a perpetual outlawry be then decreed against our poor friend. My hands are tied, if I try to act alone. But can I accept your generous offer?"

"When do you wish to leave?" asked Goodloe.

"As soon as you have safely deposited the pearls. Twenty-four hours then is all I wish," answered Mrs. Delmar. "I will fight to the bitter end for Anita's dowry."

"Then let us leave Senor Vargas here openly. I will also go on the same trains and boat to New York with you. I can easily, there, take up my role of a naval officer on his usual leave. At San Francisco we will deliberate and decide on the next steps."

"Now, my noble friend," said the grateful mother, I place all in your hands. "I will call in Andrès Vargas. He will describe to you in detail the general situation at Guaymas, and, as he will not be an active member of our invading army," she smiled brightly, "you need not tell him all our future plans of action. We will inform him later by letter of our assumed names, and he can then leisurely move on to Toulon, and after that, staunch Captain Delmar will wisely direct him."

"One moment, please!" said Goodloe, for his merry friend Wainwright's face suddenly rose up before him. In brief words, he recounted the future availability of his naval academy chum as an independent commander. "I can

already see my way clearly to several of the first moves on
the chessboard. I feel I will have from Wainwright the
most valuable co-operation in the speedy removal of the
treasure, and I can also through him protect the pretty
convent scholar under our flag. All the rest will depend,
then, on our establishing a secret means of future communication with Pesquiera. He must be patient for a time
under this persecution. We must be untiring in our secret
work. I shall ask Senor Vargas to go with me to-night to my
hotel. Then we can confer at length. It will also leave
you free to gain a needed rest for your day of final preparation.

"If you will permit me," concluded the sailor, "I will
call to-morrow morning early for the pearls, and I would
also suggest that you visit your bank alone, and make all
your arrangements for a protracted stay in New York.
In that great Babel, you would naturally be unnoticed.
People have little time for the affairs of others there."

Ten minutes later, Goodloe, with Andrès Vargas, was
speeding away towards the safe shelter of the Hotel
Athenée. Late that night, over their beloved Havanas,
the two young men conferred freely and earnestly. "I feel
as if I were already a Mexican encyclopædia!" muttered
Goodloe, as he finally sought his rest. "Sensible fellow,
this Captain Vargas! He is a type of the better class of
the Mexican gentry. Basil Goodloe's heart beat high in
anticipation of stirring adventures to come, but the warmest
throbs of his pulses recalled Anita Delmar's glorious eyes,
beaming tenderly on him, as she whispered : "You will see
my own beautiful Sonora, its blue Gulf, its grand dim Sierras

lifted high in heaven, where the heat lightning plays over the faintly drawn purple peaks. And you, dear Basil, will be at my side when I re-visit the distant land of my birth ! "

As joyous as the morning lark, Basil Goodloe was astir betimes. His servant, an old sailor, without even the slightest momentary curiosity had every detail of the voyage already arranged. When the commander returned, all was in readiness to take the night train, and join the two anxious ladies on blue water, when the great French "liner" would steam out of Cherbourg Harbour. "Madame Delmar and her daughter" had officially left Paris for New York, but it was Mrs. and Miss Woodford who, two weeks later, were the puzzle of the conservative old Brevoort House at New York City. Whether the two beautiful women were only sisters, or really mother and daughter, was known alone to the handsome and happy looking naval officer, who found a cable despatch waiting him there from Captain Delmar at Toulon:

"Your friend is here, and we sail for a long cruise to-day ! "

CHAPTER III.

MESSMATES AHOY !

"So Basil Goodloe arrives next week. It brings back the old times, Harry." The speaker was idly gazing at the hundreds of barking seals tumbling over the whitened crags of the seal rocks, below the Cliff House at San Francisco. The spirited blood horses were slowly picking their way up the long ascent from the smooth ocean beach, stretching miles far to the southward to Point Lobos. Mr. Philip May was the very type of the swell "broker," of the great era of the Californian "mining stock" craze.

It was in the culminating time of the wildest speculation, the maddest revelry, and the most daring schemes of the seething Californian mining maelstrom. On this particular sunny spring Saturday afternoon, the "social world" of the feverish Pacific money mart was on parade, all *en route* "to the Cliff," or thronging the park, and crowding the brown wave-washed beach drive. Lieutenant-Commander Harry Wainwright, U.S.N., whose vessel was now only delayed a few weeks for certain grave looking envelopes, carefully plastered with the inviolate seal of a sleepy Navy Department, soon forgot his own personal charms in noting the admiring glances often cast by the passing beauties at his handsome friend.

"Yes, Phil, old 'Regular' will soon be with us again," said Wainwright, absently murmuring "splendid eyes!" as a sweet face for a moment flashed a kindly glance at Phil May, from an exquisitely appointed carriage. Mr. Philip May, the very cynosure of all observers, kept his own glances steadily fixed between his horses' ears as he murmured: "It's nearly twenty years since we sang 'All along the coasts of the High Barbary' in the cockpit of that dear old tub, the 'Dale.'" Phil May carefully eyed his lively friend, who instinctively had observed the lovely face, the rare smile, and the glad surprise of the passing divinity. Forgetting his own faultless attire, the prim correctness of his swell park driving dress, and the rare exotic *boutonnière*, the handsomest of mining brokers gazed longingly at careless Harry Wainwright's well-brushed navy blue frock, and the gold leaf of the Lieutenant-Commander gleaming on his manly shoulders. With a sigh over the happy past, the "sailor ashore" then said warmly: "We will have two or three days together, old boy, any way. But here we are at last at the Cliff. Queer show, isn't it, Harry?"

The park and beach had given them quick passing glimpses of every kind of turnout possible, from the ambitious coach and four of the last reigning "bonanza" boor, the splendid spans of the "old timer" money aristocrats, the victorias with their fair freight of lily blossoms or full blown tulips, to the livery "buggies" of the "fast youths," and even the humble business equipage, out on a most unaccustomed lark. For the "Cliff" is open to plebeian as well as haughty patrician.

On the broad outer piazza, thronging the seaward plat-
form, and crowding the horse sheds, a tide of eager visitors
ebbed and flowed in a characteristic Californian unrest.
Flashy turf men, dissipated looking gamblers, gay brokers,
in all the wild excitement of their senseless money spending ;
doctors, grave shaven priests in the muffled Roman collar;
tired tourists and vulgar politicians, all this human circus
passed in a strange review. The Cliff House steps were to-
day a matchless menagerie of polyglot human bipeds. Jew
and Gentile, bearded foreigner, and lean Yankee, leavened the
bustling crowd of easy going wild Western pleasure seekers.
From the great drinking bar arose the wild tumult of the
thirsty, and scores of sleek "garçons" sped along nimbly
in answer to the ever clanging bells from inner rooms,
whose half opened doors gave out that wild strident
laughter of women, which is more tragic than any human
wail. All the local world, good and bad, was "out at the
Cliff."

Giving up his superb horses to an eager retainer, Mr.
Phil May pushed his way through the dense throng, and
knowingly guided his astonished classmate to a favourite
nook, overhanging the waste of surging breakers, boiling in
mad wrath two hundred feet below.

Settled now at their ease, and free from all passing intru-
sion, Phil May only nodded to a passing friend here and
there, and moodily gazed out on his first love—the blue and
open sea. His troubled heart was full.

"Do you come out here often ?" said Harry, as he
languidly watched the white-sailed fleet below them on the
sapphire zone, with a sly glance at the passing beauty show.

"Oh, yes, Harry. The sea breeze brings the old navy days back. I get mining stocks out of my head here for an hour, and I always like to look at the passing ships." The wearied broker sighed heavily.

"Are you really happy in this new life, Phil?" said the generous sailor. He was touched by the air of haunting nervous anxiety, which was deeply imprinted on his friend Phil's handsome but careworn face.

The frank blue eyes were as bright, the crisp hair curled as freely over his forehead as of old, but there were coming crow's feet around his eyes; a furtive, watchful look possessed him, and a professional paleness, as of the "croupier," had replaced the honest red brown of the quondam officer's cheek.

"Who is happy in any form of social life, old or new, Harry?" said Phil, slowly and yet not unkindly. "I certainly hate the meanness of the daily struggle of speculation. I loathe the mad men and wild women whom I have to deal with daily. In the old free life I had the flag always to fall back on. The honour of the Service. This crazy San Francisco huddle of to-day is after all only a devil's auction. But, I shall soon leave it, thank God!"

"I thought, I had hoped, that you had done very well out here!" said the rich Pennsylvanian, hesitatingly.

"Oh, If you mean that I have dropped easily into the groove of living in the very fastest set in the whole world, into a daily race of rushing from one excitement to another, and carrying alone all the cares of a reckless principal's mad plunging, then I have succeeded," said May, bitterly. "I live a whole week in every exciting day. But I can look ᴜᴛ on no fixed future. I am in a den of human jackals, and reckless Ned Battles, my chief, often clears a daily business of half a million. While I try to follow up honestly the threads of a great business which keeps twenty stock clerks and four cashiers often working till midnight; he simply saunters around with a rosebud in his buttonhole, and merely waits for some crash to tell him finally where he is."

"Is this whirl of stock gambling, then, really so exciting? Are there no solid values lying beneath those clouds of steel-engraved certificates, which I see flying around?" queried Wainwright.

"Who knows?" said Phil May, quietly. "There may be! I can't see into the bowels of the earth any farther than you. I only know that the daily fever rises and falls with our telegraphic reports from certain of the great leading mines. The real work is all done out on the frontier. But the fight for the control of the shares, the lying, the wicked luxury, the vicious and desperate scheming, all this passes under my eye daily here. Flimsy as these pictured paper things seem, they mean power; for no four kings ever handled the mountains of gold which has been used as yellow ammunition by Flood and O'Brien, Mackay and Fair, in the last four years. I have carelessly cashed a man's check for fifty thousand dollars one day, without the teller even lifting his eyes, and on the very next evening, I have seen that same signature dishonoured for ten dollars. I have known a man to humbly apply for a drudging clerk-ship, who, a few months before, had a dozen horse-troughs of the purest Parian marble, chiselled for the costly

thoroughbreds, which he had not even time to grow familiar
with by their colour. So—Ruin chases Fortune—out here
in California."

" And why do you assume so much responsibility ? " said
Wainwright.

" It is after all merely a matter of personal honour,"
bitterly replied May. " I carry the vault keys and combi-
nation, and I have had three million dollars of active stocks
often under my sole control," quickly replied May. " I
have also dabbled a little myself. I have already made and
lost two fortunes. There is no more rule in this game than
the fortunes won or lost at the rattle of the dice. I'll tell
you though, frankly, Harry, I have held on here lately, only
for a woman's sake."

" Ah ! " said the commander, gazing at a graceful white
schooner yacht dashing by, under a cloud of snowy canvas.
The green water spun away from her leaping prow, and a
dainty private signal flew at her mizzen, under the Pacific
Yacht Club's burgee. Always some woman," instantly
thought the heart-whole officer. " Why don't you marry
her then, Phil ? Go away with her. I would leave this
strange land of artistic wood-sheds and cosmopolitan
deviltry."

" Because, Harry, the gulf between us is deeper than the
sea dividing us from that peerless schooner. I am simply
selling my life for a thousand dollars a month. Why !
That's her own boat ! Constance Lee gave sixty-five
thousand dollars for that last freak of her dead millionaire
husband. It is a bagatelle to her. It is her money which
draws the honour line between us."

"She is a widow, then?" said Wainwright, his eyes kindling.

Phil May bowed assent, as his eyes followed the racing yacht sweeping by. He slowly said, "Two years ago, her husband, Arthur Lee, died, simply broken down with the strain of fighting the 'bonanza firm' off the hidden treasures of the Sierra Morena. Childless, alone, a beauty, and only twenty-four, Constance has the whole local world of swains sighing at her feet.

"That passing smile you caught was from the lady herself," said Phil May, heavily dropping his head in his hands. "I'm only a mad fool to stay, and yet I cannot go away," he concluded bitterly.

"Why do you not avoid her, my dear old boy?" said Harry, deeply touched by Phil May's evident suffering.

"Because our lives should flow together. Because I know that she is a true woman at heart. Her brief marriage with Lee was almost a separation, for he was ever on the wing to and fro, fighting for and guarding his favourite silver mine. She owns now the controlling block of the stock, and from mere habit, she trusts Ned Battles blindly. He was for years her husband's leading broker. I have to see her very often on this special business in her splendid home. The street would be too dangerous for her frequent personal appearance. Letters, messengers, and even cipher despatches are all mysteriously unreliable here. I have sworn in my heart that I will watch over her interests. She has a million at stake, and even Ned Battles is only human."

Phil May relapsed into his musing, and was moodily silent.

"Does she know that you love her?" queried Harry.

"I am sure of it," replied May. "And I would to God she were poor. Then I would take her far away from this wild menagerie. If she could be asked to share a decent poverty, I would now re-enter the merchant service. I could, any day, get the command of a Pacific Mail liner. But it is useless to dream. I will not drag her down!"

"See here, Phil! This cannot go on for ever," cried his friend. "You are, of all men, above mere mercenary motives. The whole world knows that. Your faultless record as a man of honour,—in the service, you know!"

"That is just the very thing which palsies my every thought. She has, of course, crowds of admirers—the whole local world is at her feet. If I were to-day in command of a national vessel, as you are, I would then have something to offer her. But I have sworn to keep my lips sealed in silence. Listen, Harry! There is a great fight now impending over this very Sierra Morena,—the great Bonanza firm have their iron hands stretched greedily towards it. Now I have never yet tested my influence over Constance Lee. But I shall watch over her until all this is over. If she is true to herself, she can finally force them to buy her interest out at the highest fever-heat value. If she is not robbed in this transaction, then she can soon easily draw out, in gold, the discounted value of her Bonanza. I know privately that it has been already secretly cross-cut, bored and drifted out, until these four wonderful miners of the Nevada Bank know just what she should receive, down to a few straggling thousands. If they cannot tempt her to any fatal speculation, and cannot trap her, then they will

have to buy her control at last, for they must have it.
They are the coldest gamesters of the financial world of
to-day."

"But why must you face this agony? It may be a year
before the struggle is decided," persisted Wainwright.

Phil May suddenly rose. The cold, gray fog had drifted
in, and its mantle hid Constance Lee's beautiful yacht from
their sight. May eagerly leaned over his friend and
whispered: "Because her last share of Sierra Morena
stock is locked up in our vault. As long as I hold the
keys and the magic words of that strong room, she is safe,
my helpless, confiding darling!"

"Safe from what?" eagerly asked the sailor, as they
walked slowly toward the horses. The crowd was now
moving homewards.

"There are daily dangers. Ned Hetherington, a great
broker, sold out all his customers' stocks secretly, two
months ago, in the excited week of the last great 'rise,' and
then quietly blew his brains out after a ball, where he said
'Good-bye!' in mere sport, to the fair woman whom he
was to have married in a week. Ned Battles is a reckless
lunatic also, in his frenzy of speculation. He might also
be tempted to some deed of shame. So, I never will
abandon Constance Lee in such a peril!"

There was an anxious, brooding silence as the friends
settled down in the fur robes, and the willing steeds turned
their heads eastward.

"Nice quiet gentleman! Fine man, Mr. May," said
"Irish Mike," the head hostler, pocketing Phil's half-dollar,
which he neatly caught on the fly. "Sure, he has an aisy

time. Rich, an' young, an' han'some!" The hostler little knew the surging tide of love, wounded pride, and hopeless devotion, which was this moment thrilling the heart of the man whom he envied. So runs the world away!

"Now, Phil!" said Harry Wainwright at last, as the horses trotted along steadily over the smooth, red, jaspery roads of the park, "See, here! I wish you to feel that you have someone who will stand up to your support. I know that you cannot bear up long under the double action of your loving heart and busy brain. Wait here, on guard, till this great deal is over. Then tell her all. I hate to have to offer it, but I will help you to a start in any first-class business at home which you can find. I have a whole lot of money idle. There are no good investments for me east, now. My dear old grandmother kindly left me a substantial slice of her great estate last year. Go in and try your fortune boldly. You may find your own picture in the leaden casket!—Sailor's luck, you know."

Phil May's flashing eyes were very misty, as he turned and gazed lovingly at his generous friend, "Ben Bolt of the salt sea gale!"

"I'll carry your kindness to the very grave, as the one golden memory of unselfishness, Harry, but it is impossible!" And Phil May deliberately uttered the death sentence of his own dearest hopes. Pride, a defiant pride, ruled the unhappy lover's heart.

Rollicking Harry Wainwright was almost morose when they drew up at the Occidental Hotel. "Second time in my life that I have found a man whose insane pride would

E

not let my beastly money help him. There is a new spirit born in this world. It is a modern marvel!"

"See here, Harry! I will repay you for your kind offer," May said, smilingly, as they alighted. "Dine with me in my room. I will then send up a messenger. If Mrs. Lee has no objection to the 'Service,' I will then take you up and show you a noble redwood palace on that great Tarpeian rock, whence the Pacific nobility annually hurl each other down to honest poverty, from a dream of brief, but dazzling, social glories."

"With all my heart," replied the young mariner. "I think that I will put in a little fancy Munchausen work for dear old Phil to-night, if the fair lady is visible," he mused, while they glanced over their evening mail. And the letter was dispatched.

"I am glad to see that I am not alone in the anxious boat," sardonically remarked May, when the tête-à-tête dinner had given way to a half hour's tobacco worship, and the broker lover had found strange tidings in a bulky letter from Basil Goodloe. "Old 'Regular' seems also to be a knight errant of these later days. He is coming out on a most romantic quest," murmured May, when Harry had finished a guarded recital of Goodloe's purposes. "A woman fair also leads him blindly on! Whither?"

"If you have as lovely an excuse for your own self-devotion as he has, I must then envy you both," said Wainwright.

"You can soon judge for yourself," answered Philip May, visibly brightening. "Here is Mrs. Lee's charming request for our presence to-night"—for the returning messenger boy was the bearer of good tidings.

" I can really excuse you, Phil. She is a rare beauty ! " was Commander Wainwright's guarded remark, as the friends drove away, three hours later, from the stately home where Constance Lee had most cordially received her visitors.

" Mrs. Lee is certainly a noble woman. There is a splendid charm all her own in her gracious manner, and, I think, a gentle heart in her fair bosom. She is not of the local fashionable circle?" earnestly questioned the navy gallant.

"Most decidedly not!" replied May. "Every day since she left New York has been merely an exile from the congenial early surroundings of her refined nature. Whatever has been done socially in the wild hurry here, the true home building has certainly been neglected. California, with all its varied charms of nature, is after all but a temporary social abiding place. All yearning hearts finally turn homeward."

" Phil," said the hearty sailor, as he said "good-night " to his disturbed friend, " I shall think of you often on my cruise, my old comrade, under the glittering Gulf stars. There's a sweet little bird tells me of the dim future. I feel that this fond woman will yet lean on you—will know you as we all know you—bright, honest, and true ! Stand by, on watch. Follow up your self-devotion silently for a time, and I hope to know when I bring the ' Ranger' up next year that you will have something definite to tell me. Meanwhile, I shall leave it to you to aid Basil Goodloe in

E. 2

his generous efforts. Few modern men would be willing to take up the uncertain life quest that he has assumed, and it would be a very graceful deed, by the way, if Mrs. Lee would extend her own kindly offices to the two friendless ladies under Basil's charge. They are most worthy even of her kindness."

As Henry Wainwright gazed at himself in the mirror, before seeking his peaceful slumbers, he pondered deeply over his western friend's situation.

"Phil May is surely blind! Why, I could see at the first glance that I was gladly welcomed only as his friend. Do what I would, the subject of Phil's past life always came back. I'm really thankful that lovely young Californian visitor occupied Phil so continuously. What a queenly home! What a sudden luxury of adornment called up by the magic wand of mighty Gold! Now, I flatter myself," continued the warm-hearted commander, "I did no special harm to my old friend's cause. How her tender brown eyes sparkled when I told her of Phil saving a simple sailor's life at the risk of his own in open wintry ocean."

Throwing himself back in an easy chair the debonnair Wainwright proceeded to smoke his last evening cigar.

"And I also worked in his taking off the crew of that Italian waterlogged ship in a howling gale. Phil is the very man! Young, well-born, his family long distinguished in our annals, Philip May needs only to have met her, under the fair conditions of money equality. By Jove! He shall conquer his obstinate pride! I will make him do it, even if I have to tell this dainty woman a parable which her loving heart will quickly understand. Such a form—her perfect manners—her distinguished air—and that womanly voice! Heavens! How she sings! By Jove! I must must come to a full stop. Somewhere in this wide world, I suppose, there is a sweet unknown divinity waiting for me. But it will not be on this cruise that I may hope to meet the fair unknown goddess, I'm sure of that. I will be forced to settle my young affections on the antique 'Ranger' for a season. I am glad that my old shipmate Goodloe will be here before I sail. They will both be here to see me take my first command out."

And the sprightly officer drifted easily into the future dreams of his bright manhood, as yet unhaunted by " her bright smile," whom the dim future hid.

A week later Lieutenant-Commander Henry Wainwright was one of the very happiest officers on the U. S. Navy register. Imprimis, the stout 'Ranger' lay, as bright as a new medal, out in the blue stream, and he was eagerly pacing her snowy decks, in impatience, awaiting the arrival of the steam launch laden with his first guests as a commanding officer. He tasted the sweets of command at last !

The noble bay of San Francisco stretched out before him, walled in by the picturesque coast range, and above him grim old Tamalpais cast friendly shadows towards silver snow-capped Monte Diablo forty long miles away. The blue waters sparkled under a royal sunlight backed by sapphire skies. His heart bounded !

"Launch coming, sir," reported the watch officer, as Wainwright at last stepped on deck, clad in his full uniform. He was eagerly happy, for Mrs. and Miss Wood-

ford were the two graceful supporters of that most fascinating
principal guest, Mrs. Constance Lee.   Harry Wainwright,
preoccupied with his departure, had stolen but one evening
ashore, which was devoted to "old navy days" with his
two now re-united friends.   It is true that he had not
denied himself the pleasure of frequent private afternoon
conferences with the beautiful autocrat of the Sierra Morena
mine.   He was only human.   And naval officers are not
ascetics.

"I shall have to anxiously watch your movements from
a distance, Basil," said the commander, when he greeted
Goodloe; "but our navy agent at Guaymas will instantly
send a canoe to me with any tidings, if I am away up the
Gulf.   You can count upon me."

Basil and Phil May were already deep in inchoate plans
to reconnoitre the local situation at Guaymas.   While the
three men had conferred in private, Mrs. Pauline Delmar
and her daughter had been safely shielded from prying eyes
in the hospitable mansion of Mrs. Lee.   A long conference
with the venerable Catholic Archbishop caused Mrs. Delmar
to leave the plan of action suggested by the wise prelate to
her only mainstay, Basil Goodloe.

As Commander Wainwright met the party on this
auspicious day he saw in Philip May's eyes the signs of some
present danger.

"What's the matter, Phil?" he quickly demanded, as he
artfully left the three fair women, making the acquaintance
of his gallant subordinate officers under the guidance of
the courtly Commander Goodloe.   The commemorative
feast was now in readiness.   May was evidently labouring

under some suppressed excitement. He replied hurriedly :

" I shall have only a few words with Mrs. Lee, Harry, and I then want you to send me on shore with the launch, at once. See here ! I have left the one man I can trust for life and death in the office, with my secret orders. This strange message caught me at the wharf." May then read the pencilled lines : "' Street wildly excited. Great rush in Sierra Morena. Battles losing his head. You must come. Afternoon session will bring on a crisis. Don't fail. Danger!' Now, Havens is a man of a thousand. I do not wish to needlessly alarm Mrs. Lee, but I fear to trust Ned Battles alone, to-day especially, if he has had his usual wine lunch."

May was haggard and excited.

"See here, Phil !" energetically cried the host. "You are a commander yet under the shadow of your old flag. I'll take the party at once into the cabin. You can detain Mrs. Lee here. Explain to her in private, and get her absolute order for the transfer of her stocks to you. If I were you, I would keep it private until danger comes. If she will trust you in this, I would then remove them, and deposit all in the safety vaults at once, in your own name. Should you fear Battles' future resentment, fill up the empty packages with dummy bundles and say nothing. You must outwit him ! He may lose his presence of mind !"

May stared at the quick witted commander.

" I will send my own man ashore to wait in plain clothes with you, and the launch will be in waiting at the wharf. Ten minutes will serve to bring back a messenger sent by you, and you can wait in the Occidental parlours for Mrs.

Lee, if you need her. I will bring her ashore later myself, if she must come. Basil will do the honours then for the rest of the party here on board!"

"By Jove! You are a genius! Go ahead!" cried May, his face instantly brightening. He then drew out his note book and led Mrs. Lee quietly aside.

Five minutes later, Constance Lee's heart followed her eyes as she watched Philip May steaming straight for the shore, with the launch's prow half buried in foam. The proud beauty turned away, her lovely eyes misty with unshed tears.

"If he would only speak," she murmured. "Whose pride is greater? His or mine?" The man whom she loved in her silent pride sped away, in her defence. Her tender eyes met Harry Wainwright's frankly, as that aid of Dan Cupid offered his graceful escort to the cabin, where his "first guest table" was graced by the lovely trio of fair women. And now the shadows were lifted from Constance Lee's face. "I can trust Philip!" and she blushed at her whisper of his name.

"There goes a noble fellow, Mrs. Lee," said the wily young Commander, watching May's last fluttering saluta-tion, as his merry eyes were fixed on the tell-tale roses mantling fair Constance's cheeks.

"I would trust him with my life," said Constance Lee, her slender fingers tightening in a sudden friendship on Wainwright's arm, for Philip May's last words were still ringing in her ears. "He has gone away to fight my battles to-day," thought the millionairess, with a secret joy as she entered Harry Wainwright's stately cabin.

Rocked by the rippling tide, under the growing magnetism of laughter and merry jest, the happy circle passed gaily the noon-day hours of this never to be forgotten impromptu feast. The morning tide would bear the "Ranger" past the Golden Gates, to glide down by romantic Monterey,· beyond the old Indian haunted islands of Santa Barbara, to double grim Cape St. Lucas, and pass into tropic skies within sight of the great purple Sierras, now hiding Anita Delmar's imperilled dowry.

While the happy ladies fluttered in their bright plumage, wandering over the cruiser, earnestly studying object lessons in naval warfare, under the guidance of the graceful "juniors," Basil Goodloe and the Commander sat in waiting by the open port, whence the grim "stern chaser" had been removed, and they spoke only of the blind Mexican quest. For the three naval friends now knew all of Mrs. Delmar's hopes and fears.

The Pacific Queen City was swarming with Marquez's agents and correspondents. The Mexican steamer line was now making the most of his brief lease of power, in unusual commercial activity, and a cipher despatch from Paris, sent on from New York, told them of mysterious inquiry there as to the whereabouts of Achille Delmar's widow. How had distant Jose Marquez learned of the jealously guarded story of the past? Was it by some chance slip of the tongue? Some successful bit of mean eavesdropping? The new Mexican Governor was evidently watching every portal of his usurped domain.

"I am loth to risk these two defenceless women down there, or to put either of them in this scoundrel's power," said Basil Goodloe, with the gravest concern. "If I had only a man to go down with me who knew the gulf region thoroughly, I would go on without them. If I could only frame a feasible plan to remove the treasure, I would take a schooner myself here and cruise around the gulf, as if I were only otter hunting or sealing. I would meet and bribe the pearl fishers and smugglers. I would find some sure way to safely reach poor Pesquiera: I must not fail them now! But I do not dare trust any one here. By Heavens! Perhaps Phil May can find me here some miner, prospector, or a roving skipper who knows all the lower coast. The steamers are evidently now all run in the new Governor's interest. I might go down there by myself first. But the long delay to find the boat, and to select her crew. I am helpless here now!"

"Basil, I have it!" said Wainwright, you can easily charter or hire a boat and have it cruise around near my surveying ground. Go down first alone, and cover the whole preliminaries. I will see that all your letters are covered by my official seal. Leave the two ladies here with Mrs. Lee. But do you want a companion, a man, wise, cool, brave and true? Now, if Phil May could only go. The very man of a million!"

"Ah, yes! But Phil is tied down here by this harassing business. He would soon lose his place in this fierce race of life on Pine Street," sadly said Goodloe.

"Then he must try and find you some other trusty man. As for a proper boat, there's just what you should have for this run," said Wainwright, as the bevy of laughing ladies re-entered the cabin. A half mile away lay an exquisite schooner of a hundred and fifty tons idly rocking on the glassy bay. Her gleaming white sides gave her the mien of a graceful swan, and her rakish heavy masts towering in air proved her a crack sail carrier.

"Harry! I could take that same boat around the world," said Basil Goodloe, with enthusiasm, as he peered through the binoculars which his host handed him. "Some great money prince's yacht, I suppose," said he, listlessly. "She carries a private signal, I see." A merry voice broke in upon the sailor's soliloquy—

"If you have any time for the pleasure of a cruise, I would be happy to lend her to you. I really need a gallant captain. I am afraid of these fresh water sailors of the Bay!" said Constance Lee, quietly, handing back the glasses she had accepted. Her eyes were twinkling now with gratified pride.

"Is she really yours?" said Goodloe, in blank amazement, gazing at Mrs. Lee as if she were a water nixie.

"There is my own monogram, C. L., Sir," daintily answered the beautiful widow. "I only seek a gallant captain. She is all ready for the Club races now."

"Hello! What's this?" suddenly cried Harry Wainwright, as his man hastily thrust a sealed note in his hand. The launch had glided up unobserved with the swiftness of an arrow. "Extra! Sierra Morena jumped two thousand dollars a foot! The whole of Pine Street crazy! Leading brokers ruined!" A hurried departure was made, on a signal from Mrs. Lee. Nothing was said as the natty Commander grasped the tiller. A general excitement thrilled every tingling nerve!

The whole party were a hundred yards away before Constance Lee could thoroughly understand Harry Wainwright's lightning movements. For he had hurried them, all at once, aboard the launch, and was at the tiller himself. The Californian beauty held in her hand a brief scrawl from her absent champion. Her heart bounded as she read his laconic words : "Come instantly! I am waiting for you at the Occidental."

It was signed by Philip May. It seemed an hour before the launch touched the landing. Wainwright hailed the first passing carriage. The driver had to whip his way through a howling mob to finally reach the ladies' door of the Occidental Hotel. When the excited party reached the ladies' parlour, a keen-eyed young clerk sprang forward to meet them. He whispered : "Come at once to Mr. May's rooms."

When the door opened, Mr. Philip May smiled as the ladies started at seeing two revolvers lying on his table. "Pray excuse me, ladies," he said, and, as he led Constance Lee to a chair, he placed by her side a heavy despatch box.

"All is safe, Constance," he murmured, as their eyes met. Mrs. Lee was astounded when he gaily cried : "You are eight hundred thousand dollars richer, Madame, than you were this day at sunrise ! Battles cleared everything of his own out in the afternoon session to prevent a failure. Cash deliveries. He finally then sold out all your own trust stocks 'short,' but could not deliver, as I had them all safely transferred to my own name, as trustee, just fifteen minutes before the afternoon board opened. Young Havens saved your whole fortune, Mrs. Lee," he concluded, pointing to a bright eyed Western lad, who was now guarding the door.

" And you?" said Constance Lee, with a strange light in her eyes. Her bosom was rising and falling in a strange thrill of delight. He would not speak for himself.

" I only did my duty," said Philip May, gazing steadily at the glowing beauty, whose eyes dropped under his burning glances. There was a silence which grew strangely awkward.

" Let us all drive up to my home and dine," said Mrs. Lee, finally, in an altered voice. " I wish for your protection, till I can send for my lawyer." And the word " Philip " was trembling on her pale lips.

" Certainly," said May, now master of himself, as he lightly said, " I am ' on the world ' now, for the celebrated firm of E. Battles & Co. has ceased to exist."

CHAPTER IV.

WHILE the astounded ladies congratulated Mrs. Lee upon her sudden increase of fortune, May exchanged a few words with his factotum Havens upon the safety of the imperilled securities.

"I presume you wish to see Judge Westervelt at once, Mrs. Lee," said May. "Havens, if you will permit, will find him. You know that the judge is a secret adviser of the Bonanza firm. He will probably be closeted with them at the bank, or with the other lawyers of the Big Four who happen to be here."

"Can I trust him?" Constance whispered to the man who seemed now her guide in every movement.

"I will answer for him. He is wise even beyond his years," the broker replied.

"Then, Mr. Havens, use every effort. Find the judge, and say that Mr. May will wait at my house with me to explain all. Tell him to bring a power of attorney, for I wish Mr. May to handle the whole business side of this affair."

Havens bowed and departed instantly. The sudden announcement stunned May. He gazed at Mrs. Lee, who said, " You will need some occupation, you said, I think the Sierra Morena can keep you busy."

As the party endeavoured to leave the hotel, it was only through the urgent efforts of two policemen in plain clothes that the gathering throng was traversed. Messenger-boys, brokers' clerks, news-boys screaming " Latest Extra ! Last Figures of the Market ! Further Failures !" and impromptu corner stock exchanges, crowded door-ways and pavement. Men and women of all grades, the mistress in silk, the maid in stuff, mechanic and banker, roved excitedly from hotel rotunda to street corner to catch glimpses of well-known faces and the latest rumor.

As the two carriages reached the steep ascent of " Nob Hill," May broke the silence :

" Never since the South Sea bubble craze has any State been so debauched. Homes, savings, business reserves, trust funds, the hoardings of years, all are poured into the yawning bottomless pit of Pine Street. This fierce fever of speculation has divided families, alienated friends, and debauched the social circles of this fiery town. In secret, husband and wife, father and son, play against each other. But here we are," said the still excited broker, as the ladies were ushered into the safe retreat of Constance Lee's splendid home.

Far below them, leaning on its buttressed hills, in lines of light, San Francisco lay, a huge glittering octopus, stretching out radial arms of flaming lamps, from its central vortex of the molten golden philtre crazing all, the huge granite Stock Exchange.

" I shall claim the absolute obedience of all," cried Mrs.

Lee, whose eyes were shining. "Commander Wainwright's lovely breakfast party was interrupted by this upheaval. We will dine in absolute peace. Let the grim old judge bring the business with him; until then, we will celebrate the sailing of the Ranger."

"Thank heaven, my responsibility is over," cried May, as he rejoined Goodloe and Wainwright in the ante-room. "Mrs. Lee has her stock certificates locked up in this plate safe. I can see them in the Safe Deposit vaults to-night; they will open for Judge Westervelt at any hour."

"You must have had a run for it," said his two listeners in a breath.

"Mrs. Lee's main fortune hung on the chance of ten minutes' delay. I turned a friend out of his cab at the naval boat-landing, and beat crazy Battles by a quarter of an hour. I'll tell you all after the lawyer comes. There are some further steps to be taken at once."

"Where is this reckless plunger now?" asked Wainwright.

"He may be on the Honolulu steamer. He may have caught a coasting vessel running out: there are tugs always watching for such sudden flittings," said May. "Or," and his voice grew grave, "he may be found in the scrubby bushes of the Park sand-hills with a ball through his head."

The merriest dinner-table in the city that memorable night was presided over by Constance Lee. Commander Wainwright observed that the beautiful widow showered all her attentions on her guests and was frankly solicitous for the two who wore the blue and gold. Handsome Harry chuckled inwardly: "Keeps Phil for the last morsel. I can go to sea now. *I* am not needed here any longer." With equal fatherly interest in Basil Goodloe, who was assiduously watching over Anita, the commander was careful not to obtrude himself.

"Ah! I knew Havens would find him," remarked May, as Mrs. Lee handed him a telegram marked "*Immediate.*"

"Will be with you at ten. Am now at bank.—Westervelt."

When the toast to the health of the gallant commander of the Ranger brought the blushes to Harry Wainwright's cheeks, he drank in reply, "To our next merry meeting," and added, "Why do you not take a cruise in your beautiful boat, madam?"

"I retain it only because of the interest Mr. Lee always had in the growing yacht club. The Halcyon was finished too late for his enjoyment. I cannot bear to ask Captain Warner to sell her, he was so proud when he built her, and predicted then that she would be the ocean queen of the Pacific. I had hoped to have the Halcyon take the blue pennant away from the fleet this year. But all that is now impossible. Still, Captain Warner has offered me a full price for her as a sealer or otter-hunting schooner. I cannot bring myself to see the beautiful racer make her first voyage for mere dollars. She is Warner's pet : he says she will outstrip anything under sail in the West."

Basil Goodloe's hand clasped May's arm as he asked, "Would you charter her to me, madam, for a six months' cruise?" The eyes of Pauline Delmar and her daughter were fixed on the laughing hostess, who hesitated.

"Commander Goodloe," she said, archly, "I do not let pleasure craft. No, sir; I refuse to accept money for the

F

fleet sea-racer's first voyage. I will *lend* her to you, if you will allow me, but she shall not be bargained for."

"But the risk, the inconvenience to you, madam! Can I accept such a favour? It will, however, place Mrs. Delmar and Miss Anita under lifelong obligation to you. It's the very thing. Just the boat for us. She has all the legal yacht privileges?"

"I will give you a letter to Captain Warner, who is now heart and soul bound up in seeing her speed tested. He has built a hundred fliers at his yard at Benicia, and he will give you his advice and every assistance."

The three men were exchanging nods. "Just the place to fit her out, near the navy-yard. Who is this Captain Warner, madam? Is he reliable?"

"He was a trusted business associate of my husband. He is interested in South Sea, Arctic, and Mexican trade, as well as sealing, hunting, and Siberian adventures. He is the recognized Pacific authority on yachts, yachting, and all aquatic matters. My husband used to say that when the old sea-dog was not building or sailing ships he spent half his leisure frolicking in the water. He's a quaint, bluff old character, rich, powerful, unpretentious, and a Yankee of the Yankees. He knows every sailor on the coast, and every inch of shore from Singapore to New York."

"Decidedly he is worth a visit," mused Goodloe. There was a general interest in his decision. "I may accept your kindness, Mrs. Lee, but I fear that you will regard me as an enemy if I should take my friend May away to command your beautiful boat."

Mrs. Lee started, and a bright flush dyed her lovely

cheek. All eyes were drawn to her. She was silent. A tender gleam from Anita Delmar's eyes gave Goodloe new inspiration. "We would not leave here for several weeks, and if Mr. May was joined by these ladies in explaining our secret plan, you might forgive me."

Constance Lee's voice trembled slightly, as she said, leading the way to the coffee-room, "First the Sierra Morena must be safe, then you can borrow Mr. May. Does it take *two* captains to sail one yacht, commander?" the lovely widow queried, flashing a searching glance at Goodloe.

"I think there is no other man than May who could do your swift vessel justice in her maiden cruise. What say you, Phil, to ploughing the blue water once more?"

"I am at Mrs. Lee's orders for the present," slowly answered the object of these negotiations.

"Ah! then, if you have very good reasons, I may lend you both the boat and Mr. May," laughed Constance, as the fair owners of the fabled Yaqui mine added their gentle entreaties.

CHAPTER V.

"TELL us now of the day's excitement on the street" said the Lady of the Sierra Morena. Her cheeks were crimson.

May was glad of the change of topic. "May I speak freely?" he asked, inclining his head to the hostess.

"Certainly," she answered. "All that is true will be in the morning journals, with fabulous additions. I would like to be enlightened a little before Judge Westervelt comes."

"It appears that a decision of the Nevada courts has enabled stockholders, at last, to have access to the deep levels of the mines, hitherto shut off by the leading magnates. The great bonanza was at once traced into the Sierra Morena, and the first visit of five agreed-on experts proved that your co-partners (the great firm) knew of it and had been working for months to gather in all the loose stock out, yours alone excepted. The news set Virginia City simply wild. The usual tactics of delaying telegrams would not do. Orders to buy at any price poured in by the thousand. No one thought this great find would burst on the public so soon. The dominant firm had depressed the stock only to gather it in. My one 'outing,' by fate's decree, occurred on this very day. The men at Virginia City, who had been guarded in the mines and kept from communication, spoke freely now. The moment when Sierra Morena was called, the Board broke into a pandemonium. Its price jumped from thirty-five dollars a share to seven hundred and eighty in the call. The excitement was so great that the whole detective force and reserve police, in plain clothes, were put on duty at the Exchange. The scene has never been equalled here in wild intensity of excitement. Havens, finding the office besieged by a mob, took instant action and sent for me, with orders to bring me off on a tug."

"Where was Battles ?" said Mrs. Lee. Her eyes were lit with an eager fire.

"He missed half the morning Board. His second broker handled the list. Havens tells me he rushed in, when the call was over, to the office, went to the vault, and was then driven rapidly to his bank. I did not see him then : I arrived only half an hour before the afternoon call. Battles was still at the bank. I followed your private instructions, and ten minutes before the afternoon Board, I re-entered the office. Havens was on guard at the vault. He had our two porters with loaded revolvers by his side. I had ordered that no one but Battles should have access to the securities. Yours were in a special burglar-proof compartment, you remember, Mrs. Lee ?"

The fair mistress of the great mansion nodded in silence : her bosom was heaving. She motioned for May to continue.

"Our office was filled with a crowd of madmen. The

policemen fought my way back to the vault. Then Havens whispered to me that Battles was short fifteen hundred shares of Sierra Morena, which he had sold days before, for a mere turn of a dollar a share, at thirty. Bank messengers, brokers, and our leading customers were clamouring and flourishing their delivery orders."

"And did Battles come back from the bank?" Mrs. Lee queried.

"He was forced in through a lane cleared finally, and called for me. They would not let us talk in secret. I think he would have been mobbed had he lingered."

"And the rest?" Mrs. Lee eagerly demanded.

"The rest I can tell only to you, in presence of Judge Westervelt," said May, bowing respectfully.

"What will be the sequel?" Goodloe inquired.

"Hundreds of men ruined forever, brokers swamped by the dozen, banks cleared of their surplus, and the Juggernaut of the Nevada Bank will roll over a thousand more victims," was May's answer.

"But the Sierra Morena has then a wonderful intrinsic value?" Wainwright asked, gazing at the young millionairess.

"Certainly," said May, looking Mrs. Lee firmly in the face, "but the present craze has carried it up to the discounted value of every cube of dark greasy ore in its narrow quartz-pinched bed under Mount Davidson. Besides, the Nevada Bank people must have this one large block of stock to play the public with."

"I don't exactly understand," Mrs. Lee murmured, with a glance at May at once an entreaty and a command.

" It is easy to see, Mrs. Lee, that the mine is enormously
rich. The bonanza barons wish to toy with the public as a
cat plays with a mouse. They must retain control always;
and yet, to have stock to throw in and out, so as to make it
fluctuate from four to eight hundred dollars every week,
they *must* buy out your interest. Throwing it on the open
board, you could break the market at their highest figures.
As you own it, you can feed it out either to them or to the
public at the highest price. If you break the market to-
morrow, they will lose two dollars to your one. It will pay
them, therefore, to buy your whole holding."

"Can they do so, and pay for it?" said Goodloe, in
wonder.

"They opened the Nevada Bank with ten millions in
solid gold coin in sight of the public," May quietly replied.

" And you tell me that these four money kings five years
ago were unknown men?" said Wainwright.

"They were in modest obscurity," May cautiously
answered.

" It beggars belief," cried the officer. "A wonder of the
world!"

" Do you advise me to sell at once?" said Constance
Lee, gazing at her new employee.

"Judge Westervelt!" announced the butler, as a swarthy-
faced man of sixty-five entered the grand hall with the
indefatigable Havens.

" Ask *him*. Let him decide. He is the only man whom
the bonanza kings fear," May whispered, as Mrs. Lee rose
to meet her guest.

" Let my carriage wait," cried the old judge's ringing

voice. "Ah, no, my dear madam," said the man of law, pressing the hand of his fairest client. "I have to work all night at the office, on bank papers. I can give you but just half an hour. I will now ask you and Mr. May to join me at once in the library. Time presses."

The nervous exhaustion of the great lawyer was his excuse for indulging in a strong cigar as he leaned back with closed eyes, listening, in the recesses of a huge leather chair, to May's recital of the day's events at the office. From the grand salon came the refrain of Anita Delmar's glorious voice, thrilling with the love which she dared not yet show before her parent. As Westervelt sank in his chair, he said, "Give me your stock certificates." Mrs. Lee handed the old advocate a packet. "Twenty-one, twenty-two ; good !" he muttered, as he finished counting the separate certificates. "And all endorsed to Philip May, Trustee. When did you endorse these ? " said Westervelt.

"Since I came here to-night," answered the young widow.

"But how, in God's name, did you get it out of the bank ? " said Westervelt, springing to his feet. "What terms did they make with you ? "

"I don't understand you, judge," faltered Constance, frightened at his manner, and casting an appealing glance at May, who stood with folded arms, regarding them.

"This stock was pledged at a quarter of three to secure Battles's daily overdraft at the Bank of Colorado. Cashier Alvin told me so at the club, for Battles had taken his other collaterals away at noon to break up some large

certificates to meet the rush. His account was over eight
hundred thousand dollars short when the bank clock marked
three to-day. God knows what to-morrow will bring forth.
How did you get it out? I have an offer of seven hundred
and ninety dollars a share for it from Flood. But dare I
tell him that you own it now? He would take it to-night!"
The lawyer was breathless with anxiety.

"The bank never had that stock," May calmly said, as
the lawyer and his client gazed, open-eyed, at him.

"Tell me all quickly,—quick!" cried Westervelt, seizing
his arm.

"I always feared Ned Battles. I knew for the last month
he had pledged his customers' stocks at the Bank of Colorado to get huge daily loans. When I found the bank
seals on this envelope, I knew that he had broken his trust
and taken Mrs. Lee's stock out of the vault. As much as
a week ago, I removed this stock and filled the envelope
with some White Pine wildcat, worth a dollar a ton. It
was easy for me to get Ned Breeze to seal the package
again over there. I told him the seal was broken: so it
was. I placed Mrs. Lee's stock in my own tin box. Now,
when I raced from the wharf to-day, I took my own lock-
box out and put it in my desk for fear of some attachment
or trouble. When Havens told me Battles was at the bank,
I slipped out, with this envelope in my pocket. At two-
fifteen I presented to the secretary of the Sierra Morena
Mrs. Lee's order to put all her stock in one certificate in
my name as trustee. I showed him every share, and filed
the positive order which she wrote on the Ranger. Now,
judge, the transfer certificate is signed and sealed, in the

secretary's safe, and the date 2.20 is also entered on the transfer book."

"Duped, by heaven! Battles pledged the worthless packet, then?" the lawyer yelled.

"Most certainly," said May.

"How did he get it?" gasped Westervelt, fumbling with his watch.

"He dashed in at half-past two and demanded of me the opening of the vault," May replied. "I was his mere employée. When I saw him, panting and red-eyed, open Mrs. Lee's box, I said, quietly, ' Battles, that's the dishonor line. You have no right to touch that box without Mrs. Lee's positive orders, given after full knowledge. You know that she is out of town.' ' Get out of this vault! You are discharged! You are a dead man if you are here in one minute,' he hissed. I handed him my keys without a word, walked to the cashier and drew a quarter of a month's salary, and then came to the Occidental Hotel with Havens, who brought my tin box over in his bank portmanteau. Mrs. Lee's Sierra Morena has never left my hands to-day. I'm now a gentleman at large."

Springing to Constance Lee's side, Judge Westervelt said, " Thank him for saving your fortune, and doubling it too! Will you sell to Flood at seven ninety? I'll take Havens and the carriage and bring his lawyer over here. It's the one chance of a life."

The silence was oppressive. May could almost hear his own heart beat.

"You can't fight the Nevada Bank, my dear lady, at long range. They will give you gold bullion mint receipts now for the money. They have four million lying there in twenties, coined for the rush they alone knew would come."

" What do you say, Philip ? " the lovely woman asked, as she slowly raised her eyes to his face.

" If my poor services have won your confidence, I beg you to sell this very night," he said, almost solemnly.

" You can go to Mr. Flood. There's my hand on it. We will await your return in the drawing room," was the widow's fiat.

" I will be back in an hour," the lawyer replied, "and I will bring four of the Safe Deposit patrolmen to watch here till morning. I wish this closed up before the two banks lock horns. Battles, I suppose, turned a hundred thousand or so into gold notes and is safe on the high seas. Remember, now, both of you, not a word to a soul after this without my sanction."

The old lawyer's hurry shamed his years. Depositary of a thousand secrets, the dawn would see him, dull-eyed and waxen-faced, still toiling to prepare the great bank's gigantic moves of the next day.

Constance Lee's face was lit with a shy and happy smile as she approached Goodloe, who with an improvised drawing-table was now giving sketches of the movements of his proposed jaunt with the Halcyon.

"I think, commander, that I will trust the yacht to Mr. May as my representative, and a sea-trip will do him good, while the Battles failure will be a seven days' wonder."

" Will you then give me a letter to Captain Warner,

madam," said Goodloe, "and one to your yacht-keeper?
We will see them early to-morrow. Wainwright and I and
the ladies have already planned out the whole cruise."

"We have been busy too," smiled May.

"Most certainly," said the woman who had just sold a
"slice of the great bonanza." May watched her gliding
towards the library as if she were "a dream of a summer
night."

"Don't you know any man here who is familiar with
Sonora and Chihuahua?" broke in Goodloe, ruthlessly
brushing away May's preoccupation.

"Just the man! Fred Bligh; he represented the Bank of
Colorado in unearthing the great diamond swindle. And,
by the way, there is old Professor Hackmuller, of Heidel-
berg, who went down there with him. They came out by
Guaymas,—had special passports from the city of Mexico,
—and Hackmuller is now working away at some land
colonization schemes down there."

"Can we see them soon?" persisted Goodloe.

"Why, certainly. Fred Bligh rooms at the Occidental.
He is a regular at the California Theatre. I'll have him
and the professor at dinner to meet you in my rooms to-
morrow night," May answered, his eyes lighting up as Mrs.
Lee returned with two letters.

Bowing his thanks, Goodloe resumed, "Now, Wainwright,
if you will make your invitation to us good, we will run
down with these ladies to Guaymas. That will give the
yacht a breezer, and we will find out all her paces."

"You shall have the run of the Ranger. I can lend you
my steam launch, or give you a tow up the gulf, and will try

and make it pleasant for you at the Mexican ports." Wain-wright was in high feather.

It was late when Judge Westervelt returned, accompanied by a grave-faced representative of the "Four Kings of the West." In fifteen minutes the transfer of the shares was effected. Constance Lee never knew that in the hour and a half of Westervelt's absence the records and office of the Sierra Morena had been examined, and May's story confirmed. Three directors of the hostile Bank of Colorado, hastily summoned by the captain of detectives, had also broken the seals of Ned Battles's deposit, to find there only worthless scraps.

Fifty eager policemen were already scouring the great sleepless city in search of the absconding criminal bankrupt. Guarded by two men, the lawyers departed, and an impromptu camp in the anteroom held the patrolmen watching the simple slips of certified mint receipts which called for a million seven hundred thousand dollars.

"I can get you Sub-Treasury certificates to-morrow, madam," said Judge Westervelt, as he seized his hat and cloak. "Be kind enough to remain at home every moment to-morrow. I'll take Mr. Havens with me. He is mine after this: I'll make a career for him. He shall be a lawyer."

The messmates were not loath to depart, for the morrow called Wainwright to the duties of his departure, and Goodloe, with May, was eager to arrange the maiden cruise of the Halcyon.

"I have the power of attorney, all properly executed," said Constance, as she bade her faithful knight adieu.

" You will come to-morrow at breakfast? I may need your advice. You are my man of business now." She spoke timidly.

" Your certificates are in your own name, Mrs. Lee," answered her lover, grown strangely diffident also.

" My business will demand your future care," she answered.

Three loving women sat late that night in fullest confidences, and when the Ranger steamed out proudly to sea at three o'clock the next day the Halcyon spread her white wings for the first time, in escort to the Heads, with her dainty mistress standing beside Philip May at the helm.

CHAPTER VI.

"THERE's Point Concepcion, Basil," said Captain Phil May, as he handed Goodloe his binoculars, one bright sunny morning a month after the memorable crash on Pine Street.

"All right, Mr. Navigator: I'll take your word for it. I'm only a passenger." It was daybreak, and the sun was throwing shafts of gold into the fleecy pearly mists of the Santa Barbara Channel.

The saucy Halcyon was stealing along under jib, fore-sail, and mainsail, and the leaden waters scarcely rippled as she swept onward like an ocean bird.

"Ah, yes, I was right: there they are." And May pointed to the three jutting peaks of San Miguel, Santa Rosa, and Santa Cruz, rising on the starboard bow. "I think after decks are washed I'll crack on all sail and see what the flier will do by the patent log. Here's the world's one course for a sea-race."

While Captain May gave some orders to a mate whom he addressed as Mr. Lake, Goodloe bared his brawny chest and enjoyed a dozen buckets of fresh crisp sea-water tossed over his whipcord-muscled torso by the sailors.

"You are a bright one, Basil!" laughed May, as the two

sat down on a hatch-combing to enjoy their coffee and hard-tack. "Every jacktar here can see your trade-mark anchors and American flag. You don't need the tattooing to give your character away."

"Well, I am only a mysterious passenger," replied Goodloe. "I wonder how old Captain Warner raked up such a fine crew. They are splendid fellows; just the gang I would pick for any dare-devil dash. Now, take your mates. Obed Lake is a deep one. Jorgensen has the Viking daring, and that pearl-fisher chap Diego, the pilot, is a free-booter all over. He has the devil's own eyes. Can you trust them? They are a suspicious looking lot, but sailors every inch."

"I'll watch them well, and trust them gingerly," said May. "Harry has promised to give me a good man or two, whose time will run out in the Gulf. Besides, Fred Bligh and the professor are well established there now.—Let us have breakfast for the ladies at eight bells sharp," said May to the steward. "I'll give the Halcyon a run. This breeze will be all she needs."

Clad in his yachting reefer, Phil May was braced to his old form, and the mahogany brown began to tint his cheeks once more.

"Will you stand out for Cape St. Lucas?" questioned Goodloe, now enjoying a morning cheroot and lying at ease stretched in a long Japanese chair.

"I shall run into San Diego harbour, Basil," answered the rehabilitated sailor. "You see, one week at Monterey set all the society reporters' pens at work. Mrs. Lee's cruise with her friends has spread the fame of the Halcyon abroad. Now, when she took the train for San Francisco she told me that Judge Westervelt wished me to run into San Diego. The two great banks have patched up the Battles trouble to save the market. All looks clear. But I might be needed for some explanations. I am glad to be away until the lame ducks are all gathered up."

"It was a struggle to the death for that mine," mused Goodloe. "I wonder if we shall have such a battle. Where did your old employer hide himself?"

" No one knows," said May slowly. "I hope he is not in Mexico. Battles is desperate and cunning. We should have trouble to mislead him. If he had as much character as quickness, he would be a Napoleon of finance. I am glad Mrs. Lee thinks of going to Europe for a year or two, if your mission succeeds. You will be wise, should you rescue Pesquiera or get him and a part of the treasure, to let the rest lie for a year or two. Mrs. Lee would be protected from all schemers with the Delmar family abroad. Battles would never dare to worry her. There's extradition with France."

" And you?" Goodloe said, quietly, looking at the emancipated stock-operator.

"I think that Fred Bligh and Hackmuller can establish close relations with Marquez. You see, Bligh has the prestige of his relations with Senator Warren, who owns nearly all the Bank of Colorado stock now. He has letters from Janson & Co., the great Mexican shippers, and Senator Warren will back him in any mining purchases. I will cast my lot in with them, if Bligh wishes. Hackmuller says that if Marquez can be persuaded to let him open the Yaqui country he can make us all rich. Fred is a splendid

G

host. He will capture Marquez. Harry Wainwright has a national vessel to give us a theatre to work on Marquez's love of official display. By heaven, we *must* succeed! Someway we must open communication with Pesquiera. There may be a fortune for me lying under the purple peaks of Sonora." May was strangely eager.

"And you will not remain as manager of Mrs. Lee's estate?" said Goodloe, earnestly.

"It would only be a daily torture. If I cannot meet her on equal terms, I prefer to worship her at a distance.—Here are the ladies."

Both the young men stood, cap in hand, before Pauline Delmar and her beautiful daughter.

"And was the rocking of the cradle of the deep as delightful as before?" said Goodloe, gaily.

"Every day is a sunny dream. I was never so happy in my life," cried Anita Delmar, as, leaning on Goodloe's arm, she drank in the beauty of the scene.

On the port side, nestling under its crags, the white-walled city of Santa Barbara gleamed as fair as Amalfi or Sorrento. The yacht leaped along under a stiffening breeze, and the roses of the fair girl's cheeks blushed redder under the wooing breeze from the bewitching vale of Santa Barbara.

"You should be a sailor's bride," said May, gazing in frank admiration. A blank look of conscious guilt spread over Goodloe's face, giving way to laughter as the steward announced breakfast, with a flourish, for "eight bells" was musically clanging from the foks'le.

"Love can wait, breakfast shall not," merrily replied the maid.

When the servants had withdrawn, Pauline Delmar asked May "Are we going on well in our voyage?" Her eyes were anxious.

"I have to spend two days at San Diego, Mrs. Delmar, and a week after that you shall lie behind Pajaros Island, in sight of your old home, and in face of your enemy. Are you sure that Marquez does not know you?"

"I am positive," replied the stately widow. "He was in Spain when I visited Guaymas, and I have never met him. It is sixteen years since I left Mexico, and we lived in the interior."

"Do not fret at our delay at San Diego," said May. "The archbishop wished two weeks for his letters to reach Pesquiera, that he might know of friends at hand. We will have every local bit of news waiting us, for Wainwright promised me to wait at Guaymas till we arrive. His surveying season does not begin for a month. Be patient, my friend, and trust to our lucky star." There were no longer any secrets between them as to the quest. Even Harry Wainwright now felt that the shadowy Mexican mine might prove a solid reality.

When the ladies rejoined their companions, the decks of the Halcyon were thronged with the entire crew. At their stations, the men showed the man-o'-war's discipline enforced by Captain May, who, sextant in hand, stood on the quarter-deck. The wind was stiffening.

"There's the Morro Rock, and we will try a hundred miles against time," cried May, as he signalled his sailing-master to make all sail. Obed Lake's men darted into the rigging, and five minutes later the Halcyon was buried

under a cloud of snowy canvas.   Her taper bowsprit strained
under its working sails and a great balloon jib gracefully
swelling under the breeze.

"Fifteen knots, by Jove, Basil!   She's the queen of the
sea," cried May, breaking in on Goodloe's day-dream.

Goodloe sprang to his feet and consulted the patent log
and his pocket chronometer.

"I never saw any craft under canvas move like her.   She
is the 'Flying Halcyon,' indeed."

As the long day wore on, the swift craft sped on to glide
into the evening glow of star-lit Southern skies.

In a merry group, the comrades of the quest noted the
general commotion on the decks of a San-Francisco-bound
Mexican steamer now passing.   Crowds were gazing on
the dainty water-witch.   It was no marvel that the San
Francisco journals, three days later, were filled with stories
of the phantom schooner, a wondrous vision of ghostly
nautical beauty and intimately related to the Flying Dutch-
man, that "moved faster than any human-built craft."

Alone on the deck that night, Basil Goodloe walked
with Anita Delmar.   The racing sails were taken in, for
the coming daylight would show them the sandy spit of
San Diego Hook, with its curved breakers lapping the
lonely beach trodden once by good Fray Junipero Serra.

Below, by the cabin light, Mrs. Delmar and May talked
long of their quest.   The helmsman, a dark shadow at the
wheel, hummed his sailor song, while the Halcyon swung
along easily under working sails.

The lookout at the prow, and Jorgensen, the blue-eyed
Viking, were alone on duty.   The Scandinavian puffed a

pipe and muttered, " If Lake had any nerve, what a race we could give the revenue cutters! She's the one craft of the world for an opium run." And he dreamed of a blue-eyed woman waiting for him afar, where the wild Baltic lashed the Swedish shores. He plotted and schemed in silence, biding his time.

When the late good-nights were spoken, Captain May bade his fair charges prepare for two days on shore. " The last safe chance we shall have for mail and telegraph is here at San Diego. Your letters will be in waiting, as Mrs. Lee arranged, perhaps even telegrams from the archbishop or from Paris. Don't be astonished if you see a change of toilet in our water queen. I shall put Goodloe in command as your Mentor, and the Bishop of San Diego will offer you entertainment at the convent. Remember, you are Mrs. and Miss Woodford."

Before the cutter had landed Goodloe and his charges next morning, a dozen nimble ship-carpenters were busy on the sloping decks of the Halcyon.

" It is astonishing," said Goodloe, as the party sat together on the eve of departure in a room at the old convent, " the power of the Church." In his hand two cipher telegrams, carefully translated by a reverend diocesan secretary, told him that Wainwright and his companions were safe at Guaymas, and that the waiting prisoner was now aware of the coming help.

" Are you ready now for your voyage, ladies?" asked May. " The tide serves, and we will go on board to-night. If your farewells are said, you will be a hundred miles toward Cape St. Lucas before your sleep is broken."

"I can think of nothing more," said Goodloe. "Our mail will go to the navy agent, under official seal. We have exchanged telegrams with our San Francisco allies. I am ready."

"So am I," eagerly said the newly-named Mrs. Woodford. "My Paris Banker cables the successful sale of the pearls. Vargas and Captain Delmar write me that the great house of Dupuy Frères has been notified to honour all the drafts of Commander Basil Goodloe, U.S.N. So, as no one will dare to question you, we are ready for our Mexican operations."

Half an hour after the party reached the schooner, the dashing of water against the yacht's quarter lulled both mother and daughter into a peaceful slumber. In the fore cabin, Philip May pressed to his lips a letter from Constance Lee. The sailor lover dreamed of a rosy future that night, for next his heart lay the lines traced by his lady's hand, "I shall bless the day which brings you back to me, my brave true guardian;" and the precious letter's last words were "Your Constance."

Goodloe walked the deck, on watch, till Obed Lake had safely made his offing. He little dreamed as he hummed "Larboard Watch," that Jorgensen, a constant shadow of the sailing-master, was whispering to the chief officer, not five yards away, "If you will listen to me, this cruise will lead you on to a fortune."

But the dainty Halcyon, true and staunch, fled away southward.

"I cannot understand it, Captain May," said Mrs. Delmar, as she gazed around, when she first graced the deck next day. The sea was leaden, a heavy swell was rolling, and the salt spray sprinkled the widow's cheek. " It looks like another boat."

May enjoyed the lady's surprise, and laughed at Anita's astonishment. The glowing girl was appealing to her lover (the one authority !) for explanation.

" Madame, this is now the sealing schooner Constance," replied the ex-officer, doffing his cap. Her graceful yacht bowsprit had given way to a mere pilot-boat bow, the tapering topmasts were no longer whipping the air, four whale-boats hung securely lashed to the quarter davits, and with triumph May aided the astonished passengers to peep over and gaze on the dark green hull.

" No one could recognize her now," said Mrs. Delmar.

" I am proud to say I am a very fair ship-carpenter," replied May. " And the name Constance replaces the gilt star and scroll Halcyon." A substantial deck-house amidships completed the transformation.

" I took out new custom-house papers as owner, and my clearance for a fishing and trading cruise, yesterday, while you wandered with the nuns under the old grape-trellises of the Mission. Pray betray no surprise before the crew."

Five days later the lookout sang out, " Pajaros Island dead ahead." The four conspirators were grouped at the rail, for safely past the frowning Cape St. Lucas, through tropical storms, under the sheen of sheet lightning, the Constance had reached the haven.

The " vermillion sea," its pearl-bearing depths traversed by shoals of hungry sharks, lay as silent and lone below its purpled eastern shores as when stout Ximenes first piloted

La Concepcion over its wide expanse under the mandates of Charles V. That iron soldier, Hernando Cortez, with prophetic greed, dreamed of the golden rifts whence were smelted the treasures he wrung from captive Montezuma.

There was a suppressed anxiety burning in the bosoms of the friends as Diego, the pilot, guided the beautiful racer into the island-hidden harbour. Prudence and precaution were now as second nature to each bearer of the dangerous secret of the quest.

Goodloe watched over the lovely maid of Guaymas, as her eyes were fixed on her natal land. Round the lovers

> All was hushed and dark,
> No sound except the sobbing bay,
> No light, save when some phosphor spark
> Flashed upward in the spray.

As the sea-tossed boat swung into the circular harbour, the three peaks of Trinidad towered over the star-lit waters whereon the black hull of the Ranger lay at rest, the lights gleaming from her open ports. Friends were near.

" Remember all we risk—our lives, our love, our future," said Goodloe, as he kissed the trembling girl's lips. For while the flag of their country floated from the cruiser near, they could hear across the water the hoarse call of the Mexican sentry, the minion of cruel Marquez. The new governor had already christened the Plaza de les Armas with innocent blood.

As the anchor rattled down, and the sails rasped slowly to their rest, the ladies, casting a glance at the old fort, with its two moles, and the low scattered town, sought their cabin. For on the deck Captain Philip May was now busied answering the questions of the mestizo port boarding officer.

In half an hour the papers were viséd and the formalities were at an end.

"We are now free to land at daybreak," said May, his brow grave with the responsibilities of the moment.

"Boat coming alongside, sir, from the man-o'-war," reported Sailing-Master Obed Lake, thrusting his crafty face down the companion-way.

In a few moments the merry visage of Commander Harry Wainwright gladdened the sight of the now anxious women. They met with carefully restrained joy.

He pressed the ladies' hands, and whispered, with a glance at the open stair, "All is right. Fred Bligh and the jolly old professor have a comfortable nest ready for you. I'll send my own launch and land you with due ceremony. Shall it be eight o'clock? You can send the baggage over in your whale-boat. I'll tow it ashore. We can breakfast in my cabin and safely have a private talk. I'll have Bligh and Hackmuller there. The old German is a jewel. Remember, walls have ears: we are now in Mexico. I won't linger to-night. I don't dare to take either of you over this evening: it would look too familiar. For suspicion these Mexicans beat the world."

With warm salutations, the young commander sprang into his boat and was gone. As his cutter pulled away, he called out, "See that your anchor's fast, Phil. It comes on to blow suddenly here often."

"Send me Diego, Captain Lake," sharply said May, as he swept the sky with anxious glance.

"He's gone on shore with the port captain's boat," said the sailing-master, shuffling his feet uneasily.

"Without my permission!" May was coldly indignant. "Send him to me the moment he returns. Any man who leaves this craft without permission shall never touch this deck again. Don't forget in future, sir." There was an ugly ring in May's stern accent.

"He said his wife was on shore here, sir," muttered Lake. Pausing at the foremast, as he walked forward, Lake clenched his fist. "I'll have the secret of this cruise yet!" The implied censure decided the wavering traitor.

While May concealed his uneasiness, Diego, the pilot, was seated on shore in the port office, cronying with the arrogant boarding official. "I can't make it out, Estrada, whether smuggling, revolution, or mining trip, but the boat is handled for some Gringo scheme. The Yankees are all thieves," the ruffian concluded, draining his aguardiente.

"Good, my old compadre. You have done well. Now get back at once. You can say you wished to get the port orders and send word to your wife. I will telegraph to Mazatlan for La Democrata to-morrow, and we will watch this strange craft. It's easy to seize her, and you know the pearl fisheries, eh? We can do a private turn."

"Splendid," said Diego, seizing his sombrero. "And the boat is swifter than the west wind in its flight. She can outsail even La Democrata under full steam."

"I'll put a prize crew on her and clap the Yankees in irons. I will see Governor Marquez to-morrow. Adios, mi amigo!"

The mongrel crew bent to their oars. Diego, in feigned

repentance, was soon giving every aid to the selection of a snug holding-ground, and May forgot his first suspicions.

The sleepers in the two cabins of the Constance were awakened by the morning gun of the Ranger and the bugle notes calling the blue-jackets from their hammocks. May and Goodloe, alert and anxious, caught a glimpse of Anita Delmar's face, as the maiden's uneasy slumbers gave way to her desire to see the theatre of the impending drama.

Yes, there it lay, the squalid old town in the centre of a mountain-rimmed cup. Far to the north, the Tetas de Cabra towered in air, and to the southward Cape Haro boldly closed the sweep of Cochues beach.

Around that rock lay the wild land of the Yaquis and the mystic mine. Somewhere in the rocky amphitheatre before her lay hidden the fabulous golden treasure of the dead partners. Startled by the crowded canoes filled with swarthy fruit and pearl-shell peddlers, the ladies kept below, under guard of the maid, the steward, and sleek Ah Sam, the Chinese cook, an old man-o'-war's servant.

Within an hour the four friends were seated in Harry Wainwright's hospitable cabin, safe behind the guns of the Ranger, and the launch lay alongside the Constance, where the baggage was being loaded under the eyes of Basil Goodloe's servant.

"Bligh and Hackmuller will come on board in two hours," said the commander, "and if we have any private matters to discuss, let us conclude them before then." The sentry at the cabin door cut off all listeners. "This is the only safe place of conference, and it will not do to assemble here alone too often. I have a plan."

"What is it?" cried the guests.

"I shall disarm Governor Marquez by giving him an official luncheon here. I will have Bligh and the professor as chief guests to meet him. You can be mere minor luminaries. While they draw him out, you can gradually make his acquaintance, and learn to be on your guard. I have already overwhelmed him with deferential courtesies. I do not wish him to think I have any special interest in your boat. Can't you send her away on a cruise of a few days?"

"I am afraid to trust her with Lake," May replied. "Mrs. Lee is attached to this last toy of her husband's fancy. Besides, our outfit of guns, ammunition, and trading goods might excite suspicion."

"Phil, I can fix all that," said Wainwright, with ready wit. "I wish to set up some beacons for sounding-lines. I'll send a boat's crew and Ensign Crowninshield and run her up and down for a week. He can take the launch. It will save getting up steam on the cruiser. Then your boat will be safe. They will think I have hired her for my work."

"Good!" replied May and Goodloe in a breath. "Now for your discoveries here. What is the present status?"

The ladies, glancing from the ports at the old fort knocked to pieces by the Dale in the Mexican war, could see the motley garrison proudly parading under their gold-bedizened officers. The enemy were near and alert.

"Governor Marquez is busied with pompous local display, sly intrigue, and forcing the merchants to disgorge by means of the sale of custom-house certificates. He has Mateo

Pesquiera still carefully guarded at the old castle at Ures, and has confiscated all his haciendas and portable property. He holds high state in the old government house on the Plaza. We waited here for your credentials before approaching the bishop. But Fred Bligh's fame as a capitalist has preceded him. With his aid, queer old Professor Hackmuller has thoroughly reconnoitred the town, and is the centre of a local swarm of mine-sellers, land-bargainers, and stranded adventurers. As an easy-going prospector and traveller, Bligh freely mingles with all circles, and finds the chief rumour to be that Pesquiera will be brought to trial in the near future. His friends are disheartened, for there is a strong garrison of federal troops holding Ures to prevent his escape or release."

"Then our task is well-nigh hopeless," Mrs. Delmar sighed.

"Not at all," said the buoyant Wainwright. "Do not forget that the bishop and Dolores Pesquiera are the real means of our final communication. Some way must be found to let the prisoner know that we are all on the ground ready to act. We must learn his wishes. Then when we have located the hidden funds, and they are saved or properly watched, we can use strategem, bribery, or cunning to help him personally. Ha! there are Bligh and the professor already. Now we will hear their final reports; and remember, none but ourselves must know of the treasures or the hidden mine. They only know till now that we wish to open communication with Pesquiera." Wainwright was grave as he said to the ladies, "Your special duties for the afternoon are to meet Bishop Dominguez and Dolores

Pesquiera. For us to approach that girl would be to throw suspicion on the whole party. But to-night we will assemble at your rooms, and you can give us your information. Marquez does not suspect the bishop of friendship for his prisoner. Above all, not one word of Spanish from either of your lips! Your safety rests on that. You will not be on the Ranger to-night. Be wary! Be wise!"

A breeze of good humour came with the entrance of the two newcomers. Fred Bligh, dark, swarthy, deep-chested, with massive limbs and an easy drawling voice, was a veteran in intrigue and the roving Western life. In Professor Hackmuller's pale blue eyes and simple Teutonic visage were seen the devotee of science and the quaintness of the German savant. Before the sun was at meridian, the ladies were mistresses of the local gossip of the whole revolution. The hour of action was near.

"I am sorry to say that any plan of my going to Ures is futile," concluded Bligh. "I wished to examine some tempting mines there myself, but the road is infested with murderous brigands and discharged soldiers. Hackmuller and I must wait for the human débris of the revolution to clear away. And the professor is anxious to examine the ores and deposits of this rich state."

Goodloe raised his head from a deep trance of thought. "I have it. Let the professor and yourself announce a stay of some months. The rainy season is coming on. If he apparently opens a laboratory and assay-office, you could gain all the news in safety, and suspicion would be lessened. Your apparent occupation would disarm curiosity."

"Very good," cried the delighted professor. "That is

the best plan. And we can quietly watch over the ladies here, leaving Mr. May and Mr. Goodloe free to open the serious approaches to the prison-cell of your friend."

" If you approve of our location, as soon as you are settled we will broach our plans of ore-examination and experimental work. It will give us a real character in their eyes," added Fred Bligh.

While the new-comers conferred with Mrs. Delmar, Commander Wainwright, walking the quarter-deck with Anita, whispered to her, " I'm going to win the very first skirmish of your battle with floods of champagne at that luncheon."

" How ? " the girl asked.

" If you can get me a letter from this gentleman's daughter, and a Latin credential from the bishop, I will wheedle this Marquez out of an escort to visit Ures. I can go and be back in eight days. If pluck or money will win their way to Pesquiera, I'll reach him : my national character will put me beyond even Mexican suspicion."

" Commander, you are an angel," cried Anita.

CHAPTER VII.

IT was three o'clock when Pauline Delmar's foot first touched Mexican soil on her secret quest. The port captain, curious and suspicious of the "Gringo" visit, eyed the widow askance as Professor Hackmuller aided her to leave the Ranger's launch. Beautiful Anita was in charge of a handsome middy, and Goodloe and Bligh carelessly busied themselves with the luggage towed in the schooner's yawl.

As the ladies entered a carriage, and two creaky ox-teams crawled up for the belongings which indicated a long stay, Captain Estrada flourished his gold-banded cap and was profuse in his compliments. The two ladies simply bowed and smiled, seeking the refuge of the waiting vehicle. The elder pointed to Bligh, who lounged up as a volunteer interpreter. "They speak no Spanish, captain," said he politely. Captain Estrada sighed and smiled in vain.

"Friends of mine, Captain Estrada: Mrs. Woodford and her daughter. The lady may buy a rancho, and also join me in a mining purchase. She has great herds of cattle in Southern California."

"Ah! Very good! I have an uncle who has even now a rancho to sell,—fifty square leagues," cried Estrada. His ready cupidity was excited.

" Then you must show them every attention. I will be your interpreter by and by."

It was not an hour after the ladies were ensconced in a comfortable one-story masonry house, when Commander Wainwright, in full regalia, attended by two officers, arrived with due pomp, to invite Governor Marquez to a festival, the rumours of which convulsed Guaymas. While the servants arranged Señora Woodford's temporary abode, Goodloe and May bustled about, settling themselves at Bligh and Hackmuller's bachelor head-quarters.

A round of the few stores, a few inquiries for letters, carriage-horses, servants, and other travellers' needs, set the gossips of the little town wildly agog. The great social lion of the hour, El Comandante Wainwright, was punctiliously escorted to the strand by the governor and his myrmidons.

" I can steal ashore in plain clothes, and join my friends quietly later," thought handsome Harry, as his gig cut the placid waves.

When the cicadas were singing and the deserted streets were lonely, as Orion swung up over the hills, no one saw under the mantle and shawl of the two dark figures the sweet faces of the two American ladies stealing into the priest's modest house, adjoining the tumble-down old cathedral on the plaza. Yet from Hermosillo, thirty leagues away, nestled in the great cleft of the Rio Sonora, good Bishop Dominguez had journeyed to meet poor Pesquiera's woman ally.

In an inner room, the prelate earnestly conferred with Mrs. Delmar, while from the padre's dining-room came the

H

murmur of the fresh voices of youth. Anita Delmar was
rapidly making friends with the prisoner's daughter. Goodloe and Bligh loitered around the old church, smoking and
chatting, but really acting as volunteer sentinels on the
alert.

But a busy cupid had roguishly transfixed with his golden
dart the hitherto invulnerable heart of Harry Wainwright.
For the graceful girl whose eyes were fixed timidly on him
was as delicate in her beauty as a gazelle. The native
shyness of her Castilian blood, heightened by her secluded
convent breeding, was evident in the fleeting crimson flushes
which dyed her tender cheek. Draped in the modest black
which gave an ascetic tone to her startling beauty, Dolores
Pesquiera flashed her dark eyes mournfully at the handsome
officer, in answer to his earnest queries. Clasping her
slender hands, she begged him to reach the father who might
any day be dragged before a jèfe politico and summarily
shot at a tyrant's bidding. The sight of Dolores's lovely
head resting on Anita's bosom, her silken tresses flowing
over exquisite shoulders, her arms clasping the new-found
friend, moved Wainwright to transport, as the motherless
Mexican sobbed, "Mi padre querido! padre pobrecito!"
in the flowing music of her race.

"Give me but a token, señorita, and I will reach your
father or lose my life."

She handed him an emerald ring. "It was my mother's,
—his wedding gift. That will tell him all. And I will
write three lines. The bishop will sign it."

Before the lazy Mexican bugler blew taps in front of the
cuartel, Wainwright had his full instructions from the bishop

and from Mrs. Delmar, now breathless with anxiety to see him start. A secret courier would precede him, bearing words which no layman or friendly heretic might hold in trust.

The bishop raised his hand in blessing as they parted for the night. " I will send you a man and woman to watch over your household, my daughter," he whispered to the mother. "You, dear child, can go and come as you please to meet my lamb Dolores. The Mother Superior will know you only as another one to shelter and caress. Keep Dolores from betraying excitement.—Comandante, I shall not see you till you return. You will meet my faithful messengers. They will whisper to you these two words." He bent his stately head and gave the messenger of love a secret counter-sign.

The lights went out one by one in Guaymas. The mother and daughter caught friendly glimpses of the Ranger's tall spars, and the welcome red gleam of the dainty Halcyon's mast-head light.

" I feel that our brave friend and the wise bishop will find the safe way. But prudence, patience !" The anxious mother folded her lovely daughter in her arms and slept in peace.

A stone's throw away, Diego the pilot and Estrada were plotting cheek by jowl. "You must guide me, amigo," said the port captain. "A clearance to cruise in the gulf, on surveying work, in command of a Yankee officer, cannot be refused : that is regular. But if they go near Hermosillo (the great Mint is there) they may try to smuggle a cargo of silver, who knows ? If you have probable cause, I will

H 2

board her, but only after the naval officer and his men leave. Hoist two red lights at the mast-head instead of one, if you want a visit. La Democrata will be here to-morrow night."

On the deck of the schooner, Commander Wainwright was giving Ensign Crowninshield his last orders : " Run out at daybreak. Put in a week and give me a good shore reconnaissance as far as the Yaqui River, and twenty miles beyond. Land always with your flag. You can run up the Yaqui with the launch fifty miles and see what it's like. There are great coal-fields of anthracite there. I am going to Ures, to be gone a week and examine the beds. They may be accessible by the river. Use the trading-goods freely with the natives, and stop the moment they object to your interior researches. I mean to have a look at them before our cruise is done. Be open, friendly, and hospitable. I want a report from you."

Wainwright heaved a cavernous sigh as he pulled home to his ship. His head was busied with the flitting of the Constance. " I don't wish Marquez to poke his nose into that schooner's affairs. I'll lay him out at the lunch : I'll captivate that swarthy tyrant. As for Mr. Diego, he will not set foot on shore for ten days. The ensign will nail him on duty." In the starlight, Harry kissed Dolores Pesquiera's emerald ring. " The father in chains ! I will loosen them, for his daughter's sake." The sailor's dreams were haunted by two liquid Creole eyes, his slumbers lulled by a murmur as sweet and sad as the rustling of autumn leaves : " Mi padre querido ! padre pobrecito ! "

When Wainwright's morning coffee had driven the

tumultuous dreams of night from his brain, he peeped from his cabin window. The beautiful Constance was gone.

"Good for Crowninshield! He's a bright lad, and a born sailor, like the rest of his name." Wainwright dismissed his breakfast calmly, varying the routine reports by a hurried conference with his steward. "You can serve the champagne on my order without stint. And brew a bowl of that Ranger punch which gave you the honors of the Alaskan squadron. I do not wish his Excellency to leave this vessel thirsty."

After a studied full-dress morning toilet, Harry laid out ostentatiously on his official desk a formidable array of maps, charts, some old reports on the Lower Mexican coast, and a bundle of severe-looking envelopes marked "Navy Department."

"A little cunning, some confidential flattery, and a good deal of scientific drinking, will bring José Marquez into a good humour. I'll play the great man. The ward-room can entertain his staff. I will be diplomatically confidential. An hour alone will start him on the path : the list of official toasts will conclude the good work."

The gay sailor could not see Obed Lake and Jorgensen forty miles at sea, lurking at the bow of the Constance as she darted along to the south. "There's some trick here," Lake snarled. "Curse that upstart officer ! I'll have this boat yet, in spite of him. If we leave the town again without the women on board, or these blue-jackets, I'll run away with this craft."

"Spoken like a man !" said Jorgensen. "Where will you run her to ? " he whispered.

"I'll tell you later. I have a scheme to load us both down

with gold, Jorgensen," he said.   "We have our show now."
"What is it?' whispered the mate.   The eyes of the
villains met.

"We must loosen the whole bulkhead of the arms-room
while we are out on this trip,—draw the nails, cut them off,
and leave a few boards tacked loosely. When we get our
show, we will jump these two fools, and make a run for
it. It is a secret for you and me alone. The men are
wil ing."

"And the two dandy skippers?" hoarsely groaned
Jorgensen.

Obed Lake pointed silently to the green water. "The
sharks cling to us like a shadow," he said, as a dozen green
slimy flattened shades swept along on the lee side of the
boat.

Jorgensen grinned.   "Here's my hand on it, shipmate."
And he laughed to think of the blue-eyed sturdy maid
waiting on the Baltic.

There was all the studied display which Wainwright's skill
could lend to the arrival of Governor Marquez,—a ringing
salute, the ship's company mustered for inspection, and a
personal reception by himself. In solemn procession, the
official cortège inspected the ship, and then the juniors in
a body escorted the governor's staff to the ward-rooms,
whence the sound of jollity soon arose. But in the commander's cabin, Wainwright, in deep preoccupation, communed with the delighted official. Coal-mines, future fleet
visits, growing business relations, the value of detailed
gulf and harbour surveys, his desire to visit the Yaqui River
and the tribes, a special report to the secretary,—all these

things were reviewed before the governor.   Samples of the
American cocktail were deftly introduced to punctuate the
conference.   " But I will not weary you, Senor Gobernador.
I have a few days' leisure.   I could have taken a look at the
main coal-fields near Ures, but the roads are so dangerous.
I have sent an officer to examine the Yaqui River.   It is too
shallow for my vessel to reach, so I have hired the vessel of
these mining speculators.   If I could see the mines, and
gain some real information of the Yaqui country——"

"Senor Comandante," rejoined the Mexican, now
flushing with the good humour of the ante-prandial appe-
tizers, " I will give you an escort of my own carriage.   I
have one of my best officers at Ures, in charge of that malefactor Pesquiera.   He cannot leave, but he shall tell you all,
and he will send you to the fields."

Wainwright exhausted his repertory of Castilian flourishes
in thanks.   " Does he know the Yaquis, their land, their
habits?   If we could only use this coal-supply !   Ah, what a
boom to our service !   I cannot visit their land !   I must
obtain details for my secret report "—" to Pauline Delmar :
Heaven pardon me this official humbugging !" he soliloquized.

"I have it !   Mateo Pesquiera was his father's secretary.
He knows : he shall tell you all.   I will have my carriage at
your disposal to-morrow.   You shall be there in a day and
a-half."

Wainwright cast a glance toward the red-tiled roof of the
distant convent.   He felt the emerald ring, Dolores's token,
on his finger.   " I will live to see her folded in her father's
arms : I swear it.   And then ? "   His heart leaped up

Along the future pathway of his life he saw the glances of those Creole eyes, loving, burning, tender.

" Excellency, allow me to escort you to the deck.   Our other guests are waiting to do you honor."   Wainwright led the way to the quarter-deck, while the merry circle gathered, and Mrs. Woodford and her daughter were presented in due form.   Fred Bligh cautiously dilated upon the land and mining speculation which bound them all together.   Mother and daughter learned to breathe more freely as Bligh and Wainwright courteously interpreted.

The splendour of Wainwright's feast dazzled the Mexican governor.   Seated in the place of honor, under the glances of the ladies, Marquez loyally drained each of the ceremonial toasts which dragged along during the two hours at table.   Pressing his hand on his heart, he offered his services to the visitors.   Even quaint Professor Hackmuller shared in his general outpouring of effusive hospitality.

" Permission to establish a laboratory?   Certainly, my dear sir.   I have a fine location near the governor's house, and a yard full of machinery there.   Come and see me. Ah, my friend, when I have finished the trial of this pestilent Pesquiera, I will go myself and show you mines.   I go to Ures in two weeks for the trial.   It will be pushed. When his fate is decided and the decree executed, I am at your service."

" And what will be his fate if found guilty?" asked the host, with assumed carelessness.

" He will be shot forthwith, on telegraphic confirmation of my review of the proceedings.   He is a foe of progress."

Marquez's face was scowling with passion.   A general

springing from chairs followed, for Mrs. Delmar's sudden pallor gave way to a death-like swoon.

"It is the heat, the close cabin. Gentlemen, let us retire."

Ten minutes later, on the breezy deck, the lady was able to thank the governor through her anxious interpreters.

"Rouse yourself. Be brave now. He may suspect you understood his Spanish," Wainwright whispered as he fanned her. "I leave to-morrow with his escort and permission to see the prisoner. I'll save him or die."

The invalid was soon able to promenade the snowy quarter-deck, leaning on the arm of the anxious guest of honor. It was but natural that the unnerved woman should soon accept Goodloe's escort to the shore. Mr. Philip May, the mining partners, the commander, and the governor whiled the afternoon away in the cabin. Cigars and confidence followed the celebrated punch, which sustained its ancient reputatiom. When his Excellency departed for the shore under Wainwright's escort, the circle had progressed far in a general plan to perfect an exploration of the Yaqui lands.

"These Americanos are rich, powerful. They know the secrets of art. If I only dared to bring Pesquiera here, I might force him to show me the riches of the closed-up region. I must think,—must think." And the governor's nodding head drowsily dropped on his shoulder as he gyrated to his carriage.

When Wainwright waved adieu to Goodloe and May next day, he resigned himself to the care of a wild-eyed driver, who urged the travelling-carriage along after a half

troop of lancers, the rear guard struggling after. Harry's
last glimpse in Guaymas was of Bligh and Hackmuller
earnestly orating to the governor on his portico.   The long
windows of Mrs. Delmar's house were darkened, but one
green blind was raised a moment.   A kerchief fluttered : it
was Dolores's farewell.   While the cavalcade climbed the
sierra, the officer reviewed the hours of his last conference
the preceding evening.   As his head rested on the reclining
cushions, he forgot the bishop's grave cautions, the careful
plans of the circle of friends quietly assembled.   He dismissed his official cares, his pretended explanation, and fell
into a day-dream slumber haunted by Dolores Pesquiera's
smile.   On for hours the train climbed, until the sierra was
passed.   Refreshed in mind by rest, he gazed on the half-
desert land, the mean villages, the scanty cultivation, and
the savage scenery.

Late on the second day he saw the walls of the old castle
of Ures rise before him.   Fields of maize, wheat, peas, and
beans alternated in the winding river-bottom with tobacco,
sugar-cane, and cotton.   The linen-clad peasants, shawled
women, dashing horsemen, wild muleteers, groaning ox-
wains, and long trains of pack-mules with tinkling bells gave
an air of romance to the stony road over which the mail-clad
Spaniards had wearily marched in search of gold.   Silent,
cautious, wary of all, he noted gladly the old romantic town
with the royal escutcheons rudely graven on the mouldering
castle arch-ways.   A cracked bell was clanging from a once
magnificent church, now in the last stages of decay.   The
plaza was silent, save for a few Indian women flitting
ghost-like to vespers.   A loitering crowd of the mean,

stunted, ignorant populace followed his troops into the court-yard.

With profound respect, an officer of the guard ushered him into a guest-chamber overlooking the river.

El Senor Castellan Alvarado was absent, but in an hour would return and pay his respects to the illustrious national guest, the comandante of the great war-vessel of the Norte Americanos.

Wainwright despatched in silence a bountiful repast, and sought the comfort of a hammock. The call of the sentinel on the old walls lulled him to sleep. He woke with a start, to see a dark-eyed priest bending over him. Two whispered words told that the mysterious arm of the Church was over him.

In half an hour the castellan, the visitor, and the bishop's spy were at home over a bottle of mescal. A frank and loyal old soldier, Alvarado was delighted when the padre offered the distinguished visitor his services as cicerone. "I can offer you a little better than this soldier's fare, and will bring you over to breakfast with the castellan."

The rushing river lulled Wainwright to his rest, and the moonlight, streaming into his room, showed him afar the crested sierras and the sparkling stars above them.

"To-morrow, to-morrow," he murmured, "Dolores's token shall unlock her father's heart."

It was with a beating heart that the sailor, next day, followed the castellan through a vaulted stone corridor with double guards. "I will go on before and announce you to the prisoner. He is gloomy, and has seen no one but our friend the padre. Alas, poor Pesquiera! The court meets

next week.   I fear he will never go farther from here than
to the firing-ground on the old plaza.   How many men have
died on its cruel flag-stones !   I will leave you here, Senor
Comandante," said Alvarado at the door.   " I cannot bear
to appear as jailor before a man whom I have saluted with
my regiment and the national colours as our honoured
governor.   His father gave me my first commission, and I
hope the ignominy will be spared me of witnessing the son's
execution by a platoon of my regiment.   Ah, Mexico,
unhappy Mexico !—I will send the sentinel in on his half-
hour rounds.   You can stay as long as you wish."

Wainwright entered the vaulted room where a bearded,
middle-aged man stood moodily gazing on the river from a
grated window.   A straw pallet and a chair were the only
articles of furniture in the cell.

The captive governor turned dark wolfish eyes on the
visitor, as the castellan's feet echoed in retreat on the
corridor.

"Who are you?   Speak !" the prisoner cried, gazing in
wonder at the American's undress naval uniform.

" A friend, who comes to save you," Wainwright answered.

"I know you not," the prisoner sullenly said.   "You
come from Guaymas, from Marquez?"   The eyes read the
young man's very soul.   Wainwright, without a word, placed
the emerald ring in Pesquiera's hand.

The tremulous lips which kissed it faltered, " Poor
Dolores !   An orphan, alone, and in that villain's power !"
He sank into the rude chair and sobbed.

" Guard yourself, my poor friend.   Listen !   You shall
be saved !" the sailor urged.   " Confide in me."

Pesquiera sprang to the window; with a meaning gesture he pointed to the plaza. "Marquez shot my most faithful friends there. I covered my eyes. I heard the crashing volleys. Poor child, Dolores!"

"Rouse yourself! Be a man!" cried Wainwright. "Beware the sentinel! Give me the ring back when you have seen its inscription. Save yourself for your daughter. Look at these!" The young champion of Love placed the lines from Mrs. Delmar and Bishop Dominguez in the prisoner's hand.

A gleam of hope lit up Pesquiera's face. In eager words Wainwright recounted the efforts to bring help near to him. A new life sprang up in the captive's heart.

It was after one visit of the sentinel, who found the two talking placidly of the unexplored Yaqui land, that Mateo, the father, bent his head on his breast in thought.

"Be quick in decision," urged Wainwright. "An accident might ruin all. This is our one chance to make a plan. This villain's suspicions once aroused, he might bring you to trial and execution. I must go soon, to disarm any spies. I have left my ship, for your daughter's sake, to save your life. My honour, my future, are in your hands. Would it not be well to treat with Marquez?"

Pesquiera sadly said, "He would verify the facts, seize the treasure, conquer a way to the mines, and poison me in prison. Pauline Delmar and her child would be ruined. Dolores would be in his power, her birthright confiscated. Welcome death first! Here; I will make all sure while I can."

The hollow-eyed prisoner searched the straw of his

pallet nervously. " Here is the token of the Yaquis.
Guard it with your life. It carries the pact of the idolaters:
it was on the altars of their god. The chiefs swore their
oath to Delmar. My father took it from his dead body.
Padre Francisco kept it for me. I had sworn to throw it
into the river before going out to face the rifles."

"Can I trust Francisco ?" asked Wainwright, examining
the token. It was a rude human figure, three inches in
length, carved from a single piece of the turquoise of the
Colorado River.

" You can trust him in all. He was sent by the bishop
to hear my dying confession. Then the words breathed in
the ear of God's messenger would reach alone my orphaned
child through the grace of our holy Church. I held my
secret to the last. Give the token to Pauline Delmar.
The letters at San Francisco complete the protection of
the two deposits and the mine. All the Yaqui chiefs and
high-priests know this. The idol, his feet still smeared with
the stains of human blood, lies prone in the ruined temple
at Culiacan, but the oath and pact are handed down by
every high-priest and chief of the Yaquis. Listen, my
friend. You are young, brave, true. You have life and
love before you. Swear to me by the mother who bore
you, by the God we worship, that you will guard my
daughter's rights. Justice to the friends who have crossed
a world to try to help a doomed man ! Protection to my
child !"

And Harry Wainwright bent his handsome head, and
kissed a cross the eager father held out. " I swear," he
said, and a far faint glance of Dolores's tender eyes seemed

to shine on him, as the ripple of the river alone broke the stillness.

" Now, quick to write ! " Wainwright produced a note-book from his bosom. The nervous prisoner covered page after page. " It is done," he said. " Now the rest to you. My only hope hangs on a hair. You say your mining friends are gaining an influence over Marquez. He is sly and greedy. Return at once, after a full conference with Padre Francisco. Excite Marquez's cupidity. Tell him of the value of the coal, the silver, the gold, to which I can pilot a small party on the Yaqui River. The buried treasures are safe. With the bishop's help they can be secretly removed. He has a duplicate of the letter to Delmar's widow, with the location of the hiding-places : he keeps it in his sacred archives. They are guarded by bands which are ready day and night. Should I be murdered here, Padre Francisco will bear my last sealed letter to my child. But if you could delay the fiend who thirsts for my blood, and, without arousing suspicion, advise him to bring me to Guaymas and delay the trial so as to gain the valuable news from me, then you might plan my rescue there. I might at the last make terms as to the mine. If he would accept them, I could be perhaps taken to the Yaqui frontier. They might treat for my life. The chiefs might give an entrance to Marquez's men, but only if I live. Should your friends, the miners, make promises to Marquez to excite his greed, your help as the commander of a war-vessel might make him weigh his revenge against a fortune. Once in freedom, I could dictate, I could more than satisfy him. Then my child would be safe, and Delmar's trust fulfilled."

"Senor Pesquiera," said Wainwright, "I shall tell your daughter that you will hold her on your bosom yet. I shall leave to-night and hasten. I shall take Padre Francisco this afternoon to show me the coal-fields. My hasty return will excite Marquez. I shall—I swear I shall succeed in bringing you to Guaymas. The bishop has his quiet influence. Marquez fears a Church he does not obey. It will be a request from Bishop Dominguez that you shall see your child before any final decree. Now, think all over. I will come at evening. Your trust is safe with me, and, as the order for the court is not yet issued, Marquez has a safe opportunity to assemble it there. I swear by your daughter's love that, once at Guaymas, I will save you. Trust a sailor."

"You are a brave and loyal man, comandante. I give you the charge to hand the note-book to the bishop. He can read it to Pauline Delmar, to my daughter, and to you. It contains my order to the bishop to open the secret letters alone with the widow, read them to her, and reseal them. She then will know of the deposits which, in case of my death, belong to my child and to hers. I shall die in honor," said the proud Mexican.

The clattering of a horse's hoofs aroused Wainwright, loath to leave the prisoner. It was a mounted messenger, who dashed by with a dozen lancers, and the man urging on his steed was Basil Goodloe.

The heavy tread of Castellan Alvarado resounded in the

corridor. He entered, casting his eyes in sympathy upon the prisoner. "A despatch for the Senor Comandante. The officer is with Padre Francisco."

Wainwright's heart beat wildly. Was it a wreck, an accident to his vessel? He tore open the envelope. It was a long blue strip with a cabled order from the Secretary of the Navy: "Remain at Guaymas, subject to the orders of the minister at the city of Mexico. Your ship may be needed at Mazatlan. Report receipt."

"Ha! I shall use this on Marquez to excite his fears. I'll leave Goodloe here to make the pretended examination," Wainwright mused. "I may come back and say adieu to Senor Pesquiera," said the commander. "I must return to Guaymas to-night, but I will leave an officer here to close up my explorations." With a meaning glance at Pesquiera, Wainwright dashed away to join his friend in the priest's secluded home.

When the lancers wound down out of the forgotten old city of Ures that night, Pesquiera knew that another friend was near, that Padre Francisco had an ally.

"I bear your daughter a father's blessing," Wainwright had said. "Remember that I shall not rest until you are conveyed to Guaymas. I can send a courier to my fellow-officer here, and through Padre Francisco you will have the tidings instantly. You can have any message despatched to me at once by him. Let the priest write it in Latin. My officer will forward it as an official despatch. The bishop shall decide and act for you."

With grateful tears, Pesquiera saw his strangely consti-tuted champion ride out on an errand of life and death.

1

Basil Goodloe and Father Francisco roved unchallenged over field and glen, and waited, counting the hours, for tidings of Wainwright's mission.

When the commander dashed into Guaymas, waking the sleepy plaza to unwonted life, he drove straightway to the Governor. Half an hour later, Marquez called an extraordinary council, and ere night the courier who bore the order for Pesquiera's removal to Guaymas carried a huge despatch with the navy seal to gladden the prisoner's heart.

CHAPTER VIII

BISHOP DOMINGUEZ was in deepest thought when Commander Wainwright, muffled in a boating-cloak, was admitted at the side wicket of the priest's house on the evening of his return. The hour of action drew near.

"My son, do you bring us good tidings?" anxiously queried the prelate. He led the officer into an inner room, where Pauline Delmar sat waiting, her fair face haggard with intense emotion.

"All is well, reverend bishop. The 'Constance' has returned. My ship's affairs are arranged. Bligh, May, and Hackmuller are dining this evening with Governor Marquez, who is now eager to enter into the great speculation of the coal-fields, the future opening of the Yaqui River, and secretly into the acquisition of the mysterious mines. My friends have promised me to keep him in a fever of growing enthusiasm : it will divert his brooding revenge. Commander Goodloe will return to-morrow night. I shall then expect May and himself to remain apparently busied on the yacht, in actual readiness for any movement. My ensign has had several friendly parleys with the Yaquis and obtained their permission to enter the river with the steam

I 2

launch for an examination. I now submit myself to you. We must devise at once our final plan of action."

"Hasten, my brave friend," cried Mrs. Delmar. "I will make any sacrifice to save Pesquiera's life."

"We must have one guiding mind," said Wainwright. "I will act at the right time. I will answer with my life for May and Goodloe : we are one in heart. But time presses. Let the bishop guide. He would never be suspected ; he cannot be punished ; he is safe. The voice of the Church is powerful here even yet."

"Then, my children, hear me," the bishop gravely began. "There must be no suspicion of united action or any friendship not growing from our daily life. Above all, Dolores must remain in the convent. Your daughter, madame, can take up a temporary residence there. It is natural these young girls should seek each other's society. Your daughter will be safe there. The commander can protect them both ; I could trust them to him to go on the war-vessel to Mazatlan in case of trouble here. A chosen nun could go with them : that will blind Marquez. He will be forced to apply to me to communicate with the prisoner's child. If the trial comes on, I can work on Marquez, and keep a priest in Pesquiera's cell. Thus we will have a line of safe communication open to him always. You can receive your friends, singly, on your vessel, and come alone to me at any time. You, madame, must remain as you are, surrounded by my faithful domestics. Now the mining promoters are free to range the town and watch the exterior, as well as spy on Marquez's official circle. We have one great question before us : shall we try first to save the treasure, or Pesquiera's life ? "

" The prisoner first, the treasure later," cried the widow and the sailor, mindful of loving Dolores, hungry for a father's love.

" Yes, you are right," said the bishop. " Under the extraordinary power of a Mexican state governor, martial law being in force, Marquez can convene the court at his will, control the proceedings, and send the condemned to immediate execution. If we had an agent at the city of Mexico now, we could, by sharing the future proceeds of the mine, get an order to have Pesquiera sent there for trial. But Marquez, sly and adroit as he is, would delay the order, which would come to him, rush the trial, and report the victim as summarily executed. The hidden mine alone delays his speedy vengeance. If we could effect Pesquiera's rescue, nothing easier than to treat at a distance. Marquez would come to terms ; for in that case we could either intrigue at the capital or bargain with him direct. We must work at the mine. Yet there is a tremendous risk of property to consider. Shall I tell the commander our secret ? "

" I trust him as I do Commander Goodloe. Tell him." Mrs. Delmar placed her hand in Wainwright's. " You bear own country's golden leaves on your shoulders. You will be true."

" In life and death," said the sailor.

" My son, there is a cave, submerged at ordinary tide, under the middle island of Trinidad. In it, sewed up in raw-hide ore bags, is the secret hoard of the great governor

and my dead friend Achille Delmar.   There are one
hundred sacks of five thousand eagle dollars each.   This
treasure, too considerable to conceal in the city, was
accumulated to meet state needs or the unusual demands of
the Yaquis.   The entrance is possible only for a light boat
at the lowest monthly tide.   Its secret is safe."

"I will answer for its removal to my vessel if needs be,"
said Wainwright, resolutely.

The bishop continued : "That is not all.   The annual
tributes of the Yaquis, in golden bars, lie concealed under
the stone flagging of the main council-hall of the government house.   There is a pillar supporting the central span
of the roof, in a direct line with the two great doors.   It
rests on a masonry foundation of burned bricks.   The
flagging has been removed and recemented.   Bricks have
been loosened from the foundation prism of that pillar.
There are eight hundred and seventy-three bars walled in
in that underground recess of masonry.   One-half is
Pesquiera's fortune, the other half the dowry of Delmar's
child.   It is a fortune, this golden hoard.   To reach it
there is almost impossible.   The house is guarded ; it is
thronged with Marquez's brutal soldiery, and his staff hold
riot there day and night.   If we had it, we could use a
part to bribe Marquez, and hold back the secret of the
mine."   The bishop sighed.   "You know all, my son."

"I'll get it.   Remember Franz von Trenck's journey
through Vienna from his dungeon-cell in a coffin.   All is
possible.   We must save Pesquiera, and reach the treasure
too.   If we had either, we could save the other.   Stay : I
will reconnoitre this place.   I will tell the governor I may

be ordered away, and we must hasten to act as to the
Yaqui River project the moment Goodloe is here. Wait
for me." Wainwright seized his boat-cloak, sword, and
cap, and cried, "I have an idea I dare not breathe
yet!"

His springing steps led him to the government house.
"If it is not rock, then we may fool this fellow. I'll ask
him to go on a cruise with me as far as the Yaqui River.
Then our friends could work in his absence. This golden
hoard once in our hands, the secret of the cave would keep
safely."

The lights were gleaming in the governor's council-room.
With a hasty word to an officer in waiting to request a few
moments' conversation, Wainwright sprang around the
corner to where Professor Ernest Hackmuller's experimental
reduction-works and assay-office were temporarily located
on the lot volunteered by the governor. A rapid survey of
the site proved the practicability of the daring scheme
burning in his brain.

Masses of machinery lay around, the *disjecta membra* of
old importations. One or two foundation-pits were already
excavated. The sailor sprang down into one breast-deep.
"Glorious!" he muttered. "It is a soft clay."

His brow was unruffled as he was ushered into the
presence of the great man of the hour. Seated at a long
table covered with papers and maps, Bligh and Hackmuller were deep in a conference with the governor.

Wainwright held his breath as he crossed the hall. His
nervous tread rung on the stone-flagged floor. His heart
beat quickly as he glanced at the one great masonry pillar

based on a dressed gray stone in the centre of the hall.
A rudely-framed pine truss rested on the pillar. Two
similar ones occupied central points on the median line of
the long hall. "Twenty feet at most! Hackmuller's lot
adjoins the room!"

Suppressing his excitement, he said, " I beg a thousand
pardons, my dear governor, but I am called suddenly to
make a cruise to the mouth of the Yaqui and below. As I
have secret orders from the Department, which may change
my head-quarters, I wished to invite you as my guest on
this short cruise. As my cabin is of moderate size, and the
ward-room crowded, I ask you alone. I should like to have
the chance of privately advising with you as to the Yaqui
project. Our minister at Mexico will be instructed by the
State and Navy Departments, and the President of Mexico
shall hear of your public-spirited plans."

"When would you sail, comandante?" inquired the
governor hesitatingly.

"As near noon as your Excellency would honour me.
My steam launch will await you at that hour."

"To be frank, comandante, I am anxious to go with
you. But one important matter claims my attention. The
state prisoner, Pesquiera, will reach here to-morrow. I have
to examine the charges and summon the court for the trial
of the unhappy man. However, in my absence, the public
prosecutor might perhaps arrange the charges and prepare
his evidence."

The Mexican smoked in gloomy silence. Wainwright
breathlessly awaited his decision.

"You will not be absent longer than a week?"

"About a week, your Excellency," replied the sailor, with quick mental estimates of tunnel-digging.

"Then I will accept your offer. I will be ready at noon."

Happiness gleamed in the sailor's eyes as he bowed himself out, carelessly saying, "Bligh, bring the professor and stay on board to-night. My boat will wait till midnight for you. Don't fail, as I wish to talk mines with you."

The anxious bishop was electrified at Wainwright's flush of triumph. In a short half-hour the commander had formulated a plan.

"Dear lady," he said to Mrs. Delmar, "I will be here at eleven to-morrow. I wish to see you and the bishop then. At twelve I go on board with the governor for a week's trip. Pesquiera will be here to-morrow. I will secure the golden treasure, and the prisoner is safe a week longer. Now sleep in peace, and hope for the best. If I only have sailor's luck, I will bring you out safely. Bid Dolores be of good cheer. Her father shall not die if I have to raid the town. Tell her I say so."

As Mrs. Delmar said good-night to the eager sailor she read in his kindling eye his secret.

"His heart is interested," she said. "He has a secret plan already. Ah, he is in the royal season of love and hope."

The good bishop sighed. The roses of his own dead youth bloomed again.

Long after midnight, the untiring Wainwright walked his quarter-deck with Bligh and the old German.

"I understand you now, commander. I will have a

little working-plan ready before you are on shore. The governor will easily understand that I wish to drain my arastra out into the main street channel, and that I must have a fall to clear my débris. His permission will be easily gained. I will have the passage-way ready on your return."

" It will secure your fortune. I can say no more. Now, gentlemen, let us sleep. We must meet Goodloe and May to morrow early."

" And I will be a general outside guard and utility-man," said Bligh, as they spliced the main brace.

The morning gun brought the commander to his feet. His cutter lay ready when his coffee was despatched, and a dozen bronzed blue-jackets bent to their oars as he approached the Constance.

An hour later he left the yacht. " Phil, this is a life-and-death matter. I depend on you. All Bligh and the professor can do is to watch and make ready for my later work. To you and Goodloe I entrust the ladies, and the execution of the bishop's plans. He will find a way of secretly communicating with Pesquiera. Get on shore, bring Goodloe quietly to the bishop's house, and wait there for me. The blue-jackets on shore will be under Goodloe's command. The Constance is your special trust."

There was undisguised astonishment in the eyes of the bishop and the anxious widow when Wainwright detailed before them his daring plan. Goodloe and May agreed as to its feasibility. " It is our only chance," was the chorus of the allies.

" Now I will escort the governor on board with due

pomp. Before we return, I will work on his mind to have Pesquiera sent to the border for a conference. Give me that idol and your husband's picture, as well as Pesquiera's. I will try to influence the chiefs."

" You will find my missionary priest awaiting you at the river mouth. You can trust him," said the bishop, significantly. He approached Wainwright and whispered in his ear, " I shall at once see the governor and obtain permission to visit the prisoner alone on behalf of his daughter. Also I will learn the exact side and location of the opening to the crypt under that pillar. Go, in God's name, my son. You will say adieu to the young ladies? They are in the adjoining room."

Anita Delmar found a few words to exchange with her returned lover, while in the farthest corner of the room Wainwright kissed the white hands of Dolores.

" Do you trust me?" he whispered; and the maiden dropped her eyes under his burning glance, and murmured, " You are my only hope. My life is yours if you save my father."

At high noon, while the tall mast of the Ranger shivered under the jar of the bellowing salute announcing that his Excellency José Marquez was approaching, a haggard prisoner looked out of the grated window of his dungeon on the hill, and saw the flotilla escorting his foe in state to the national vessel.

He dropped on his knees, as the iron door swung open, and a gentle voice whispered, " Be comforted, my son. Rise. It is your friend and pastor." For the bishop stood by his side.

As the Ranger swept out majestically between the islands of the entrance, a score of brawny blue-jackets marched jauntily into Hackmuller's enclosure and reported to Commander Goodloe. The German had easily gained the governor's permission for the excavation. Marquez, flattered by the public honours so liberally showered on him, was unsuspicious, and had even forgotten to direct the preparation of the charges against Pesquiera.

The Ranger's absence restored the dreamy quiet of the town. No signs of life appeared on the dainty Constance save the unloading of the bulk of her heavy coarse trading-goods, which were publicly deposited in the warehouses of the navy agent.

" What are these devilish Gringos hanging round here for ? " grumbled Port-Captain Estrada to Diego the pilot.

" I cannot fathom it. But there is some villany in the wind, and I will unearth it. They are getting ready for some cruise."

" Remember your signal—two red lanterns. La Democrata will give chase and seize her. I will entrap these fellows as soon as the Yankee war vessel goes away."

The Ranger lay securely anchored in the bay at the mouth of the Yaqui River, a week after her leaving Guaymas. Under an awning on the quarter-deck the commander and his guest were intently watching the shore.

" Will they never make the signal for the conference ? " grumbled Marquez, as Wainwright laid down his telescope.

" Patience, my honoured friend," said the sailor. " These wild natives are cautious. Your presence is known to them in some way : their canoemen may have recognized you. I trust to the missionaries' influence. Ah, there goes the signal at last. Call away my cutter," said Wainwright to the watch-officer, as a dense column of blue smoke rose from a point at the mouth of the river. "They are ready at last. Let us prepare to go on shore."

The governor was eager, for he had come to a private arrangement with Wainwright, representing his mining friends, to push on every plan of co-operation. No flicker of doubt harassed the greedy ruler's mind. "If we can only make these strange beings tractable, I can soon discover the location of the mines," said Marquez, as he seated himself in the boat. "Then I will hold those points with my soldiers, rush in a column of troops, and privately denounce the land and mines in our joint interest. But I am anxious to get back to Guaymas, for I must question that fellow Pesquiera. He knows much of these secret matters, and I will put him to the test. I will give him one chance. If he does not yield up the information, I will push his trial and shoot him like a dog. He *shall* yield."

"But if he does, what is his reward?" asked the American, with assumed indifference.

"Oh, I might ask the government to commute his sentence to life-imprisonment and relieve the confiscation in favour of his daughter. She's a beauty," said Marquez, with a leer. "She would be rich then."

Smothering his disgust, Wainwright thanked God that the missionary had delayed the chiefs. They knew well now that a messenger was coming in secret, under the midnight oath sworn on the idol, to treat about their future. For they were loyal to the son of the great Pesquiera, and their traders and spies had told them that he was languishing in the prison at Guaymas: so a secret council of their high-priests and chiefs had been called to his aid.

"Here we are," cried the sailor, as the boat ran high up on the silvery sands of the river bay. At a distance, grouped under the mahogany trees, a weird assemblage of the glittering-eyed and defiant Yaquis watched the disembarkment of the unarmed boat-party. A black-robed priest came down the strand to welcome the head of the state and the secret agent of the powerless prisoner. It was an anxious moment for Wainwright. How could he meet the chiefs alone? One misstep would ruin all. "They are a peculiar people, your Excellency," softly said the missionary friar. "I will bring three or four of the war-chiefs to you. You can talk alone with them here, in sight of your boat's crew and these people. All is safe. The commander and myself will withdraw and spend half an hour with the others. It will reassure them.

"Do they know my power?—that I govern Sonora?—that my flag is the national ensign of Mezico?" said Marquez, with some pomp.

"Your Excellency, they all know of your power, and several of them have been in Guaymas and seen you at the head of your troops. You will be treated with the respect due your rank. The chiefs will confer alone with you."

Marquez nodded his head. "Bring the chiefs down, padre. They speak Spanish?"

"Quite well, your Excellency. They are bred to Spanish as a second tongue. Only to the born Yaqui is their sacred birthright, the unwritten language, ever confided. They use it only with each other. It is the key of their mysterious life, handed down from generation to generation."

Striding over the pearl-shell-strewed beach, Wainwright kept pace with the black-robed agent of Bishop Dominguez, who said, "They will hear him and demand a conference with Pesquiera, whom they know still as the rightful governor—their friend, the son of their great protector. My dark friends think Mateo Pesquiera an hereditary ruler."

"Then he is saved!" cried Wainwright. His blood was tingling in every vein. "Did the bishop instruct you how to act?"

"Yes," replied the priest. "I have given Marquez three or four wary old chieftans, who will insist on a free conference here with Pesquiera. I will take you to the high-priests and the real leaders." Drawing into the forest amphitheatre, Wainwright was led to a circle of silent seniors gathered round a gray old headman. "I will leave you now," whispered the missionary. "Be brief."

While Wainwright made his salutations in Spanish, he could see, as he turned his head, the doubtful embassy surrounding the governor.

"The black-robe has told us you have a message from him who is dead,—a token to show us," quavered the aged spokesman. "Our friend, his son, sends you to us? What sign did he give to you?"

The officer extended the idol, to which the circle bowed in sudden awe. With reverence, Wainwright held it up. It was taken by the high-priest, who kissed it, and handed around the dusky circle. In silence the old Indian returned it. Wainwright solemnly restored it to his bosom. He exhibited the picture of Achille Delmar and of the dead magnate, the great war governor Pesquiera. A murmur of astonishment ran around the circle.

"What would you with us? We are faithful to our friend. We would look on his face again."

Casting furtive glances at the council on the open beach, the sailor told his story.

"Beware of that man. He would take your land from you. He holds your friend in his power, and, unless you hinder, he will take his life."

To the high-priest the commander rapidly unfolded his plan. "I will have help here. I will know of his coming. The black-robe will be here. He will give you the signal. We will bear him away from you, to the sea." Wainwright pointed to his ship. "And he will come again and serve you. The black-robes alone will know."

"It is well! Tell him my young men will aid. Now, my son, send the black-robe to me. The sun passes the line : we have a long way to our homes, and no one must know our road. Our tongues are silent until you send us the black-robe or bring us the token. Tell him the Yaquis will save him, even if we take him there." The old priest pointed to the towering blue mountains. Far in their dim gorges the Yaqui trails, with infinite doublings and hidings, lead to the fastnesses where no Spaniard ever trod. Cave and gorge were traversed by the way. The path led over trees left to be rolled into the chasms at a signal, and where ladders of twisted vines were drawn across by a cord wrapped around a stone ball.

Placing his hands on the American's head, the high-priest cried, "Go in peace, friend of our friend. We will keep the faith never broken since our brother left us at Culiacan to go to the great lakes in the valley."

Wainwright saluted the dusky chieftains, who disappeared in the forest shades. When he turned from gazing at Marquez, the aged high-priest was gone. It was as if the earth had swallowed him.

The embassy filed past the officer as he retraced his steps. The governor was already in the cutter. The priest pressed Wainwright's hand silently. "I rejoin the bishop by land. I will be there before you," he whispered.

Marquez sat in the stern-sheets, eyeing the lonely shore with a malignant scowl. "If I had my way I would hem the whole nation in with a cordon of troops and carry fire and sword to their innermost haunts."

"What ties your hands?" queried the commander.

"The general government has ordered me to keep quiescent. Ten thousand soldiers' bones are scattered over the yet unconquered Yaqui land. We have sent in small columns, and never seen a return, save a few frightened and wounded stragglers. The rest lie cold in those dark fastnesses."

He dipped his hand in the sparkling water and mused gloomily till the quarter-deck wooed him to its comforts.

Over a luncheon served *al fresco* the baffled statesman told the story of his defeat. The screw of the cruiser was slowly revolving, and the Yaqui Point was soon a blue hazy cloud as they sped southward. Wainwright begged for a day's run farther south to complete a personal reconnaissance. "It will give time for the priest to return, and for this brute's anger to cool," he reflected.

Marquez walked the quarter-deck in indecision before he confided in his American friend. "I hardly know how to handle these fellows," said he, after a second cigar. "They will not acknowledge me as governor, and until they have seen Pesquiera in my power they doubt my authority. The chiefs agree that if he will sanction my proposals they will consider the privilege of entry to the river regions, but no settlement in their reserved territory. It would be an opening wedge to hold the river. I might introduce a force of men, gradually increasing them. But, if armed, the Yaquis would oppose them; if unarmed, they might fall on them and massacre them. The great point is to open the river. I would like to know how far up a boat drawing five feet can enter. Can you not send your steam launch to explore the river quietly? Your people will be safe. Then we might make the coal-mines and the river trade a means of discovering the gold-regions. I could hoodwink them. After I had located these, I would march in a strong body of troops and hold them by the sword; but I must have the river as a base. We could never cope with them in the woods."

"Will you use this man Pesquiera's influence?" asked Wainwright, with an appearance of unconcern.

"Yes. I have made up my mind to telegraph for La Democrata. I don't like to risk her on the cape coast, for she is our only war-vessel on the Pacific. Her engines are weak, and she is slow, only seven to eight knots. But I can trust her commander. I dare not let the central government know of my plans. They might send some man to replace me."

"Seven knots! My launch makes fourteen easily," Wainwright said to himself. "I think I have a bit of work for mad Jack Crowninshield."

CHAPTER IX.

BUSYING himself with suddenly discovered important affairs, Wainwright ignored his guest, save in the duties of ceremonious hospitality, until the Ranger was speeding back to Guaymas. The governor smoked and mused upon his dark plans.

"I think there is no further need of elaborating my idea," soliloquized the commander. "I will post May and Good-loe, and send them out of port. My launch can coast down in ten hours. This adept in deceit would use Pesquiera as a decoy, gain a foothold on the river, murder Pesquiera when the secret was his own, and butcher the Indians. I think I can show him a Yankee trick. I'll try."

The officer's latent disgust never pierced the veil of his punctilious politeness. "It will take a week for La Demo-crata to arrive," said Marquez. "My good friend, you can have your exploration party on the ground and at work before then. Your boat can go up fifty or sixty miles cer-tainly, and the Indians with their canoes can take them farther up. Call on me at the government house. I will give you every facility. I do not wish my progressive ideas to be used by others to endanger my power."

The city of Guaymas was *en fête* as the American cruiser proudly steamed in and with due display gave back the ruler of Sonora.

May and Goodloe sprang on board as the anchor rattled down.

"What cheer?" whispered Wainwright, his heart in his mouth.

"All is well! We are ready for you. Bligh and Hackmuller have fenced in their premises, shutting out the curious. Our boat is clean and clear, ready for any service." Goodloe was radiant as he spoke.

"See here, old man; something has happened to you," said the commander. Basil wrung his hand as he whispered, "You are to be best man, for my reward waits only our arrival at San Francisco with Pesquiera."

"I suppose you will get it, Basil," laughed Harry. "Sailor's luck! But, by Jove, old fellow, you will have to earn it. I'm going to escort his Local Majesty to the shore. Bring Phil at once to the bishop's. Take another boat." The swift oarsmen were all too sluggish for the lover of Dolores.

"I am happy as a man can be!" cried Wainwright, entering the room where the friends were gathered. "Marquez has given me exemption from all port regulations. I have *carte blanche.*" He failed to mention his most recent happiness in a few whispered greetings with the dark-eyed beauty sitting with beating heart, listening for his footstep.

"We must not lose a moment. To-morrow I send off Jack Crowninshield with the steam launch. My engineers will warrant her condition. Your priest, reverend bishop

may slip on board my vessel at a word from you. I will
answer for the Yaquis. To-morrow I land a party on
Trinidad. It will be dead low tide in three days. I will
put some triangulation parties around the harbor to occupy
the gossips. I will take my own boat's crew, and you, Phil,
can busy yourself with getting ballast for your boat, for a
cruise. I will see that you have barges. I can give you
sixty days' water from my tanks, and extra supplies.
Leaving your trading cargo here will hoodwink them. I
will personally handle this affair on shore. I have the excuse to be with Marquez to await the Democrata. Then,
reverend bishop, if God grants us the grace to see Mateo
Pesquiera landed on the beach, he will sleep a free man on
blue water the same night."

"But will not Marquez's rage be violent? I fear him!"
Mrs. Delmar shuddered.

"First, my dear lady," said Wainwright, calmly. "the
news will not reach here till Pesquiera is safe. Goodloe
and May will be on the high seas, and the young ladies in
the convent. The bishop is invincibly fortified in his rank.
If there is suspicion, it will fall on me : I can bear the brunt
of the storm. I ask now only the utmost prudence. We
must not pay the faintest attention to the case of Senor
Pesquiera, for the governor confided to me that the guarded
visit would be kept a secret. The moment the Democrata
is ready, the prisoner will be smuggled on board. He is
safe until he comes back here."

"And must this attempt be made without a farewell between the father and daughter?" asked Mrs. Delmar, her
eyes filled with tears.

"We are in God's hands. It must be so," said Wain-wright, as he drew the bishop aside.

"Tell Pesquiera to give you now the secret of the cave; for to-morrow night I go alone, and the next night the treasure must be removed. The tide serves then. We have but six hours to do it. The boat might be shut in the cavern and the men lost. That would lead to discovery. Tell him to have no fear. I will be the first to take the risk."

Long after Dolores had sobbed herself to sleep in Anita's sheltering arms, Wainwright sat in conference with the man who thirsted for her father's blood.

"Your friend Professor Hackmuller is a wonderful man, commander," said Marquez. "He is gathering ores and samples of every lead in the State. Ah! you Americanos! I see through all your designs!"

Wainwright started.

"Your amigo Bligh, with his great bank behind him, uses this old scientist to test all these ores, and then you and his friends will buy the mines on their real valuation. We are a simple people. You know all. But we will hold the sovereignty of our land."

"You can certainly see, governor, that it is to your interest to aid these men of money and science," artfully interposed the sailor. "In making their fortunes you will be enriched."

"What more can I do, my friend?" said Marquez, drawing a cup of mescal from an exquisite old Chihuahua flagon. "I give them the password every night. I have allowed them to work night and day. I give the officer of the guard orders to let them pass without question. I am always at home to them. You see, commander, there is a prejudice against Americans here since Walker the filibuster stormed La Paz in '56. He and Raousset de Boulbon ravaged our fair Sonora. But when Henry Crabbe and his invaders were destroyed at Arispè, your adventurers took warning from the pile of heads around the old adobe. Ah, yes, the Mexican eagle fleshed his talons there. But drink with me to the success of the professor,—it will build up my power, —and to your own !"

"Most heartily !" cried Harry, with a strange gleam in his eyes. He drained his glass.

"And now, a glass to your lovely Sonora ladies. I am told the city of Culiacan has the purest type of Castilian beauty in Mexico," Wainwright gayly answered.

"Yes and no," spiritedly replied Marquez. "There's one here whose loveliness is unmatched,—a bride for an emperor ! In two years, Dolores Pesquiera may rule the richest domain of Mexico."

"Your enemy's daughter !" ejaculated the horror-stricken Wainwright.

"Oh, I'll find a way to dry her eyes. I may hold her father after sentence. The sly old bishop can arrange it. I could build up Church and State again. She is a pearl of loveliness."

"I must be off," cried Wainwright, hastily seizing his cloak and sword. The heat-lightning was playing, and a storm was brewing in the mountains.

"Be my guest," said Marquez.

"Ah, no, my dear governor. I shall have steam

raised. A tornado may visit us. My ship's safety is my honour."

As Wainwright went out into the night, he clutched his sword. "I could have cut him down for his insolence. To-morrow I will win the first trick,—Dolores. I will bear her out of this wolf's den. She is mine alone. Now to the work."

The Ranger's boats were everywhere next day. Parties with flags and signals moved from crest to headland, from point to island. Foremost in activity, the busy commander darted in his swift launch from station to station.

A brief visit to the bishop concluded, Wainwright stood, chronometer in hand, on the lowest crags of the central peak of Trinidades. His boat's crew was sounding every quarter of the compass around the deserted rocky isle.

"Facing the north, the Tetas de Cabra in a line, two tongue-shaped rocks running out into the sea," he read from a little slip of parchment. "An immense boulder like a helmet, the entrance open behind it from either side."

"'Tis the very spot! At eleven to-night it will be dead low water; to-morrow night the lowest of the month. Yes, I'll have a rope ladder, lights, port-fires, lanterns. The party, Phil, Basil, and my own man, no more. I'll soon find the truth of the fable. I don't like to take Basil away from that blossom of love, Anita, but he must help me to success."

"Ten o'clock, and all's well!" the Mexican sentinels cried as "Four bells!" rang out. It was a star-lit night, and the bay lay smooth as oil, for the storm had passed over.

"Now for the cave!" said Wainwright, as he beckoned to May and Goodloe. The three friends left the cabin together. Clad in rough garb and booted high, each man carried a knife and revolver under his boatswain's great-coat. At the side, Wainwright's man sat holding the lightest gig at the gangway.

At a nod from Harry, Phil May, who had grasped an oar, gave way with his mate, the old factotum. The boat glided over the swelling glassy green bay like a phantom.

"All the things on board, Davis?" questioned the commander.

"Ay, ay, sir, right as a trivet," answered the old salt, rolling his quid, as he grumbled, " A night expedition ! Blast me, it's a queer lay-out !"

"Look here, Goodloe," whispered Wainwright, "to morrow you see that all is ready to get the Constance in racing trim. You can send up your topmasts and step your bowsprit in half a day. All that house business can be knocked down flat and thrown overboard, and your boats swung inside and lashed on deck. You may need every inch of canvas if you have to run for it. There's but one chance in this whole scheme, and it will never return. Pesquiera's instant death would follow an alarm. Then Marquez would call it suicide."

" All right, Harry : we will be clean as if we raced for the Queen's Cup."

" Another thing : I don't like that fellow Diego. I'll call him on board the Ranger and keep him there, as if by accident. I'll tell him I want to have him guide my harbour-parties."

"Good !" nodded Basil.

"Way enough ! Here we are !" cried Wainwright.

Springing to the bow, he flashed a dark lantern. "Two feet of water yet. All right."

The party landed at the crag. In the calm night the boat rode just afloat at the outer edge of the little bay.

"Phil, you stay here with Davis," he whispered. "Basil will come with me. Secure the boat with the painter."

Springing out on the sand, Wainwright saw at a glance that the helmet rock was dry. Attaching one end of a ball of light spun yarn to an oar laid across the bow in the rowlocks, he said, "If I want you, we will give three pulls ; then follow up the line. Be careful."

May was all excitement. "Look out for yourself, for God's sake, Harry!" he cried. There was a laugh as the dauntless sailor disappeared, a dark lantern in one hand and a boarding-pike in the other. Goodloe was at his side.

Once behind the helmet rock, the explorers flashed their lanterns. Before them lay a burrowed entrance, beneath which a man by crouching might enter. "The cave's here, anyway," cried Harry, as he disappeared in the narrow passage.

Ankle-deep in pools of water, the cautious comrades followed the turns of a cleft in the soft rock, where the wind-lashed waves had eaten their way under Trinidades. Groping over slippery sea-weed, the sailors noted the deepening pools and the enlarging cavern. After an easy turn they stood in a vaulted room some fifty feet in height and double that in irregular extent.

"Turn on all the light," cried Wainwright, as their eyes roved over the cave.

"Give me a port-fire." The commander flashed it, and

the brilliant steady glare lit up a great black pool in the centre of the cave and revealed a series of irregular ledges around its sides.

"My God! what's that?" yelled Goodloe, as a terrific agitation of the water lashed its black depths into foam. They had sprung to a high shelf for safety. A huge, greasy-looking, greenish-white body gleamed out of the shallow pool, and with a terrific swirl threw the brine over them.

"Keep away! It's a big devil of a basking shark caught in here by the tide!" cried Wainwright, springing to a more remote place. Goodloe followed him, and stumbled over an irregular object.

"Here you are. It surely is true. See here, Harry!" Goodloe's voice was triumphant as he ripped a stout hide sack with his boat-knife and held up a handful of broad Mexican dollars.

Wainwright was eagerly roving from place to place. Piled high above the blackened sea-stained level of the highest tide lay the heavy sacks, with the mouldering hair clinging to the tough hide.

"Thank God, this part is done." They crouched behind a ledge and watched the frantic shark tearing from side to side in his impotent rage. "I'll settle that fellow with a stick of dynamite to-morrow night."

"Don't venture," cried Goodloe. "It might bring down the loose rocks of the roof. A couple of men with spears and lights will keep him away. The long-boat's crew can carry this out,—four men to a sack. Leave one of the ballast barges over here, and the launch can tow it to the schooner. I'll give the men leave. You can have a ballast-barge towed alongside, and we will have these sacks piled away on the keelson of the Constance, and covered before they return."

Throwing the expiring port-fire into the pool where the hungry shark lurked, Wainwright said, "I will not leave this a moment till the work is done. My men can blast off a hundred tons of stuff to-morrow afternoon."

Picking their way out by the cord, the friends groped in the semi-darkness to the waiting boat.

"It will be lower yet to-morrow night. We will bring a couple of rifles and shoot his sharkship. But he has been a good sentinel. It's a rare night's work," said Harry, as he passed his flask and lit a cheroot.

"I am distressed not to be able to dine with you to-night, governor," answered Commander Wainwright, as he sat at ease the next day with Marquez. "But I have some star observations to take. I have some ballast-parties working over at Trinidades. If it were to-morrow night!" The sailor's voice was politely regretful.

"Just the thing. I have a despatch. La Democrata will be here by noon, and I shall ask her officers to meet you and your gallant subordinates."

"On behalf of my juniors I thank you. I accept gladly," said Wainwright, bowing.

"If I succeed to-night, to-morrow morning I will burrow under my host's dining-hall. It's a rare chance. The whole town will be *en fête* to welcome Mexico's only Pacific war-vessel. And I can get a good look at her. If international courtesy permits, I may judge how fast they can push her. Pesquiera's life may hang on that."

"My son," said the bishop, when Wainwright had finished his brief recital, "I shall be on my knees imploring Heaven's protection for you to-night.   The governor will have a private interview with Pesquira to-morrow.   He has confided to me that he will send him to the Yaqui land, but with orders to the commander of La Democrata to shoot him forthwith if he betrays Mexican State secrets or stirs up sedition.   He will be landed with a guard."   The bishop's voice trembled.   "Our hopes, our hearts, all hang on your wisdom and energy."

Wainwright told the prelate of Marquez's dark plans to consolidate his fortunes by a forced marriage with his victim's heiress.   The old man leaned his silvered brows on his thin hands and moaned, "Ah, the tiger !   Barrios did the same in Guatemala, and God's vengeance overtook him. You must thwart the plan."

"Shelter her, reverend bishop.   Watch over her.   I will rescue her by force if you ask me to."   Harry Wainwright's fighting blood was up.

At ten o'clock, a flotilla of boats left the Ranger's side. From the shore was wafted the sound of flute, violin, and guitar, for a grand fandango was delighting the crew of the Constance.

Philip May, sweeping the bay with his night-glass, noted the launch, towing a substantial barge, glide by.   Another lay moored at the beach of Trinidad.   The cutter and the captain's gig bore Wainwright's men.   In half an hour the twinkling of lights around the beach at Trinidad proved that Wainwright was at work.

Two hours later he sprang on board the yacht's deck.

Behind his fleet gig, the sturdy little steam launch was towing two heavily-laden barges. The cutter's crew ranged up alongside.

"Let the cutter report on ship, boatswain," said Wainwright, and he whispered a few words. "Tell 'your men they'll have a three days' liberty next week and a twenty-dollar piece to liven it up for each. Silence as to our boat affairs."

"We give no points up to them greasers," said the stout sailor, as he sprang to the yacht's side and steered his tried men home.

"All right, Phil! Quick, now, to the whips. Tumble up, men," cried Wainwright, in a ringing voice. "Is your whip all rigged, Phil?"

"Yes, and both hatches open. All clear for you," replied the yachtsman, throwing off his coat and calling his two men.

The steam launch safely swung the two barges alongside. Wainwright's cutter crew lashed them securely to the yacht's side. After a brief inspection of the yacht's hold, the alert commander mustered his forces. Goodloe, his man, and Wainwright's sprang to the dangling tackles.

"Here goes the first," whispered Harry, as two stout men swung up a bulky sack, which disappeared in the dark hatch, to be seized by Ah Sam and the other faithful retainer below.

"We had to empty two dozen cartridges into the white shark to quiet him. Did you hear us?" said Harry, pausing for a rest, for May and himself were aiding now.

"Not a sound. Is all unsuspected?" May asked.

"Not a hitch anywhere. My men may think it is ore, or salt, or some smuggled goods. They are trusty."

Before the strains of the dance-music ceased and lights began to drop off one by one along the squalid beach-row of the port, the hidden treasure was ranged in a double line of sacks on each side of the keel.

"I can breathe freely now!" cried the commander. The steam launch had towed away the empty barge. May, Goodloe, and the triumphant Wainwright smoked their cigars in wakeful occupancy of the deck, as their hearty servitors covered the precious lines of specie-bags with broken rock and gravel from the ballast-barge. In an hour the rock covering was trimmed even and smoothed with loose sand and gravel.

"Now, men," cheerily cried the commander, as he served them with a generous flask and a pocketful of cigars, "if you can spread those dunnage-boards over the hold and cover the gravel surface we will knock off."

The faint streakings of day were in the east when Wainwright regained his vessel. May and Goodloe, with their retainers, were sleeping, save one watching the yacht in his turn.

A Wainwright saw the empty barge moored by the Ranger's side and his skeleton crew turn in, he waved his hand lovingly toward the silent convent where Dolores slept. "My darling!" he murmured, and as his tired head fell in slumber his last words were, "Outwitted, you Mexican scoundrel! Now for the Yaquis' tribute."

"Not a minute too soon, by Jove!" he exclaimed, when his servant handed his coffee next morning. The sun was

pouring a golden flood on shore and sea, and two cable-
lengths from him lay the patched-up lumbering Mexican
gun-boat La Democrata.

" The commanding officer will visit you at noon, sir,"
Ensign Crowninshield reported.

" Have the ship's company ready for inspection, officers
in full dress. Call away my boat lively. I have to go on
shore first."

With a hasty toilet, he sped to the shore as fast as his
crack crew could hurry over the smooth bay.

" I'll just have time to tell Mrs. Delmar the good news,
for I must hasten back and see the Mexican Captain. After
that I shall find out what the inside of a Mexican gun-boat
is like."

The lazy street-strollers wondered at the springy strides
of the Gringo captain. Without a glance at beautiful
Anita Delmar, Wainwright sprang to meet the widow, whose
eyes told of a night vigil.

" It's all right. The treasure of the cave is safely hidden
on the yacht." As soon as he could escape from the con-
gratulations of the two delighted women, he stammered,
" I can't wait. See the bishop and warn Dolores. And let
none of you show the faintest interest in the game I play
now. I go to receive the official visit of the Mexican
officer, to return it, and examine the Democrata. Let the
bishop inform Pesquiera. Has he seen his daughter ? "

" Alas, no ! " Mrs. Delmar faltered; " but Marquez has
promised an afternoon to them together, in presence of the
bishop, in the prison."

L

" I must go," cried Harry. " The governor can keep his tardy clemency, for Pesquiera will wait for Dolores at San Francisco."

" God speed you ! " cried the ladies, in a breath, as the lover sped away. In half an hour, Dolores hid her blushing face in her friend's bosom, as Anita told her the tale of Wainwright's deed. " You love him, Dolores ? " Anita questioned, and the fair girl murmured, " More than my life. He fights for my dear father ! "

The motley populace of Guaymas thronged the old piers to see the interchange of stately courtesies between the war-ships. Clouds of rolling smoke, flashes from the red-mouthed cannon, and the speeding of boats filled with decorated officers, made it a day not to be forgotten. For the governor's great feast was to be the signal of a local *festa* never before equalled in splendour.

At five o'clock the three Americans were gathered in Wainwright's cabin.

" You can answer for Bligh and Hackmuller Phil ? " Harry asked, anxiously.

" I have as much to lose as you," said May, " if I am caught. Besides the love of a life, I should lose my liberty."

" Then listen. I will take all my officers on shore to this dinner but the two watch officers. Such a night will never offer itself again. You tell me the passage is clear, Basil, and you are ready ? "

" Thoroughly. All is ready," Goodloe answered.

" Of course I don't know the size of the golden bars.

The thin side of the foundation is the one toward the bay. A short crowbar is all you need."

"Thanks to Hackmuller's mining outfit, I have everything," Goodloe replied.

"Then when you hear the music of the dinner, as soon as it is dark, put Bligh and Hackmuller on guard. Do you two alone go into the tunnel. I need give you no directions. When you have finished, send Bligh in to the banquet-room. I will leave him and join you. If I can escape, I will come sooner."

"All right!" answered the comrades.

While the wassail din was at its highest in the banquet-hall, the streets were filled with an enthusiastic multitude. Above, on the hill, one gleaming taper shone from the postern gate of the prison. Laughter and music filled the narrow stony causeways. In the priest's house Bishop Dominguez calmed and cheered Pauline Delmar, who started at each unfamiliar sound. Speechless, in a corner, Anita and Dolores watched the wicket-gate.

Pacing his cell, wringing his hands in impotent rage, Mateo Pesquiera listened to the shouts of the rabble cheering his conqueror. "And to-morrow, to-morrow, my God, I sail without a word, a glance, one loving kiss, from my child! I may be stretched a corpse on the sands of the Yaqui River! Who knows but he may sacrifice me there and report an attempted escape!" The defeated governor was on his knees, pressing the crucifix to his lips, when Wainwright's anxious eyes caught sight of Goodloe's tall form forcing its way through the crowd of spectators at the

L 2

opened doors. Welcomed with effusion, the American strode up to his friend. His face was pale, and he was haggard and weary. Two hours in a cramped tunnel had stiffened his muscles. But triumph shone in his eyes.

Wainwright read the signal aright. " Trick number Two!" he muttered, as Goodloe whispered. " It is done. Phil waits for you in Hackmuller's little office. Join him at once. I will occupy the governor."

Before Wainwright could enter the enclosure of the assayer's premises, Goodloe was eloquently responding to a toast to the American Navy.

The town's clamor of feast and fandango quieted. Even the drunken sentinel in front of the governor's house leaned his gun against a pillar and slept.

But three resolute men sat, weapons in hand, waiting for the dawn, in the little room where Hackmuller concealed his crucibles and alembics of the metallurgic trade.

"We had no trouble," said Goodloe, in answer to Wainwright's eager questions. " The soft brick filling yielded easily. The bars were piled together loosely. They are small, for hand-carrying. We threw them out in heaps, and carried them out in a hide ore-bag. And now what will you do with them ? "

" I can tell you," said the jovial Hackmuller, who was smoking a long German pipe. The golden ingots lay covered with sacks and in chests and boxes in the room.

" Did you get all? Are you sure ? " interrupted the excited commander.

"We cleared the crypt," Goodloe answered, "then threw the broken rubbish in and walled it up with loose brick, smeared over with quick-drying adobe mud. We then threw up earth against it."

"Good! Now, professor, your plan?"

"I know you have ten or twenty tons of soft pig lead on the Ranger. Your engineer showed it to me. I wanted some for cupelling bullion. Let me have forty bars of it early to-morrow. I can melt it here. I will make some rough sand moulds, and run six or eight of these gold bars into one pig. The pigs can be put on board the yacht to-morrow afternoon. No one will step inside these gates till it is ready. Send me your man Davis. Bligh and I can do the rest. I will jacket your treasure so that no one could ever tell it."

"Professor, you are a genius," Harry cried. "Now I will hasten to my ship. I wish all our friends to be quiescent to-morrow. No one is supposed to know of Pesquiera's being smuggled on board. Marquez has put twenty of his trusted soldiers on board the Democrata. I must trust to Jack Crowninshield to outwit them."

The burning sun poured down next day on deserted streets, for the *fiesta* had demoralized high and low. The blinking sentinel never lifted his eyes as three creaking ox-carts dragged along under heavy burdens of dull-looking pigs of lead. Pauline Delmar from her green-shaded windows watched the heavy barge reach the Constance with that precious freight. The harbor was soon free of a hull, for the beautiful Constance spread her white wings and bore out to sea.   There was silence in the priest's house.   Three women watched the stars together that night.   The Ranger had stood up the gulf under half steam, and La Democrata, lay at the point with her engines broken down.   One precious day was gained.

CHAPTER X.

BISHOP DOMINGUEZ sat under a spreading vine in the walled garden of the Convent, where the timid dove, Dolores, was momentarily safe from Marquez. It was in the early freshness of the morning after the feast, and he anxiously awaited the return of a special messenger. There was a settled look of grave anxiety on the good prelate's brow.

His thin gray hairs waved in the morning breeze stirring the vines, and the gentle plash of the fountain in the paseo lulled him to repose. In earnest vigils of the anxious night he had prayed for the safety of Mateo Pesquiera. While the shouts of the revellers reached his ears he implored the Blessed Virgin to soften the stern heart of tiger-like Marquez.

From the streets, the din of fandango and cries of the brawlers added to the feverish unrest of Guaymas "en grande funcion." When those prayers were ended, as the convent bell boomed the solemn hour of midnight, Bishop Ignacio Dominguez laid his tired head to rest. His last thoughts were centred upon crafty Marquez. "He is at his cups to night. The fiery brandy will add a new madness

to his tiger-like blood. Day by day he has put off my plea
to bring my lamb Dolores to her father's bosom. I know
the dark strain of the merciless Marquez blood. He may
yet have a lingering fear of the terrors of the anathema of
Holy Church. But, his old way! He will prolong my
suspense—Dolores agony, and I may look from the
window and see La Democrata speeding to sea. When
she returns without him (if that is the tyrant's plan), any
easily forged tale of accident or suicide will satisfy the
ignorant masses here. Or the old fable—killed while trying to escape! Shot by the guard! A few doubloons and
a little aguadiente will silence every tongue. I must act
to-morrow. I will face the worst. I shall urge that I must
return to Hermosillo."

The Bishop longed for the unbroken peace of his ruined
old Episcopal palace, under the shadows of the crested
cliffs of the Rio Sonora.

"If Pesquiera were there—among the faithful, I could
myself compass his escape. Alas! The Church has lost its
secular arm. The good old days!"

And Ignacio Dominguez fell asleep, his thin fingers
clinging to his golden pectoral cross, and dreamed of the
grand Church which held the keys of palace and prison,
before rebellious priest, Hidalgo, broke down the power of
His Catholic Majesty.

"Spain! Spain! Always faithful!" lingered on the
devotee's lips as he fell into slumbers of unrest.

But a calm had settled on his mind, as he sat in the
pleasant garden where a cloud of white-hooded sisters
timidly watched his morning self-communion. He had said,

with fervent zeal, his matin mass, and now only the tinkle
of the bells of a passing mule train, or the cry of the pulque
seller disturbed the morning hour.

The sun mounted higher, and its fierce golden rays beat
upon the white paved paseo. Still his trusted messenger
came not. Touching a little silver bell, the old ecclesiastic
sent away his untasted morning repast. A roll, a draught
of the delicious Mexican coffee, a few grapes, were the only
inroads made upon the good sister's luxurious provision.

"Madre de Dios! Esta enfermo!" murmured Sister
Agatha, as she hastened away in search of the Mother
Superior.

"I will see the child. I will prepare her for the worst,"
sadly decided the anxious Bishop. "The war vessel may
sail any moment. Will he dare to break his promise?"

Five minutes later, as Dolores Pesquiera's graceful form
was seen at the end of the long corridor, with heated face
and radiant brow, the bishop's private secretary hastened
through the guarded stone archway.

Kneeling respectfully, he kissed the prelate's withered
hand, and presented a sealed letter.

"Pardon, my lord!" he humbly said. "El Gobernador
was not to be aroused after his carnival. He finally allowed
me to be admitted. I waited two hours in the ante-room,
while the various morning reports were made. Good
Carbajal, his adjutant, told me that an important mail had
arrived from the city of Mexico, and that several express
riders came in last night. There is some tumult in the
interior. I hope no injudicious effort of our friends!
Believe me, my lord," said the anxious subordinate, "this

villain, at the fresh sign of a revolt, would have Pesquiera shot. My good friend Carbajal kindly held back these matters until I should see Marquez before any rage would be added to the fierceness of his debauch. Ah! Unhappy Mexico! Half the officers of the Democrata are still stupefied from wine. So I was not astonished when Governor Marquez told me, gruffly, to say to your lordship that he will not send the Democrata away until to-morrow. To my pressing but diplomatic urging for a definite reply to your request, he only replied, after glancing at your note 'Mañana! Mañana!' I ventured to plead, and he finally said, 'I will send for the Council.' So I was forced to await his breakfast, and I lingered with Carbajal in the Presidio ante-room. While there, the Capitano Americano came in. In a moment I told him all.

"What a man! What energy! what wit and quickness! 'This usurper wishes the friendship of my government. He promised me to give the bishop this privilege. Wait here! I will remind him of it now.'

"After we had listened to a war of words for a half an hour, the handsome Capitano Wainwright went in to Marquez alone.

"I sat with beating heart. Thank God! in five minutes the door was opened and the American came out laughing.

"'Go in now,' he whispered as he passed me. I knocked at the door. To my astonishment, I was graciously received. The governor gave me the order, good for this afternoon only."

"Go now, my son! Take your rest! You have done

well ! " cried the overjoyed bishop, as he bestowed a benediction upon the kneeling ambassador of hope. " I will
take the Sacristan and the Mother Superior with this dear
child."

And as he raised the beautiful Dolores with a fatherly
hand, in his joy the happy bishop almost shouted, "You
shall see your father this day, this very hour, my poor
child ! " The strong arms of the Mother Superior closed
around the swaying form of the Pearl of Guaymas, for
the sudden happiness smote the motherless girl like a
blow.

As she re-opened her eyes, she whispered, " Take me to
him, now ! Ah ! my father ! No ! no ! I am very strong."
She smiled through her happy tears. " Let us go at once ! "
the eager maiden pleaded, " for those bad men are not to
be trusted."

In a half hour the great cumbrous convent carriage
drew up at the doors of the grim stone jail where the ex-
governor lay in duress. Below them, the party could see
the star flag of the American gleaming in the morning sunlight, at the mizzen of the heavy Ranger.

Though she shuddered as the sentinels rattled their
muskets in a ringing salute to the Bishop, Dolores paused
on the threshold of her father's prison. Her light foot
lingered a moment, and casting a glance tearfully at the
Mother Superior, Dolores gazed to where the American
ship danced on the sparkling tide. A kiss was wafted from
one rosy palm, which the Castilian maiden sealed with her
glowing lips. Its destination was the immediate whereabouts of that dashing officer Henry Wainwright, U.S.N.,

whose heart would have leaped up could he have listened to the words trembling on her lips.

"Help me! Help me! Brave Americano!" was the girl's despairing plea.

With a heart fluttering in fear, the timid Dolores brought the splendour of her beauty to light up the gloomy guard-room, where a wolfish-eyed officer sternly scrutinized the official order handed by Bishop Dominguez. The revolutionist dared not meet the prelate's eye, as he sharply said, "Only two, the order says. Admit the bishop and the prisoner's daughter only." And so, while led by the aged ecclesiastic, Dolores shrinkingly penetrated the gloomy vaults whence so many had been led to death, the stout sacristan remained in the guard-room defiantly gazing at the brutal soldiery.

Crowding eagerly around, the half naked sentinels leered at the good Sister whose eyes were fixed upon her beads, as her thin transparent fingers swiftly moved over the emblems of prayer. On her noble, shaded face, the humility and resignation of her fraternity rested with a hallowing dignity. A silence fell upon the guard-room. Rude jests were hushed, the sandalled feet were stilled, and, leaning on their loaded rifles, the fierce adherents of Marquez paled before the power of defenceless womanhood.

The gentle hands of the nun moved unceasing in prayer, and from her pallid lips fell the accents which have soothed the death bed of thousands, which have braved danger and pestilence to linger in unselfish love beside the bed of pain.

For all the slips of womanhood in a world of sorrow and

sin, these gentle and devoted Sisters of the Church of
Christ would alone atone. Into a life racked with the
storms of passion, woman has brought also fortitude, meek-
ness, charity,—the kindling eye and ready touch of loving
charity.

So, with this slender guard, the pious bishop led the
patrician girl, motherless already, to the side of her father,
now standing in the very shadow of death.

The callous turnkey who had often seen unmoved a
score of shrieking wretches dragged to the parade yard,
to be shot without warning, turned away as with an inarticu-
late cry, Mateo Pesquiera folded his sobbing daughter to
his bosom.

And there, his noble face lighted with peace and love,
the old bishop with outstretched hands called down the
blessing of an almighty God upon the reunited. For the
thrills of a love beyond all earthly bounds pulsed through
the veins of the devoted sire and the beautiful child clinging
to his breast.

The turnkey gently touched the bishop's arm, and
motioned him into the corridor, where a feeble pencil of
light reached the flag-stones from a loop hole. In the cell
of Pesquiera, a single candle lit up the gloomy interior,
whose shadows seemed to whisper of awful deeds.

"When you are done, my lord bishop," humbly said
the jailor, as he bent a knee, "if you will sound upon
the wicket I will open. I will leave you now alone in
peace."

"Can you not give this poor gentleman another cell?"
compassionately said the bishop, his gentle voice alone

breaking the silence, for the father and daughter were yet clasped heart to heart in silent agony.

"Alas! It is the cell of the condemned!" cried the jailor, who hastened away with haggard eyes, hastily picking up his keys which had fallen with a sudden clash.

"The cell of the condemned!" whispered Bishop Dominguez, in a sudden affright, for his aged heart was sorely shaken. "Ah! Sanctissima Virgen!" I must pray for light, for wisdom, for help. And he fell upon his knees on the cruel flag-stones of that "via mala," whence the departing only journeyed to an unknown grave.

As he rose to his feet, he thought of an old law still in force that no Catholic could be executed, save when caught red handed in rebellion, without the last rites of the Church. "It is my right, as bishop, to know of this in time." With a sudden fear, he strode along the gloomy passage, and tapped at the wicket.

The astonished jailor, re-entering, gazed in eager wonder at the sudden summons.

"Pablo!" softly said the sorrowing Bishop. "You were once a son of the Church. Listen! I fear that I may not be warned in time. If an order should arrive for you to deliver up Mateo Pesquiera for execution, you must arouse me at the Convent. There is a hundred doubloons for you there in the sacristan's hands. And from me—my blessing and my protection.

"If it should be at night," murmured the shaken recalcitrant, falling on his knees.

"He must not die unshriven! More than by day! You must watch. Ring the Convent bell boldly. If you cannot leave the prison send your most trusty man. He must see me himself. He will be admitted at any moment. And no one will ever know !" added the aroused Bishop.

"I will send my son, Jayme," muttered Pablo, gazing around in fear. "You must be ready at any time, even to-night." The old prelate's ashen cheeks were even paler than their wont as he fixed his tranquil eyes searchingly on Pablo, who hung his head.

"You know something?" sternly said the bishop.

In a torrent of remorse the superstitious turnkey unloosed his heart. He feared the awful thunders of the excommunication. "A grave is already dug !" he faltered. "There is an uprising in the mountains. Captain Villareal has doubled the guard. And he told me, this morning, that the prisoner would either be sent away on the gunboat to-morrow—or—or—" he hesitated.

"Speak !" commanded the Bishop, whose high courage overcame his weight of years.

"Or shot—at midnight to-morrow night !" the jailer answered, as he insisted on fleeing from the old priest's presence. "They may see me! I could not then help you !" urged Pablo, as he disappeared.

Ignacio Dominguez stood riveted to the spot. "Shall I tell them now?" His bosom heaved in the keenest suffering. And, standing there, near the door of the cell, he could hear the voices of father and daughter mingled in loving converse.

They were reviewing all the happy days of the past. The bygone years, when the gentle mother's splendid eyes shone on the one in devoted love, and on the other with he infinite tenderness of motherhood. The strong man

clung to the gentle girl in his arms as if his warm
embrace would shield and guard her in the shadowy years
when he should have passed beyond the gate which opens
never again! Dolores was seated beside the wasted
prisoner, her fresh beauty lighting up the gruesome chamber of the adjudged dead. Her rounded white arms were
clasped around him as if she would shield him with her
delicate body against the messengers of death. All the
love and kindness lavished on her early years returned to
Dolores, whose warm blood was bounding in her veins
with the intensified emotion of a tropic nature.

The bishop paused and gazed from a distance. Though
dead to the world, this pure and touching devotion melted
his chastened heart.

"I must find a way,—with the help of the blessed
Virgin!" the grand old man murmured. "The Church
has given me a childless life. I will save the father for this
child's sake. And God will find the way!"

And as he paced the corridor, casting his eyes upon the
two loving ones, unconscious of his presence, his thoughts
reverted to the brave young American. He started as the
convent bell sounded the passing of two hours. "I must
not lose time!" And, with a reliance upon the young
stranger which he could not explain, he summoned Pablo,
and sent the sacristan at once to the landing to bid Commander Wainwright repair at once to the convent to await
his own return.

The shadows of the afternoon were falling before the
bishop dared intrude upon the last interview of the father
and daughter. His plan was now perfected. "I will my-

self go to the Governor this night, and will urge the sending of Mateo Pesquiera to the city of Mexico, or make a demand for a commission to be named by the General Government for his proper future trial. It would be composed of strangers; and Pesquiera's money, with the power of the Church, would suffice to save his life! Delay— delay, now, is our salvation! Marquez will not dare to sign an order for his execution in my presence." And another expedient occurred to him. "Marquez dare not offend the American Commander. I will urge the Comandante Wainwright to go at once, as if by accident, and spend the late hours of this night with Marquez on some pretext. If he does not become brandy-crazed, or fall into some panic, we may effect the rescue of Pesquiera on the cruise. And I will claim my right to-night to prepare the prisoner, in any case of sudden emergency, for a Christian death."

And so, with trembling knees, the old Bishop approached to tear away the loving and beloved daughter from the heart which beat nearest and dearest to her. "It is only mercy," he murmured, for the sound of passionate sobbing was heard in the narrow cell. His noiseless foot did not arouse Dolores Pesquiera, who, clinging to her father's knees, her beautiful loosened hair streaming over her shoulders, cried, "There is one way to save you, Padre querido! He will not dare to kill you—if—if—I am his wife! I will save you! You must not die! I will throw myself at his feet!"

And Ignacio Dominguez paused, awed by the solemn dignity of the prisoner, who laid his hand in a last caress upon the devoted girl's head. "Not that way, my own

M

darling !" he said. "I will not take my life at his hands
if such a price is paid. Never !" And the sound of three
beating hearts in all the unison of tenderness, witnessed the
noble girl's offer of her beauty in its flower to save the dear
and reverend head of her sire.

"Wait, my children ! Wait yet on the mercy of God,
and the intercession of the most blessed Virgin," said the
Bishop, as he raised his hands over the heads of the loving
pair. "The hour is not yet come. But it is time to part.
You shall meet again—I promise it in the name of the
Holy Church !" There was that in his tone which brought
conviction to the listeners, who parted in the silent rapture
of an embrace hallowed by the purest love on earth.

Even rude Pablo was lifted beyond his brute level of
feeling, as he gazed upon the face of the Pearl of Guaymas,
when she passed out of the gray gateway. "Pobrecita !"
he muttered,—but the girl's wan face was lit with a smile,
as her eyes rested on the "Ranger's" flag.

Mateo Pesquiera listened to the retreating footsteps of
his motherless child, and for the first time felt the full
power of his relentless enemy. He threw himself on his
rude pallet in an agony of grief.

Yet though he stood in the very shadow of death, he
would not buy his life at the price of his daughter's un-
happiness. "My noble Dolores !" he fondly murmured.
"Shall I buy this villain's clemency?" He paced the
gloomy den with tiger-like tread, lost in a whirl of burning
houghts.

He was still in the high tide of life. His daughter ! To
live and see her future happiness—to gaze upon the royal

womanhood, recalling the dear one, loved and lost—it was the temptation of a life ! He wavered, but across his disturbed mind drifted the thoughts awakened by an unsullied honour.

"No ! I would sacrifice Pauline Delmar and her child ! And Marquez, once master of the treasure, or inflamed by the richness of the mine, would assassinate me ! And Dolores—she would be helpless in his power. I am lost !"

And, clutching the iron bars of his prison door, he shook them in a mad delirium of frenzy. His strength failed him, and he sank on the stony floor.

There he lay, until the vesper bell boomed from the convent. He sprang to his feet in a transport of emotion.

"My darling child ! My only one ! She is under God's roof. They will not dare to tear her thence !" And once more the unfaltering trust in Him who raises up the fallen brought a strange fortitude to the man whose firing party was being warned by Captain Villareal, while Pablo shivered as he secretly thought, "I must send the message !"

As the evening shadows fell, Bishop Dominguez was seated again in his favourite arbour in the convent garden, for there alone was he safe from the prying eyes of Marquez's spies. Beside him, Commander Henry Wainwright eagerly listened to his every word.

The missionary priest and the Bishop's Secretary paced the garden in earnest converse.

"I must soon leave you, my son !" said the anxious prelate. "I shall occupy the time of the Governor until you arrive. When the convent bell strikes ten, you must leave here, and arriving at the Presidio, insist on an interview with the Governor ! Detain him, flatter his cupidity, dilate upon his future grandeur ! He may fear a public exposure of his cruelty ! You tell me that the ' Democrata ' is now ready to sail ? "

."It is so, your Eminence !" answered the naval officer, whose thoughts strayed to the parlour where Pauline Delmar and her child were vainly trying to cheer Dolores Pesquiera. "The Commander made his farewell visit this afternoon, and expects to rally all his crew and subordinates to sail as ordered."

" Then Marquez must be occupied and distracted every moment ! I will take the stranger ladies down in my carriage, and send it on an evening drive with them, to divert suspicion ! Remember, my son, the Sacristan will instantly bring you the messenger from the prison, should he come, which God forbid; and my Secretary will wait here on watch. You can remain in the convent parlour with poor Dolores until it is time for you to go to the Governor. Try to divert her from this awful suspense ! I must now go to the presence of the enemy of God ! I shall use every artifice of the priest, and you, generous man, have promised to throw your national influence into the scale. Fear him not, for he, too, is afraid of the Mexican central authorities. Perhaps all is quiet—there is no messenger from Carbajal, who promised to warn me of any exciting news at the council room ! "

" Trust me, Reverend Bishop !" warmly cried Harry, whose heart was moved by the pathetic glances of the frightened maiden's eyes when they met for a moment.

On the step of the carriage, the hopeful Bishop started

in sudden fright, as a breathless messenger from Carbajal accosted him. Wainwright had placed Pauline Delmar in the vehicle, and he led Anita and Dolores artfully aside.

" Quick, quick, my son!" gasped the Bishop. "There is an extraordinary council ordered for nine o'clock. It is reported that a band of Pesquiera's friends are marching from Hermosillo!" The Bishop was trembling, as he drew Wainwright aside. "Remember! not a word to the child of her father's danger. If the messenger from the prison comes, hasten to the council room! I will go from there to the prison and watch for treachery. I will there demand my rights to prepare him for death. In a respite of a few hours you may win him over to delay!"

And as the carriage rolled away, Henry Wainwright led the gentle girl back to where the Mother Superior watched the scene with an intense sympathy. Alas! she knew too well the dark clouds menacing Mateo Pesquiera's evening hours. The brutal vengeance of the tyrant's hate might come at any moment!

The young Commander paced the garden in a fever of unrest, till he should be summoned to the gentle presence of the woman whose father he vowed to save at every risk. "If it were possible, I would even land a party," he vainly soliloquized, "but—the flag must be respected!"

While he spoke, the Secretary hurried through the portals. "There is great excitement," he cried to the sailor. " Guards are hurriedly being doubled, and mounted videttes are galloping out to take post! I fear that under cover of some local excitement, Governor Josè, in a tyrant's sudden impulse, will order the instant execution of our helpless friend ! " There were tears of helpless rage in Wainwright's eyes, as he cried, " Impossible ! It must not be ! Is there no humanity in Mexico ? "

"Alas ! My amigo Americano ! " the young priest answered. " Mexico was once loyal and devoted to the church. We had law and authority. But the temple of Faith has been shattered ! All is overthrown ! I am but a poor priest, and yet I see that each succeeding Liberal wave of modern progress bears us farther on towards a moral chaos. The world drifts thither. Unhappy Mexico ! When religion and morality are not preached, are not respected, are not practised, the waves of human error overwhelm the simple-minded ; the helpless innocent are ground under the heel of the armed spoiler. All pull down, none build, in the age of license, the era of free-thought. But see, Comandante, the Mother Superior beckons you. Remember ! I will wait at the postern, and you shall have instant tidings ! " The sorrowing priest bowed, as gallant Wainwright, his heart thrilling with love and a sudden sympathy, went into the presence of the defenceless girl now grown so strangely dear !

CHAPTER XI.

THE young officer was preoccupied as he entered the long room, whose windows commanded a view of the superb bay. It was growing dark, and the lights of the " Ranger " gleamed in a friendly welcome from her ports ! Her black hull was softened into the purpling blue of the hushed bay. A few cables' lengths away lay the improvised Mexican cruiser, the " Democrata." Some unusual bustle agitated her crew, for twinkling lanterns wove strange patterns on her decks, and the nervous blare of the bugle reached even the lofty convent gardens. The room was dark, save for the gleaming tapers before an image, from whence the mystic benediction of the Blessed Virgin's open arms thrilled the thoughtless young officer. An open door indicated the absence of the good nun whose mission was evidently to order lights.

Though he could not see her, the virginal presence of the young girl thrilled her knightly champion. He softly said, " Dolores !" He started at the sound of his own voice. For in that blessed atmosphere of love-haunted anxiety, the two bright young natures were drawn by the invisible chords of Love into " Life's song without words "—the sweet apture of first love !

"Senor !" was the softly-breathed answer, and Wainwright sprang to her side, forgetting, madcap as he was
known in the service, that sage advice of Calderon : "There
is no playing tricks with love !"

The Pearl of Guaymas was seated in the deep window
embrasure, and with her hands clasped over her exquisite
bosom, gazing out into the night.

Through the open window the sound of galloping horses
was heard, and the ominous rattle of carbines. Far down,
in the straggling town, the sharp notes of a bugle corps
broke out in a Moorish fanfaron march.

"What are you watching, Dolores?" kindly said the
American, as he took her unresisting hand. The frankness
of maidenhood was in her answer, almost the trust of a
child, as she clasped his arms with her nervous fingers in a
transport of anxiety.

"You will not let them kill my father! See! Your
great ship! So many cannons! So many brave men !"

As the blood leaped into Harry Wainwright's heart, the
Mother Superior entered, followed by an Indian maid
bearing candelabra.

A sudden impulse seized Wainwright to go himself on the
launch and leave his ship in port. "They would never dare
to kill Pesquiera in my company! But the service,—my
ship—our government might be embroiled ! And no one
could handle the situation here !" His eye sought the
harbour once more, and he noted the gleaming lanterns of
several boats, moving in regular order to the shore! "Ah!
an armed landing !" the quick-witted sailor cried. "Why is
this ? "

As he spoke, the tramping cadence of heavy feet sounded in the street, and the marching music broke out under the convent walls.

Dolores sprang up as lithe as a deer! "Madre de Dios! They go to the prison! My father! My father! They will kill him!"

"Never! I swear it by the flag I serve! I will face this madman! I will demand delay—a regular trial! I will open my guns on the 'Democrata' if this midnight butchery is attempted!"

But Dolores heard not the wild words of the rash young Commander, for she tottered, and with a feeble wail sank into the arms of the startled Mother Superior. The frightened nun gazed bewildered as the stalwart officer grasped the swaying burden, and bore the fainting girl to a cushioned window recess, dashing open the casement to admit the cool night breeze. In her paleness, as clearly lined as marble, her drooping eyelids feebly fluttering, the lovely girl moaned, all unconscious, that the excited champion was showering kisses on her slender hands! That burning words of tenderness fell from the lips of the ardent young American, who vaguely muttered, in impatience. "Will help never come?" For the Mother Superior, in her fright, fled away from her retainers. In the soft language of her native clime, Wainwright, on his knees, called her the endearing names springing to the lips of youth. The sound of shuffling feet was heard as Dolores heard, at last, his impassioned pledge. "I will go to the Governor myself. I shall demand delay! I will protest! Fear not, Dolores, my Dolores, your father shall live!"

And, in a transport of delight, the fair young head rested sobbing on his bosom.

Wainwright sprang to his feet as a heavy knock resounded at the hall-way door, and the Secretary rushed into the room, followed by the excited Professor Hackmuller. The good German was strangely moved, as he strode to where Dolores was now the centre of a group of eagerly sympathetic Sisters, "all bearing gifts!" The gentle women were in a nameless tremor of fear, for only the appealing Cross of Christ might stay a wild mob sweeping in. Revolution had too often turned loose a band of wild marauders to terrorize the patient dwellers by the beautiful Guaymas bay.

The Secretary drew Wainwright aside, and his face was ashen pale, as he whispered to the American : " Carbajal has sent me word to go in my robes to the prison, and the Bishop will have the acolytes and his vestments ! I fear we can only delay the murder a few hours ! He will venture his very life—the good Bishop !" And with a frightened look he glided away, as Hackmuller pounced upon Wainwright.

" Quick, quick ! You must hear all. I was waiting," gasped the Teuton, "to show the Governor the returns of some wonderful ores from his estates, when the Bishop tottered from the council room ! Adjutant Carbajal was dispatching troops outside, and giving orders, so that we were alone, save the sentinels. There has been an alarm, and all the troops, with the sailors, sent to hold the heights and occupy the prison. Marquez has been drinking again! He is in a deadly mood, and his recklessness grows hourly. He fears his own downfall. The Bishop will delay him, and no order will be sent to the prison for the execution, until

Carbajal has given the Bishop time to reach the prison. It must be delivered through the Adjutant! Ah! God! what a brave old man! He will demand his rights to shrive the dying man, and he vows they shall not take him from the cell save over the body of God's anointed. There he will protest, and demand an appeal to the city of Mexico, and a confirmation of the sentence extraordinary!"

"But what must I do?" stammered Wainwright, with a glance at Dolores, whose mournful dark eyes were intently fixed upon the two foreigners. Around her stood the defenceless band of the gentle Sisters of the Church, meekly ready to share any fate meted out to the daughter of Marquez's proscribed enemy.

"I am to return at once, for I warned Bligh, who is now mounted. When the Bishop is warned to leave, he will send Bligh to you. You must take Bligh's horse, and force your way to the presence of this beast. Then threaten, cajole, charge him flatly with the desire to murder Pesquiera; and tell him you will officially report this barbarity to your government, and send a protest to your Minister at Mexico."

"Gott in Himmel! what inhuman fiends!" groaned the peace-loving savant.

"Go, go, my good friend!" huskily cried Wainwright, his voice choking with impatient rage. "Tell the Bishop he can rely on me to the last gasp," and the good man was soon lost in the darkness. It was now nine o'clock, and yet no message from Pablo. The Commander's honest eyes sought the face of the maiden, who instantly read the burden of new sorrows and nearing doom in their pitying glances. Gliding like a spirit to his side, she murmured, "It has come—the worst! You have heard that which you conceal?"

Wainwright steeled himself to a pious lie. "Nothing. It was nothing, my Dolores! The Bishop is still pleading with the Governor."

"On your honour! You hide nothing?" the impassioned beauty demanded, fixing her wistful eyes on him with a glance which pierced his very soul.

The American bowed, and murmured a denial which his eyes would have gainsaid. Dolores, like a wraith, sought the shelter of the Sisterhood, but stood in rapt expectancy, her eyes fixed on the door.

Her American lover was lost in uncertainty. "Shall I send for Pauline and Anita to break this news to her? My God! I cannot! And the summons to action may come at any moment. Alas! the poor darling! She will know too soon that she is doubly an orphan!" Under pretence of a necessary question, he led the Mother Superior to the farthest window recess.

"Reverend Mother, can you not induce Dolores to retire? There may be excitement, some grave emergency, and we may spare her innocent young heart one night of agony!"

"Ah, Senor Comandante," sighed the Sister, "there is the old Castilian spirit in that gentle girl. My own lamb! Last night I stole into her cell at daybreak, to mark if she slept! There, upon her knees, she had fallen asleep exhausted before the little shrine. Trust her in all. You cannot deceive a daughter's instinct. I will guard her.

But the dreadful deed may occur any time. Come with me," she softly said, and they passed into the garden. From the open doors of the chapel a light as of the Holy Grail streamed out into the oppressive blackness of the night. Wainwright shivered as he saw the grave face of the Secretary, clad in his priestly robes, bearing before him the monstrance with the host. A half dozen Indian youths clad in the robes of the acolyte preceded him, and across the garden the little procession solemnly moved. The fragrance of the roses was wafted from the clambering vines of the arched paséo, and a chill breeze of night smote the heated brow of the sailor.

He stood as in a dream. The grave-faced Mother Superior dropped on her knees as the little throng entered the arched convent portal, awaiting the unfolding of the doors by the Sacristan, lantern in hand.

A sudden clamour at the outer door drew all eyes thither, and a tall youth clad in the uniform of the Rural Guards sprang into their midst. It was the turnkey's son.

"Quick, quick ! The Bishop !" he cried, as his wondering eyes turned from the tall priest, ghastly in his robes, to the astonished nuns who crowded around.

"Your tidings ! Speak ! The Bishop is with the Governor even now," said the Mother Superior, in a voice thrilling in its accent of command. A human life was trembling in the balance, a life dear to the girl whose voice rang out in a piercing scream, as the young soldier sullenly replied, "Too late ! The firing party is paraded under arms now ;" and he dropped on his knees, as the resolute priest, standing with the flaring tapers lighting his stern face, cried, "Hasten! Take us over the hill to the prison. The shortest road. Lead on!" The quick clatter of a horse's hoofs resounded on the stony street, as a man dashed up at frantic speed. The foaming steed reared high in air as a ringing voice called out through the wide-open door, "Here, Wainwright! To the Governor! The Bishop is half way up the hill on his way to the prison. Carbajal is holding the order back till you can get there. But it is signed," and as Fred Bligh swung lightly out of the saddle, he cried, "It is for twelve o'clock."

"My father, my darling father! I must see his dear face once again," cried Dolores, springing to her startled lover's side and standing between the two men, a vision of thrilling, entrancing beauty, all the eager bravery of her race shining in her sparkling eyes.

"My child, you cannot. It were death to the one you love to delay now. Go, go, brave Americano!" cried the Mother Superior, as Wainwright strove to free the clutching fingers from his arm.

"Hasten, Harry, for God's sake! Leave the poor child in God's hands. You may frighten him into a respite till to-morrow. If we could only get him on the steamer."

Wainwright gazed around in wonder, for as lithe as an antelope, Dolores Pesquiera sprang towards the tallest acolyte and tore the white robe from his shoulders. Resolutely throwing it over her black dress, she seized the candle from the amazed youth's hands.

"Quick now, Diego," she almost screamed, as she called to the nearest nun; "a knife, someone! Twist up my hair and cut it. They will never know."

Wainwright broke away from Bligh, who strove to drag him to the door. "Go, go! I will walk with her pistol in hand!" he yelled.

As a peon shore the beautiful tresses which Dolores had freed with one sweep of a rounded arm, Wainwright clasped her in his arms before them all.

"For my sake! For your dear father's sake, do not venture! It is madness!"

But the maiden, casting one glance of appealing love, glided from his grasp and led the way down the steps into the dark street.

"God will protect her! Away!" eagerly urged the Superioress, as the night swallowed them up; and before the echoes of her voice rang back, Wainwright was dashing madly down the causeway, his horse's hoofs striking fire.

"To the chapel!" commanded the nun, as she stood in the arched gateway, with one uplifted arm pointing to the pavilion of the Most High.

Fred Bligh, dazed and excited beyond his wont, stood a moment irresolute! By accident his hand fell on the butt of his heavy revolver; with a start he sprang forward, and drawing it from its sheath, ran lightly up the hill after the little toiling band, lighted on to a father's prison by the taper held by the devoted Pearl of Guaymas!

"The bishop must be there already," shouted Bligh, as he gained the head of the little column. And the priest's lips only paused in their prayers for the dying to murmur,

"It is well! The Sacristan is there now to robe him!"

While Wainwright was pushing his way through the ante-room of the Presideo—far above—Mateo Pesquiera sat with his head buried in his hands, and vainly striving to recall the beloved face of his child. In the gloom of his prison cell he could only catch a gleam of the flickering palm-oil lamp at the farther end of the corridor. All hope had fled. For the weary hours had crawled on with no sign. In the haunted silence of the prison, whose awful secrets he knew, alas! too well, the deposed Governor awaited the stroke of fate. The unusual noises of night had reached him, and the mysterious thrills of the unknown spirit nerves, vainly struggling to warn him, told him of an impending doom. Standing on the very brink of his grave, led by the overmastering tide of his love, he saw again the fair wife of his youth—the dead mother of Dolores! Again he seemed to wander with her through the groves, where the moonlight lingered lovingly about her!

The face of a laughing child beamed upon him, as he peered into the darkness. His heart beat with proud love and tenderness as he recalled every incident of the unfolding girlhood of beloved Dolores. It was as if in sad but sweet review, all that was dear in his days of happy fortune was vouchsafed to him once again. "Ah! God!" he cried, suddenly, "it cannot be! I must, I shall see her again!" and the clash of the sentinels' muskets recalled him to the miseries of the present moment. "To leave her, alone—my own darling—in a cold world—none to guide, to guard,—" he clenched his wasted hands in impotent agony.

The deep-toned convent bell struck eleven, and he piously crossed himself, as a ray of light parted the blackness of his mental torture.

"The good bishop! The brave Americano! They will save my child! they will protect her! Yes, yes! But to see her dear face once more! If it must be—to hold her once again in my arms!" He did not fear to face the loaded rifles. A soldier's blood coursed in his veins, but the strong man was bowed in an infinite tenderness for the motherless child who had nestled in his bosom.

He sat in a stupor, the scalding tears trickling through his thin fingers, and never lifted his head until a hollow voice had called him thrice.

"Don Mateo! Don Mateo!" was Pablo's husky whisper. "It is for to-night—at twelve! Sea por Dios y la Santissima Virgen.'

"Hold, Pablo! How know you this?" eagerly cried Pesquiera, his wild desire to live for his child returning in nature's vehement protest against an untimely death.

"The Captain Villareal has loaded the guns of the firing-party himself, and he only awaits the order in writing. There are troops posted all around the prison!"

"Pablo! Is there no way? I have gold! The Bishop! He will make you rich!" and the frenzied father's voice rose almost to a shriek.

"There is no hope! Alas! Don Mateo, I am only a poor jailer! I can do nothing!" groaned the turnkey. "I must go. Villareal would hang me if he found me here! May God go with you!" mournfully said the jailer, as his light spluttered and went out.

"Then, for the love of God, on your faith as a Christian, give this to my darling child! Tell her I bless her from the grave. That I die with her name on my lips!" and unwinding the slender cord from his neck, the once mighty governor kissed the little crucifix which had been his prison solace, and passed it through the grated door to the man, who fled away from the haunted corridor.

In the guard-room of the prison a strange scene burst upon the startled jailer's eyes. The venerable bishop, in his full robes, stood facing dark-browed Captain Villareal. Behind him a crossbearer held up the sacred insignia of the Redeemer, and gathered around the young priest, whose lips were moving in prayer, was a crowd of frightened acolytes. But to Bligh, who stood between two sentinels, in the open door there was one who, robed in white, seemed to bear the face of an angel! It was Dolores Pesquiera, who, hidden in a shadow, had given over her torch and clasped in her fingers the chains of a censer. Her eyes were fixed upon the heavy iron door of that corridor of the condemned, whence her father must come to be led into the prison paséo.

And there, through the open passage, Bligh could see a lounging platoon of men, whose papelitos gleamed red in the darkness of the death shambles.

The cold drops beaded the watcher's brows as he felt his heart ticking off the seconds. "Will Wainwright stay that madman's hand?" The very thought burned into his brain as he gazed at the resolute face of the beautiful girl hidden under the rebellious tresses of her silken hair.

"My God! It must not be! It will kill her!"

For there was the light on the brows of Dolores Pesquiera which shines from the world beyond! The spirit alone upheld the delicate maiden, who lingered, rapt in love, to gaze but once into her father's eyes before they would lose their light for ever.

The bishop's grave tones mingled with the reluctant accents of the fierce captain, who, fingering his sword-hilt, kept his roving eyes turned toward the Presidio.

" I can only suspend the execution long enough to send a courier down to ask if I can admit you to the prisoner's cell. I will do so! But, reverend bishop, if the order comes to proceed forthwith, I must do my duty!" This was the final decision of the disturbed soldier.

" Then, in God's name, send at once," the aged bishop pleaded. For in his heart of hearts he wished to gain the coign of vantage for his spiritual protest—a place in the cell of the prisoner. "Let us lose no time, my son." And while the captain despatched his courier, at a nod, Pablo threw open the iron door, and the bishop in his robes led his humble followers to the cell of the doomed man.

Even Pablo, following with a lantern, did not see the graceful beauty of the face of the acolyte who now held a taper in her slender rose-shaded fingers.

Down below them, a thousand feet, with all his high-souled courage shining in his eyes, Commander Wainwright sat playing a game of human chess with the crafty and bloodthirsty Marquez for the stake of Pesquiera's life. He pleaded only for a respite until a court could be sent from the city of Mexico. The tyrant's glittering eyes gave no sign, and he gloomily watched the hands of a clock hung beneath the national insignia, "God and Liberty." In the unsteady glances of the usurper no indication of his real purpose could be gleaned. A horseman galloped up to the outer door, and as the silent governor listened to a few words from Carbajal, he said, "No answer! Let him wait."

Through the open door the adjutant seated, at his table, regarded the strangely-assorted pair.

Carbajal was a secret friend of the prisoner, and clutched in his hand was the fatal order, which Marquez had signed, handing it to him without a word.

"I will wait—will wait till twelve!" the generous soldier thought, as he noticed the growing agitation of the tyrant; for never did man more earnestly plead than Wainwright, facing the despot of Sonora.

"There is rebellion in the interior! The city may be at any moment attacked by his friends," was the stubborn response of the governor. Harry Wainwright sat watching the hands of the clock, which had slowly crawled past the half-hour mark. Well he knew it only required ten minutes to reach the prison guard station. "Dare I try to frighten him?" thought the sailor. "These haughty Dons are sudden and quick in quarrel. One burst of rage and the fatal die would be cast!" In a sudden nervous fear the commander paced the room, and as he turned cast an eye at soldierly Carbajal seated at his table, his face giving no sign. And yet Josè Marquez was silent! Wainwright's heart was far away. It was with the high-spirited maiden who now risked her own life to see her father's face once more.

"If it were not for international law I would risk my future, and threaten him with the guns of my ship. But he knows I am chained. This cruel wretch is no fool." Still the· pleading face of beautiful Dolores lingered, haunting the excited man, her wistful dark eyes pleading, and he could hear her voice, in its ringing wail, "My father, my father!" The chains of an international love were riveted, now binding him in weal and woe to the daring girl whose graceful figure, robed in the acolyte's gown, her slender hand grasping the heavy candle, came back as when she led the way boldly out into the night.

With a patient air Josè Marquez rose as he glanced at the dial. "Excuse me, I will consider, and soon give you my answer. I must think of other matters—the night guards! my great trust."

The governor silently vanished through a side door, leaving Wainwright, his heart thrilling with love, hope, and a nameless fear of the unexpected, gazing to note the appearance of the returning dictator. An ocean breeze swept in through the open door. The commander thought of Jack Crowninshield on his cruise to meet the Yaquis. He sprang to his feet. "I have it. I will threaten him with the vengeance ot the Yaquis. The broken compact. They may join with the avengers of Pesquiera to hurl this brute from his place." And still the governor came not. The commander's eyes were fixed on the side door.

Suddenly the convent bell boomed twelve, and as he heard the sound of a horse madly dashing away, José Marquez entered from the adjutant's room.

His face was ghastly pale.

One glance was enough. "Tricked, by God!" shouted Harry, as he sprang to the door and gazed with eager eyes.

Carbajal was gone.

"You fool and liar!" shouted the American. "You have deceived me, coward that you are! I will warn the Yaquis myself of your broken faith—of your murder of their friend. I sail to-morrow, and shall call the tribe together! You will find fire and sword sweeping Sonora! Liar!" the sailor shouted. "You will lose all. They will overwhelm you!"

Governor Marquez sank helpless in his chair of state. He was speechless before the American's rage.

"It is too late—too late!" he gasped. "Carbajal is gone. Why did you not tell me?"

"Here!" yelled Wainwright, as he thrust the pen in his hand. "Write!"

The frightened tyrant obeyed, wrote one word, "Suspend."

"He shall have due trial by law!" Marquez cried; but, his heart bursting with agonized love, the sailor had reached his horse.

"For Dolores' sake!" he cried, as he urged the fretting steed up the rocky path to where the prison frowned from its blood-stained heights.

CHAPTER XII.

IN THE CONDEMNED CELL.

FRED BLIGH sprang to the gallery door, and, unmindful of the sentinel's rude protest, watched the little procession vanish in the gloom of the long passage towards Pesquiera's cell. The twinkling tapers of the acolytes dimly sparkled in the distance, as the timid bearers shuffled along. Behind them the red glare of Pablo's lantern lit up with fitful gleams the rough arches piled up by the patient Indian slaves of bygone years. Following all, his clanking sword scabbard waking strange echoes in the damp corridor, Captain Villareal strode along, his hand clenching the army revolver, whose sheath he had thrust to the front on his belt.

"Is there any trick in this?" he growled. "I must watch. My life would be forfeit to 'El Tigre de Sonora' if he is balked of this man's life." Hardened by scenes of pitiless guerilla warfare, a mere thing of the cruel governor's caprices, still, the captain sorrowed to see his old chief, the son of Sonora's greatest governor, led out to die like a dog.

But, accustomed to scenes of revolution, and doubly endued with the Mexican callousness of heart, Enrique

Villareal simply sighed, "Pobrecito," and grimly watched the hasty preparations of the acolytes for the services.

At a sign from Villareal, who nodded his head as he turned away, stout Pablo opened the heavy iron door, and the bishop, splendid in his vestments, entered the cell of the condemned.   Of all the throng, one candle-bearer alone entered, while a solemn chant arose, which curdled the half-breed captain's blood with superstitious awe.   Rudely taught, only a master of his horse, the use of arms and the simple horn-book of his drill, the soldier feared the un-waked power of the mighty Church of Rome.   He had seen her fanes thrown down, her altars pillaged, her priests driven out, and the gentle sisterhood scattered over the un-happy land of Mexico.   He knew not that Time always showed a stronger Church, a subtler power, a vaster influence.   It was only from personal terror that he humbly retreated as the old bishop, the flickering lights gleaming on his silver hair, silently entered the cell.

"Valga-me-Dios! I dare not face his curse!" mumbled the soldier, as he listened to the voice of the young priest now raised in the solemn words of that mighty Church, the first and, perhaps, to be the last bulwark of a threatened civilization !

A sergeant clattering clumsily down the passage rudely saluted, and demanded orders from his superior.   "Shall the men be formed in the paseo?" he stolidly demanded, peering with brutal curiosity at the little throng beyond.

Enrique Villareal started.   "Has the courier returned?" he sharply questioned.

"Not yet!" was the reply.   "Then gather your men in

loose order. Report the moment that he enters the guard-room!" As the man hastened away his captain wiped the beads from his brow.

"The order is not yet come! Perhaps—perhaps—it will not be for to-night!" And a gleam of compassion entered the soul of the minister of bloody Marquez. Yet, with memories of sudden popular revulsions in his dull mind, Villareal walked slowly to the other end of the corridor and, mechanically, lit a papelito. "He is a fool if he does not make sure now!" mused the guardsman. "Once only the serpent comes under the foot! Marquez will not dare to keep him, a constant menace in Sonora!" "Es muy rico!" thought Villareal, wondering who would fall heir to the scattered possessions of Mateo Pesquiera.

"There is a daughter!" he murmured. "But she will see nothing left after José Marquez has taken toll!"

It was now nearing twelve, and the captain gazed from a loop-hole at the winding road leading up from the Presidio, which was still gleaming with lights. His wandering eye rested on the tiled roof of the massive old convent.

"She is there! I wonder if—if she knows?" he thought, as he turned his glances towards the bay dreaming under the stars far below him.

The "Democrata" was now warped in closely, command-ing the plaza of the town. A suggestion of moment came to the soldier.

"What a fool to excite the town with this execution! El Gobernador could have sent him out to sea! A pistol shot! Then, overboard! and no one would have known! Yes! that were better!" And he regretted the lack of finesse of his dark chief. "No rumours! No grave to be seen! No talk about a hasty trial! They could have said he tried to escape! Ah! He will never leave these walls alive!"

While the soldier waited for the fatal order, on his knees in the cell Mateo Pesquiera had murmured his confession with bowed head. Over him, in a last benediction, the bishop spread his hands, and his solemn voice intoned the words which fit the passing soul for its flight! In the nervous exhaustion of his self-torment, Pesquiera had not broken the silence, but cast himself at the feet of the prelate.

He marked not the trembling form of the graceful girl swaying unsteadily as she stood behind the bishop. Her lips were sealed though the heart was beating wildly. A daughter of the Church, she was in a trance of exaltation and fear combined. Two armed sentinels stood at the door, to see that none but God's holy messenger might reach the man whose very minutes were now numbered. The bishop turned and in a loud voice commanded, "Make your peace, my son! He took the heavy candle from the half-fainting girl's hand and stepped to the cell door.

"Now, my child!" whispered the prelate, "speak low!" and at a sign the attendants raised their voices in a chant. The sentinels retired a few paces, while in the open door of the cell the ghostly father stood, his hands folded in prayer.

Was it a dream, a mocking vision of the night, which tempted Mateo Pesquiera to a wild cry: "Dolores!"—for the words were on his lips, but two clinging arms almost smothered him in an embrace of womanly tenderness and childish alarm.

" It is I ! Whisper ! They will drag me from you ! I will stay with you to the last ! " And shielding him with her brave young breast, the Spanish maiden clung to the bewildered hidalgo. Passing his hands in tremulous rapture over her face, the prisoner faltered, " It is my Dolores ! To hear your darling mother's voice I go ! From heaven she leans to bless her child ! " His strength failed, and on her sustaining bosom, he bent his head in an ecstasy of bliss.

"Padre ! Mi padre querido ! " the rich young voice breathed, recalling him to the world of pain. " I crave your blessing ! Would you aught of me ? Your wishes— your child must know all ! " And as the condemned father strove to whisper words of parting cheer, the great convent bell solemnly boomed out on the night. Pesquiera started: " It is the fatal hour ! "

"There is yet hope," breathed Dolores. " The good bishop is here ! And the brave Americano struggles even now to save you ! He swore to me he would not fail ! " Above the solemn intoning of the chant rose the sound of a bugle calling the " Alerta ! " Too well the prisoner knew its meaning. The scattered garrison was forming up. The bell had rung out midnight ! and with a clash the doors at the end of the corridor opened.

" They are coming, Dolores ! " huskily said Pesquiera. " The Americano has failed ! It is a gallant youth ! He may aid the bishop to bear you far away from this fatal shore ! The Church—the Church will guard and guide ! They dare not rob you of all ! My lands will be yet yours ! The bishop will protect——"

A soft hand, burning in love's fever, was pressed over his mouth, and the girl's form nestled closer to the parent she would shield, as Captain Villareal's voice interrupted the old prelate in his prayers.

"Senor Obispo," cried the guardsman in a muffled voice, "I must do my duty! The time has come! In five minutes the guard will be here to remove the prisoner."

There was a silence, for even the chanting acolytes divined the grim import of the visit. "Has the courier returned?" queried the old prelate in a voice of august authority. "I have appealed to the governor for a respite until the morning. The law grants the condemned this right. He is not a malefactor—a prisoner of State! I claim my rights as titular Bishop of Sonora to an answer."

The girl's head nestled closer to her father's bosom, and her arms strained him nearer to her gentle breast.

Villareal stammered, "Lord Bishop, the adjutant of the governor is here. He has the written order for the immediate execution of the prisoner Pesquiera!"

"Bid him come hither. I will not leave a soul but half prepared for this last hour. I claim the right to finish the prisoner's confession. There are matters of State, there are tidings for the governor's own ear, before you proceed to your task." The solemn tones of the bishop dismayed Captain Villareal. Well he knew that, with the consent of the penitent, the spiritual guide could speak of that sealed otherwise to all. As the officer clanked away, Dolores, in an agony of longing, cried: "He will come! He must come! There is yet time!" and Pesquiera, whose heart was quickly nerved by pride of race when the sound of the half breed's voice reached him, passed his hands fondly over the bowed head of the devoted girl.

" My Dolores! My brave child! May God and the Blessed Virgin shield you !"

Down the flagged passage the tramping of feet resounded, and Dolores dragged her sire backward into the remotest gloom, as Adjutant Carbajal, in a reverent voice, spoke earnestly and pleadingly with the now resolute bishop.

"I will read your eminence the order," slowly said the adjutant, who vainly tried to prolong the long waiting for the fatal signal of exit.

It was soon done, and Villareal, when the last echoes died away, in a strained voice cried, "Sergeant, bind and bring forth the prisoner !" and turning to Pablo, whose lantern hung idly at his side, the captain motioned to the cell with his unsheathed machête.

"Go in !" he roughly cried. But not a foot stirred, and the stolid-faced guards turned away their heads as Bishop Dominguez seized the cross from its bearer.

Firmly planting it before his intrepid breast, the brave old prelate stayed them at the door.

" In the name of the Church ! Over my dead body only will you enter ! I will have my response first ! Where is the courier ? "

" The governor himself holds him back. He bade me say there is no answer," faltered Carbajal, as the captain of the guard turned fiercely on him for an answer.

"I will not yield," the undaunted bishop cried. " I believe you not ! He would not dare——"

" Stand back !" yelled Villareal, goaded into action by

the wavering faces of his excited guard, and he sprang upon the aged bishop, vainly trying to wrest the staff of the pastoral cross from his hands. A woman's scream, thrilling, piercing in its wail of woe, rang down the corridor as the soldiers strove to aid their commander.

But all started back as a stranger voice cried, "Hold! By the governor's order!" and in the flickering gleams mingling with the shadows Harry Wainwright sprang down the narrow passage with a paper in his outstretched hand. Close behind him, struggling with a sentinel vainly trying to retard him, was Fred Bligh, whose strength was lionlike in his wrath.

Carbajal sprang to meet him. "It is the Senor Americano. Give me the paper!" and he bounded to the side of Villareal, who had drawn his pistol.

"Madman! Beware! It is right!" and Carbajal rushed to the open cell door. He was too late, for in the gloomy cell, the sailor had clasped Dolores to his throbbing heart. "Look up!" he cried, "the governor comes! Be brave now!" And as Carbajal seized the lantern and entered he started in wild surprise, for there, in the white garb of an altar-boy, the Pearl of Guaymas was sobbing on the stranger's bosom!

"Senorita Dolores!" was his cry of astonishment, "how came you here?" But no one answered, as the bishop led the girl to where her father had sunk upon his pallet.

"It is too much!" he said, and turning to the excited officers he gravely said, "Let us await the governor."

Bligh quickly drew Wainwright out of the press and whispered in his ear, "Now is your time! When he comes

make him swear that Pesquiera goes on the Democrata
to-night. The bishop can join you in urging a delay of a
week, to await a confirmation from Mexico. If I know
Jack Crowninshield aright, there is hope for us all yet. Do
not leave him, see him embark yourself."

Wainwright's nervous hands closed on Fred's in a grip of
iron. " If there is foul play, by heavens, I'll run her down
at her moorings! "

And as they ceased a sentinel darted towards them with
the cry, " The governor comes! " The two officers hastened
to the guard-room, leaving Bishop Dominguez standing, a
faithful soldier of the Church, on guard over his spiritual
children.

"That girl is worth a king's ransom, Harry! " the miner
eagerly said, but Wainwright heard him not. Softer than
the sighing breeze of the forest came the echoes of the
impassioned voice of the girl, now by her father's side, and
Harry Wainwright heard that gentle voice alone.

" Now is your time to frighten this scoundrel, while his
nerves are shaken. Remember, Pesquiera's fate is in your
hands alone," said Bligh, as he laid a heavy hand upon the
entranced lover's arm. The sound of breaking ranks and a
clamour of surprise reached them as the tired soldiers
thronged out of the pasèo. Oaths, exclamations of rage and
joy mingled were heard, with a few perfunctory cries of
" Viva Marquez! " The largess in aguadiente, which usually
followed extraordinary services, was forgotten on this
eventful night by Governor Marquez, who was deep in an
earnest conference with his two subordinates.

Harry Wainwright bowed as the young priest and his

train filed down the deserted hall way. It was long past
midnight, and only the bishop remained in Pesquiera's cell,
where the beautiful acolyte was clinging to her now excited
father, and showering kisses on the man who dared to hope
for reprieve, if not a regular trial.

The sailor watched the two low-browed sentinels mechanically present arms as the robed secretary passed out into
the night bearing the blessed emblems on his bosom
meekly.

"I must now bluff this wretch in every way in my
power," reflected Harry, as he stepped forward and sought
the presence of José Marquez. He turned as the door
closed with a clang, leaving staunch Fred Bligh the
companion of the party in the cell.

"Never mind me," cheerily cried the miner through the
grating. "I have my pistol, and I am in the safest place in
Guaymas. Don't forget your guns shoot far! Put on the
pressure strong."

"Can I trust this wretch a moment? I must browbeat
him!" mused Wainwright. "If Phil and Basil were here, their
wit would mend mine. They will wonder at this delay."
His responsibilities as a commanding officer returned to his
mind. "Ah, I have it!" he smiled as he entered the
jail commandant's office; "I will fly the eagle a bit first—on
general principles!"

Walking up to José Marquez, who rose with a guilty air,
Wainwright doffed his gold-banded cap with an easy
deference.

"Pardon me, your excellency, but the hour is late! I
will ask you to accord me an audience on a very grave

matter to morrow, as I wish to move up the Gulf! One of my first duties is to make an official report to the Navy Department of my Government, of all serious political occurrences in my immediate cruising vicinity. Your Government shares with the whole civilized world in the peaceful explorations of the Gulf survey and chart work. I will not expose my men to revolutionary brawls! Will you kindly inform me, officially, at once, of the presence of armed bands or reactionary movements ? "

"There are none such at present!" quickly replied José Marquez, caught off his guard.

"Then it must be some private resentment which would cause you to execute, without a trial, an ex-governor of your great Sonora. The name of Pesquiera is well known at Washington, as the great governor was the constant friend of all American travellers and explorers. Would you have me officially report the hasty punishment of his son? It would look as if you feared to disclose your charges against him. I must warn you that I protest against such violations of law. I have been asked by Bishop Dominguez to say that he has special state reasons to disclose to you. He has begged my interference."

Marquez gazed blankly at his two officers. Villareal, now glad to be relieved of a burdensome tour of duty, had whispered to the governor, "Ah, Mateo has great secrets! The bishop alone knows, you must hear him first; and Dominguez could raise the Yaquis with his missionaries and throw them on our borders. You know Mateo was thei best friend."

"Right, right! Leave us, Enrique! But, let Carbajal

o

wait in my carriage." José Marquez turned to the American
naval officer with a vague attempt at a smile, as they were
left alone, and proceeded,—

" You will write no report, commandante—I beg of you,
at present. I will give you a whole memorial to guide you.
Pardon me, I was too hasty ! "

" Let me show you why you were about to make the one
error of your new administration, General Marquez ! "
cordially answered Wainwright, gazing intently at the
would-be statesman. " I have served here before as a
junior. I know the power of the bold Yaquis ! You will
be hailed as the regenerator of Sonora if you develop its
vast resources ! Now the mines, the coal fields, the interior,
the forest wood trade, can only be developed by the un-
trammeled use of the Yaqui River. If you had to fight the
man's friends and the Yaquis at once, you would be overwhelmed, for they have coped with your whole national
army. Pacifying the Yaquis, you are free to stamp out all
political disaffection, and you can easily rid yourself of this
local enemy by sending him to the city of Mexico for trial,
after you have formulated his charges. Do not let it be said
that you, a great governor, palsied your hand by a personal
act of tyranny."

" But he is rich, dangerous ! He might use his money to
bribe the court at the city of Mexico. Then he would plot
to overthrow me ! " Marquez was doubtful.

" But you must keep faith with the Yaquis to show your
power. You must appear to have Pesquiera under your
control. Send him down there to pacify the groundless
fears of those superstitious natives. Listen now ! Pesquiera

will try to save his life by doing your will! He will plead with the Yaquis. During his week of absence you can prepare such changes as will break Pesquiera's political power forever! Sent to the city of Mexico for trial, he cannot communicate with his Indian allies, you can prevent his return—for I presume you will confiscate his lands and movables!"

The greedy governor's eyes twinkled as he bowed an assent.

"Then he can never injure you, even if they acquit him. The poor man has no friends in this world! Money is the very root of political power! Once this man's property is in your hands, he sinks into the common herd!"

There was a triumphant ring in Harry's voice as the doubting tyrant's brow lightened.

"You are wonderful! You enter into the very spirit of our land!" answered the enlightened scoundrel. "If you will only take a local interest!" he eagerly added, dreaming of the great Yaqui River Improvement Company.

"I propose to. I certainly shall!" seriously replied the sailor, and the handsome fellow's cheeks reddened as he thought of Dolores, holding her father's trembling hand now in the memory-haunted cell! "I must free them all!" Harry resolved. "Now for the grand coup!"

"Again, your excellency, you know well that nothing resists a counter-current of the great Church! This good old bishop seems to be attached to Pesquiera. He is a temporary guardian of his beautiful daughter! He knows all Pesquiera's secrets. You can rivet all the clerical party to you by affecting to grant this reprieve as a favour to the bishop. In this way you divide your enemies, rally friends, pacify the Yaquis, and open the road to your private fortune, as well as future political control!"

"I will do it. You are right, mi amigo!" cried Marquez, "you shall be made rich too, for a thought comes to me. The Senorita Dolores—if I married her! I would be the richest man in Sonora. For the land must come back to her finally!"

"Good! Will you send for the bishop and pledge him that Pesquiera goes on the Democrata?" Wainwright's face was ghastly pale as he spoke.

"I will write the order of reprieve for two weeks now!" said the governor complacently, dreaming of the future greatness of the house of Marquez. "And the bishop is old. He needs rest. He can come to me to-morrow!"

"Carbajal, capitano!" the governor called, and the adjutant strode in. "Let Captain Villareal take twenty men and escort the prisoner Pesquiera to the Democrata to-night. You can attend me to the Presidio. Is the escort there?" The shaken tyrant feared the night prowlers of Guaymas. Some prowler might revenge Mateo Pesquiera's downfall.

"It is all ready, your excellency, and the carriage waits."

"Take a copy of this order, Villareal," said Captain Carbajal, with a meaning glance at Wainwright. "I will send his excellency's carriage back for the bishop, who can wait on the governor to-morrow."

"One moment, general!" cried Harry Wainwright, as the governor passed out of the door. He dared not face the bishop, fearing the burden of the secrets disclosed by l'esquiera. "Can I verify the embarkation of your prisoner?"

"Certainly, commandante! and come to me to-morrow afternoon. I would speak with you alone."

Harry Wainwright scarcely dared to breathe as the lancers rattled away in a close column around Marquez.

He gazed on the burning stars of night—lamps of love—and saw the mast headlight of the Ranger flaring over the blackened waters of the bay.

"I will kill him with my own hand, if he drags that brave girl to the altar!" so the sailor registered his oath silently before high heaven.

"Take me to them!" cried Wainwright, as he turned to Villareal. As they passed through the iron door, the captain whispered, "Senor Americano! we said naught of the presence of Senorita Dolores. Guard this secret. I wish not the death of Don Mateo. It is Carbajal who told me to warn you."

Wainwright grasped his hands. I will pay you for your kindness. Come to my vessel—alone!" And the old soldier nodded significantly.

"All right, Bligh," huskily gasped Harry. "He goes on board to-night!" Fred was standing by the cell door.

"I go to get my mantle!" suddenly whispered Villareal. "The escort will be ready when the carriage arrives!" and he darted away.

"Dolores!" eagerly cried Harry, as he convulsively grasped the stout miner's hands.

"Asleep in her father's arms!" answered Fred, as the bishop joined them. The moments seemed an eternity until Villareal returned. "To the convent first, and then, the embarcadero!" ordered Villareal, as he sprang on his horse. Bligh had enlightened the bishop, and he disappeared on foot in the darkness, as Harry Wainwright bore the exhausted girl wrapped in the soldier's mantle to the carriage of her foe. She moaned faintly, and clasped in her arms the beloved form she would still shield, but as the carriage dashed away, it was on Harry Wainwright's breast her tired head lay, and his heart leaped up in a wild ecstatic joy as her gentle bosom first throbbed upon a lover's heart.

At the convent steps, with one last kiss upon her pallid lips, Mateo Pesquiera saw the doors open, and the American bearing the precious burden of the night.

"You shall not die! Trust the American—to the death," whispered the bishop to the prisoner. "I will foil José Marquez yet!"

And when, on the deck of the Democrata, Wainwright parted from the agonized father, his last whisper was, "For Dolores' sake!"

"Gentlemen," said Harry to Hackmuller and Bligh, as he strode to the landing an hour later, "with this treasure in safety, Pesquiera can buy the national courts. It is in Jack Crowninshield's hands now to make me the happiest man in the world. I must save that man's life!"

Dark Marquez, brooding on his couch, swallowed a fiery draught to quiet his shaken nerves. "I can have him

killed on the way to Mexico! I will outwit the Yaquis.
They will charge it to the bandits. And the girl, her
fortune, his heaped-up riches will be mine at last !"

But Harry Wainwright, pacing his vessel's deck till the
Democrata stole out of the harbour, saw in the brightening flush of the eastern skies the dark roof where Dolores
slept in peace. The golden sun leaped up in the happy
lover's eyes.

CHAPTER XIII.

ENSIGN JACK CROWNINSHIELD leaned over the stern of the Ranger's launch, sweeping her wake with his binoculars. The boat glided easily along just outside the breakers coasting the mouth of the Yaqui. It was three hours from sundown. A half-dozen men lay under the awning, and the little boat was loaded deep with arms and stores. By the dashing young officer's side sat the missionary priest, calmly poring over his breviary.

"There she is," said Crowninshield to himself, as wing and wing the swift Constance swept around the headland. "Now I'll reach the point in an hour and camp. The Constance will round the Lobos Point and anchor by midnight. As the Democrata will not leave till to-morrow night, the council will not assemble till next day. So I have a whole day to fix up my scheme with the Indians. I'll run around the point to the Indian camp in the river, and leave a man at the point to answer the signals from the Constance. If I had that fellow Diego I would know the river better; but I'll get a Yaqui canoeman to pilot me. Thank God, Diego can't watch me, if he pilots the Democrata. The commander was right to get him off the yacht."

The sunset hours gave the ensign time to run in and examine the river for a league. When the lights of the Constance showed fairly abreast of the point, Crowninshield burned a port-fire, which was answered by a Roman candle for a signal.

For an hour the gay young sailor chatted from his hammock, swung from two tree-limbs, with the grave missionary.

"All you have to do, padre, is to move your Indian friends around the bend a mile or so. I'll station my launch so that the soldiers will not be able to reach the gun-boat before Pesquiera is out of danger."

The shades of the next evening wrapped the tropical forest in gloom when the Mexican gun-boat dropped anchor a mile outside the point where the sailor and the priest awaited them. A fire kindled on shore brought off a boat with the executive officer of La Democrata. Coldly saluting Crowninshield, he paced the beach an hour under the stars with the priest.

When the plash of oars died away, the missionary returned. "God be praised! we shall save him! They will land Pesquiera at noon to-morrow. A strong guard will be landed on either side of the point. I am to conduct the prisoner to the meeting. An unarmed officer and four men are to go with Pesquiera : their orders are not to leave him. I will let the high-priest select the spot to station the canoes. You must come ashore when I give the signal. Leave all to me then."

As the sun climbed to meridian the next day, the glancing bayonets of a dozen Mexican riflemen could be seen at

either side of the sixty-yard current of the swift Yaqui.
A heavy boat with a dozen occupants laboured against
the sweeping shore-currents. When its prow grated on
the strand, the passionless face of the priest greeted the
unarmed officer who bade Pesquiera leave the boat. Two
sentinels stepped to his side. In a loud voice the officer
in command addressed the guard: "Should the prisoner
attempt to escape, shoot him at once. In two hours the
guard will march up to the council-place to escort my
return."

Over the sands Pesquiera followed the officer and the
priest: a fatiguing walk of ten minutes followed. A group
of Indians with a white flag was seen gathered on a point.
The officer halted his armed guard and motioned the two
men with him to advance. Six unarmed sailors followed.
The priest eyed the prisoner carefully: "Yes, it is right. A
broad palm-leaf hat, a long linen coat, a flowing white sun-
kerchief around his neck." Not a word was exchanged
until the party halted before a clump of Indian huts on a
clear space near the bend selected for the conference.

The aged high-priest strode out to meet them. In eager
curiosity his copper-coloured followers thronged around the
Mexican. The priest fixed his eyes on the river and carefully watched its placid surface. While the suspicious
Mexican officer conferred with the priest, the prisoner stood
grave and mute. The missionary walked out to the extreme
point of the bend, leaving the party alone with the Yaquis.
An Indian canoe glided swiftly over the quiet river to the
point, and Ensign Jack Crowninshield stepped ashore. His
sword was belted on, his glistening double buttons sparkled

in the sun, and his cap with the gold anchors well became a handsome face, on which an easy unconcerned smile played. The Mexican officer respectfully saluted him. At two yards' distance, the old Indian priest and the prisoner were earnestly talking.

" I will sit down in my house, and I would see El Gobernador alone," said the priest.

"It is well," the Mexican answered, as the Indian disappeared with the prisoner into the frail shelter of bark and twigs thatched and plaited with broad palm-leaves. At the distance of a few yards, the officer fixed his eyes on the door of the tent. His men were stationed so as to observe the river-banks.

In ten minutes, with a cordial salute to the Mexican, Crowninshield bowed to the missionary, stepped into his canoe, and disappeared around the bend. The curious Yaquis crowded around the tent. Ten minutes later, the launch of the Constance passed down the river. In her stern the young officer sat guiding the boat. It rounded the river mouth in plain sight, skirting the southern shore, within pistol-shot of the guard on either bank.

When fifteen minutes had passed, the Mexican officer, with an impatient gesture, strode up to the door of the hut. The old high-priest was seated on a mat, bowing to an idol set up in the centre. Raising his voice, he gazed at the Spaniard and calmly said, " Why does he not return ? "

A yell of rage brought the Mexican watchers together. "Search the camp! He has escaped! Caramba! It shall cost you your heads."

The astounded sailors ran hither and thither like mad.
The wondering Yaquis crowded around their high-priest,
who pointed to the river, uttering some words in their
strange tongue. The simple pagans fell on their knees. A
single canoe was stemming the river a hundred yards above;
an Indian was wildly paddling, and a man, clad in a long
linen coat, a broad palm-leaf hat, and a glistening white
kerchief, leaped ashore and waved his hand in defiance.
Drawing a pistol from his bosom, the infuriated officer
dashed at the old Yaqui priest.   In an instant all was a wild
tumult.   The Indians, like tigers, sprang upon the unarmed
Spaniards.   The officer's pistol-muzzle was pressed against
his temples.   Down the beach, in frantic fear, one of the
Mexican sailors raced for the guard.

In half an hour the score of soldiers, arriving at a run,
found the officer and his six men bound to trees. The
forest was silent : the resentful Yaquis had departed. The
missionary, fleeing in apparent fear, had joined the new-
comers on the way.

"What has happened?" cried the sub-officer as he
released his senior, who could not speak for rage.
"Explain ! Can you explain, padre? We may be attacked
at any moment. Let us march to the boats. We must
communicate with the ship. I sent one man to order the
guard at the river mouth to build a fire, discharge their guns,
and call for help."

"I fear the soldiers are crazy," replied the missionary.
"The prisoner entered the little hut alone with the Yaqui
priest. These men tell me the American officer came out.
There is madness or magic. He left me on the point and

Went to his boat in a canoe. He is now on his boat outside the river bar."

" To the boats, to the boats ! We have been tricked !" roared the officer; and the party hastened out of the uncanny forest shades.

" Who was in the canoe ? " meekly asked the missionary. " You certainly saw the prisoner in the boat with the Indian who crossed ? "

" The devil, or his double ! Hold your peace, you shaven fool ! Some of us will be shot for this," snarled the baffled Mexican, as they emerged on the strand. Two boats were nearing the shore, and the guard from the other side was crowding into the cutter left on watch. Yells and cries resounded, for a signal-gun boomed over the water, and clouds of black smoke were pouring from the funnel of La Democrata. An impotent storm of cursing met the defeated officer as he clambered up the rope ladder to the deck.

Before the whole crew, the naval commander raved at the outwitted soldier: " Marquez will hang you for this, you idiot ! Can't you see where he has gone ?—Full speed !" he yelled, springing to the engine-room hatch.

For swarthy Diego, at his side, pointed to a little steam launch, a league away, standing out to a beautiful white schooner sweeping round the distant headland. The officer's glass showed him the American flag gleaming against the sun.

" The scoundrel is safe under that flag. Cast loose the four-inch rifled gun. If I can overhaul that schooner, I'll sink her, with all on board. She is a pirate."

In the wild excitement of the chase, the missionary seated himself at the side of the vessel and addressed himself to his breviary. In answer to a storm of abuse, he replied to the naval officer,—

"Senor Commandante, I am not responsible to you. I was not in charge of the prisoner. I know nothing. I shall fully report to my bishop, and Governor Marquez shall be informed of your brutality. Scold your subordinate : I am not under your orders."

"Never mind the priest ; listen to me," cried Diego. "I see the whole trick. These fellows have sent up all their racing spars and trimmed that boat for this race. Crowd on all your steam."

The white hull of the rebaptized Halcyon was hardly visible as she came up to the wind. The launch swept alongside, and, slowly swinging, the matchless racer stood off shore. The afternoon sunlight gleamed on her snowy flying jib, and aloft the topsails added to the gathering speed.

"All ready, sir," cried the master gunner, as the Democrata leaped forward, every timber quivering with the twist of her heavy screw.

"Load and fire!" yelled the infuriated captain. "Try to bring down her masts." As the steel bolt screamed away on its flight, the stars and stripes fluttered in the peak.

"You may regret this, sir," said the second in command, touching his cap. "We have no proof that the prisoner is on board."

"There goes the proof," cried Diego, his face in a scowl, as the last available stitch of canvas crowded the fleeting ocean queen. The bellying spinnaker gleamed as the Halcyon darted seaward.

"She is going three knots to our two, captain," the chief engineer reported, "and I am carrying more than our safety-limit of steam. It is of no use."

At the sixth shot, even the commander was forced to admit that they fell farther and farther astern. With a last curse, he ordered the vessel about.

"Slow down the engines," he growled. "We will steam back and anchor for the night. I will land a boat's crew to pick up our stragglers and property." He cast a glance at the Ranger's launch, leisurely steaming toward Yaqui Point under cover of the shore.

"You may consider yourself under close arrest," cried the naval commander to the sullen soldier. "I shall hardly need to prefer charges against you. Marquez will probably shoot you by a drum-head court." He signed to the watch-officer to deprive the luckless man of his sword.

When the morning sun broke over Yaqui Bay, the slumbers of the Mexican commander were broken by an official visit from Ensign Crowninshield. His launch lay alongside, ready to steam back to Guaymas.

"I deem it fit to inform you, sir," said the young American, sternly, "that I feel justified in abandoning my projected duties here and reporting at once your gross outrage in firing on the American flag."

"You know the character of that vessel," the angry Mexican retorted.

"Governor Marquez will learn everything I know, through

my commander. Meanwhile, I warn you to be ready with some explanation of your behaviour."

The young ensign stiffly touched his hat, and, springing into his cutter, sped away towards Guaymas.

The Ranger's launch was swinging alongside the cruiser at anchor while the Democrata slowly crawled up the coast. Springing lightly on board, Crowninshield entered the commander's cabin. A glance at the gallant boy was enough.

"Call away my gig!" shouted Wainwright to the sentry.

"Do not leave my cabin a moment till my return," said the commander, when he had listened to the report. "You shall never forget this day." The light of Love was in his eyes, and he carried the tidings of a father's safety to the sweetest maid in Sonora. But he trained his face to gravity, for he well knew a storm would break over Guaymas when the duped tyrant heard the tidings. He sauntered easily up the stone-fringed drive-way toward the silent old cathedral. A few Indian women bowed in the dusky corners at their prayers. He passed into the little sacristy. The sound of his voice awoke the bishop from his siesta.

"Pesquiera?" The old prelate's voice thrilled in an agony of entreaty.

"Safe, and now two hundred miles at sea," said Wainwright, sinking into a chair.

Tears of joy were raining down the bishop's cheeks. He raised his hands in an ecstasy of thankfulness.

"But, reverend bishop, there has been a fracas! The

Democrata lived on the yacht. Our dearest hopes depend on the prudence and self-control of our friends. Despatch your sacristan to Madame Delmar and her daughter at once. Let them remain at home. You can yourself break the news to Dolores : give her this." He dropped the emerald ring of her dead mother in the prelate's hand. " I have kept my word. Now, Marquez will rage, for—see there !" He threw open the casement. The Democrata was swinging round in the harbour, and a double-banked cutter was speeding to the shore. " You must stay at the convent until the storm blows over. I will go at once on my vessel, and will be ready to use force, if necessary, to protect Mrs. Delmar and her daughter. Should there be a demonstration in force, or a tumult, I will land my blue-jackets at once. I now go to Hackmuller and Bligh. They are free from all suspicion : they have not left the town a moment. I shall send one or two of my young officers on shore to watch quietly the gathering of the storm. Either Bligh or Hackmuller will be at the works, the other watching the convent. Let Mrs. Delmar go at once to the convent. Then do not leave the ladies. Silence, patience, courteous ignorance is our cue. We know nothing. The Yaquis are supposed to have carried him away. Keep your missionary at your side : he cannot then be forced to talk."

From the arched doorway at the convent, casting a glance over the little harbour, the bishop saw Wainwright's boat gliding back to the Ranger, whose long pennant and great national ensign swung lazily on the gentle breeze.

The mother superior touched his arm. " Come," she

whispered, and as he entered the convent parlour, where three women in the excitement of an unspeakable delight awaited him, the boom of an alarm-gun and the rattle of drums, with the barbaric wail of the singing bugles, broke on the stillness of the dying day.

"It is discovered! Hasten, my daughter; lead these three ladies into one of the safest cloisters. Do not leave them an instant. Now, my daughters, silence, and trust in God. Remember, you must know nothing."

"Do you fear violence?" Dolores anxiously asked.

"No. Our gallant friend Wainwright will prevent any violation of the sanctity of the convent." He did not see the blush which transfigured the loving girl when he handed her the ring. "He sends you this. Go, my children. Here comes the mob."

With unwonted activity, the prelate ordered the fortress-like doors of the convent to be closed and summoned the faithful male retainers to their posts. It was high time. From barrack and cuartel the fierce soldiery swarmed to the plaza: aides were hurrying through the street, and a tipsy crowd were howling before the barred doors, "Death to the Americans!"

"Sancta Maria, here they come!" murmured the old ecclesiastic, as the ringing tramp of a company of Mexican troops sounded on the stony street. At their head, the port-captain marched by the side of the officer in command. Diego the pilot, with a wolfish leer, led the two soldiers up the broad stone steps and unceremoniously clanged the knocker of the convent door. Half the superstitious soldiery fell on their knees as the doors swung wide and the old bishop, clad in his robes, mildly asked, " What seek you here ? "

The officer hung his head and said, " I have an order for the arrest of a Mrs. and Miss Woodford, two American women concealed in this convent."

" You will enter God's house only over my body," answered the unawed prelate. " I warn you of the madness of your act. The American cruiser's guns command the town. Be warned."

" Give them up ! " hotly cried the officer. " I shall enter by force ! "

" May the curse of God rest on the man who forces his way over this threshold ! " The bishop slowly wheeled and stepped into the shadow. With a clang the great doors swung in place.

" Here, lieutenant ; to the governor. I will have his last orders." While his subaltern sped away, the soldier posted his troops around the convent.

Wainwright, pacing his quarter-deck, swept the shore eagerly with his binoculars and exchanged a few words with Ensign Crowninshield : both were in full uniform. " There goes the signal," said the commander. " Order the executive officer to land his division on our signal from the roof of Bligh's assay-office. You will accompany me ashore." The two officers descended the gangway into the ship's launch, now filled with well-armed blue-jackets.

" Capital ! " said Wainwright, as they sped on the waves. " So you sent ashore a suit of your old uniform for Pesquiera

to masquerade in?   And the native who wore his clothes,
how did he get them?"

"It was a lightning transformation.   The missionary had
warned Pesquiera.   When he stepped out of the loosened
side of the tent, I wandered round the point.   A canoe was
there, and I lay down in it.   The few steps from the hut to
the bushes enabled the prisoner to walk into the shrubbery.
The Spaniards were watching the door of the hut.   I
boarded my steam launch on the off side, and he was concealed.   The Indian who received his cast-off clothes when
they were thrown out of the open thatch-line of the hut
slipped them on, and his companion paddled out into the
river when I was well away."

"And if that plan had failed?" said the amused commander.

"The Indians were to surround the soldiers while the
prisoner made a break to the canoe.   Once on board my
launch, I knew I could run him out.   The Democrata's fires
were banked.   I would have landed him around the point
out of sight.   The Yaquis would have protected him."

"You are a daring fellow, Crowninshield.   Here we
are!" cried the commander.   "Make your way at once to
the convent, see the bishop, and then report to me at the
governor's."

Wainwright marched across the plaza to the door of the
National Palace now crowded with officers in uniform.   A
yelling crowd followed, and he turned his head to assure
himself that his armed boat's crew was a cable's length out
in the green tide.   Four companies of troops broke away,

marching to the embarcadero, and the Democrata's boats
waited them. " Evidently a landing to punish the Yaquis.
Thank heaven," he mused, "the forests will be deserted. I
pity them if they force their way into the fastnesses."

Raising his hat in courteous salute, Wainwright strode
into the council-room. Marquez, in speechless amazement,
swallowed his wrath. Without waiting for a welcome, the
commander began :

" I have called on you, Governor Marquez," he said, in
a ringing voice, " to demand the reason of the gun-boat
under your orders firing at an American vessel. Before
sending an official communication, I felt I might save you
the consequences of making this a diplomatic matter."

The tormented governor turned to the Democrata's commander ; but Wainwright went on : " I will drop the
incident on your personal explanation. If you seek to
make it official, I will send my boat's officer's report with
my despatch to the Secretary of the Navy. Your
case can be made through the Mexican minister." He
turned as Ensign Crowninshield hastily entered, chapeau in
hand. On hearing a few whispered words, the commander
seemed to grow in size. He tore open a letter handed him
by his aide. " I am informed that there is a riotous mob
besieging the convent, and that you have dared to issue an
order for the detention of two American ladies. Bishop
Dominguez sends me their plea for protection, and requests
me to give them and the daughter of your fugitive enemy
protection on my ship. I shall do so. As there is no
American consul here, I shall ask Mr. Frederick Bligh to

act as such until I can communicate with our minister at
Mexico.   I go now to convey these ladies to my vessel."

"I shall prevent it! they are conspirators : they arranged
the flight of the villain who is gone," snarled Marquez.

"Ensign Crowninshield," said the commander, "remain
here.   If there is an insult offered to me, signal the ship."

"What would you? What is your purpose?" cried
Marquez.

"I shall land my division.   If you oppose, I shall order
my vessel to open its guns for our support."   There was a
breathless silence as the speaker strode through the open
door.

As he sprang up the steps of the convent, the troops
parted right and left.   When, ten minutes later, Bishop
Dominguez led out a beautiful girl dressed in deepest black,
and Wainwright proudly escorted the two American ladies,
there was not a soldier in sight.   Ensign Crowninshield
drove up with a carriage and assisted Madame Delmar and
Anita to enter.   Slowly moving through a hostile mob on
the plaza, the party embarked.

"The governor is going to lead the expedition to the
Yaqui River in person.   He has ordered a company of
troops to protect Bligh and Hackmuller."   Wainwright
laughed as the steam launch sped away.   "I'll send ashore
for them.   All the American citizens here are entitled to
the protection of the flag."

There was a strange light in Wainwright's eyes as he
assisted his gentle visitors to the quarter-deck.

"I shall give you the cabin, and your maid can give

my steward any orders you may have," the host merrily said.

While the women, in a delicious realization of the safety assured by the flag above them, rested from their haunting fears, the commander conferred with the bishop.

" You are right, my son," said the prelate. " I will consult with Madame Delmar. You could not extend this national protection to Dolores. It is the only way."

After a dinner at which a spirit of tender expectancy imbued even Bligh and the professor, under the starlight, before the assembled officers, the bishop gave the blessing of the Church to the commander and his Mexican bride.

CHAPTER XIV.

MUTINY.

" How did Marquez appear to relish your communication ?" asked Commander Wainwright, seated in his cabin, as the Ranger daintily picked her way out of Guaymas Harbour. The sound of happy laughter echoed from the deck, where the three ladies, with waving kerchiefs, turned their faces towards the convent.

" He groaned," replied the subordinate. " The last thing Bligh told me was that Marquez really wishes only to make a show of reprisals upon the Indians. He believes them to be his friends. And his real object is to discover the mines. What will Pesquiera do next ? "

" I think he will take the steamer from Honolulu to San Francisco, remain quietly there, and displace Marquez peaceably by intrigue at the city of Mexico. The Yaqui question alone will cause the governor's downfall. Well, we shall see how he will behave on our return. To-morrow night the ladies can sleep at Mazatlan, and the steamer touches next day. It is chiefly to avoid the sickly season that I wish them to go to California. Pesquiera can determine their future movements. I shall take the Ranger on a cruise up the Gulf until it is time to hear of his safe arrival.

It might compromise the owners of the Halcyon if he returned on her. What a cruise home May and Goodloe will have! I think I can hear the echoes of wedding bells."

The commander walked the quarter-deck with his bride. "And I shall really see my father's face again? And you will come soon?" The girl wife was gazing up at her stalwart husband.

"Why, alma mia," Wainwright answered, "they may reach Honolulu in eight days. Phil May will crowd all sail on the yacht, for I think his duties near Mrs. Lee need his whole attention now. As for Goodloe, you know from Anita that her mother and herself count every hour till they can reward the man who has saved their fortune. We agreed that, in case of failure to bring your father, the yacht should return to San Francisco to place the treasure in safety and to leave me free to take him away when the Yaquis could manage to smuggle him on my boat; then I would have put him on a California-bound steamer at sea. As it is, to diminish the risk, he will return to San Francisco with his share of the precious freight of the Halcyon. The other half, under care of May and Goodloe, will be delivered to Mrs. Delmar on the arrival of the yacht. I shall look daily for the telegram announcing your meeting, after you have been ten days at San Francisco. I can get leave in two months and come to you. Your father will undoubtedly recall Andrès Vargas to proceed to the city of Mexico. He can pour a golden shower on the scale there which will turn it in his favour. But not a step on Mexican

soil must he venture until a special judgment of his case has
been rendered."

While the married lovers followed the course of the
Halcyon in their thoughts, that elusive vessel was flying on
the friendly stream of the North Equatorial current. Phil
May and Basil Goodloe plied every device of the sailor's
art. The yacht's sails hummed in the singing breeze as she
sped on, leaping forward through bluest rolling surge, under
the tropic skies of sapphire, flecked with pearl and gold at
the prow. A restless watcher walked the deck in all a
father's anxiety.

The brethren of the sea cheered the exile. " Have no fear
for your daughter's safety, governor," cried May. " Wainwright will protect her. And with the bishop and Madame
Delmar you know she is safe."

" I know Harry Wainwright's golden luck and dashing
way. There will be a welcoming group awaiting you at San
Francisco," Goodloe added. The lover was counting each
day reeled off the calendar as one less in the fast diminishing
period of the eclipse of Anita's bright eyes.

The yacht was in racing order. Lake and Jorgensen
marshalled the crew daily to restore every dainty embellish-
ment of the Halcyon.

"Captain Lake," said May, as the sea-drift and land-birds
told of their journey's approaching end, " we may make land
to-morrow. I shall dock at Honolulu and refit the boat for
the home run. The crew will be paid off, but I wish to
hasten our departure by every minute. I shall not forget
your energy and activity at the end of the cruise."

Obed Lake bowed and walked forward, as May, bronzed and the picture of glowing health, rejoined Goodloe, who was listening to Pesquiera's stories of the quaint shadowy history of Mexico.

By the foremast, Lake and Jorgensen lingered in converse under the stars.

"Are you all ready? Can you depend on the men?" Lake whispered, his keen eye never leaving the group at the stern.

"Ready on the moment," rejoined the mate. "I can bulkhead the arms-room in a minute after our entry. The pantry-man will guard the cabin. The men are all right. It is a great scheme. Will the Chinamen trust you with the cargo?"

"Certainly. I've made runs for them before. And at San Francisco I am safe behind the associates of the secret trade. They will protect us all," Lake answered.

"This Mexican general may make trouble for us," added Jorgensen. "Why can't we do it now?"

"What could we do without stores? Let him catch his steamer: we'll have one less to watch, and, if we have to throw them over, one less to fight," Lake growled. "His arriving safe will throw the home folks off their guard: they will think we have been driven out of our course or gone down in a storm. I wish we had Diego. But we are safe. We have nothing of value on the yacht. Our men must be true, to earn their money. Only a few days!"

"Now, General Pesquiera, in half an hour you can tell your plan of action," said May, as the pilot-signal fluttered from a little schooner dancing out of Honolulu Harbour, while the setting sun shone on the fragrant groves, dreamy valleys, and wooded peaks of Oahu.

Goodloe hailed the pilot as he sprang over the side. " The California-bound steamer ? " he anxiously inquired.

" Due here to-morrow, captain," was the answer. Joy beamed in the refugee's eyes as May translated the good tidings.

" I will go on shore with the governor, Basil," said May briskly, as the anchor rattled down. " You can watch here. To-morrow I will haul the yacht up on the dock, and our precious ballast can be placed in safe hands. We will see the leading shipping people. Let not a man leave the ship when we haul out. I will give them all three days' liberty. By that time our bullion will be in safe hands."

On the deck of the yacht Goodloe walked alone, thinking of Anita Delmar's eyes. Hour after hour struck from the bells of the clustered foreign men-of-war lying near. The quick plash of oars roused the dreamer as May leaped on board.

" All right, Goodloe. The tug will take us in at day-break. Pesquiera can dispose of half his Mexicans with the syndicate of Chinese merchants. The rest will be boxed and sealed by the Oriental Bank. They will give him San Francisco bills. Pesquiera will be there in nine days, and I'll wager my head the Halcyon shows Mrs. Lee's signal at the Heads not a week later."

" You are sanguine," said Goodloe. " Come, let us drink the health of the absent ones."

" It seems like a dream, my brave friends," said Pesquiera,

as he wrung the comrades' hands in farewell the next day. A score of dusky toilers were busied on the hull of the Halcyon, and a throng of admirers watched the ocean beauty in the dock. " Your letters, your commissions, all shall be my sacred trust. How can I ever repay you? To you my fortune, my life, my daughter's safety are all due."

"Ask Commander Wainwright. He will claim the reward for us. Wait till we meet on the shores of San Francisco Bay. But when you pass the old fort, with the American flag flying, think of us as you near your daughter, and wish us a swift homeward run. There goes the gun! Now, governor!" The boat in waiting bore the happy exile to the huge ocean liner straining at its buoy.

As the great steamer swept out on the blue waste of waters, May clasped his friend's hand. " Now for our own departure. In two days I am promised the stores and our last outfit. The boat will be in the water to-morrow night. Then for a hand-over-hand homeward run! There is already enough gossip and mystery about our sudden appearance here. Thank heaven, Pesquiera and his share of the treasure are off our hands."

"Do you think any one suspects our cargo's value?" Goodloe asked.

"Not a soul. The bags were supposed to be selected Mexican ores, and the boxing and counting were secretly done in Wong Lee's warehouse. All the banks handle these Mexican dollars through him, for they finally drift to the far East for Asiatic use."

" Well, certainly no one has suspected the secret of the lead bars. That was a rare idea of the professor. I will take a run in the town," Goodloe went on, "and hunt up Captain Lake.   We had better gather in the crew."

Mr. Obed Lake was at that moment enjoying the luxuries of the Chinese merchant prince's abode.

While Wong Lee studied, through his circular horn spectacles, a chart of the North Pacific coast, the sailor marvelled at the richness of the Oriental interior.   The old Chinese added lines of undecipherable characters to the last of a series of letters in the strange language of his land.

"The time is right.   When you reach Nagasaki the cargo will be ready.   It all depends on the San Francisco orders."

Wong Lee strained his almond eyes after the disappearing Halcyon as she swept away from his sight.   At the helm, Philip May watched the shores of Oahu recede.   "It's a fair breeze, Basil.   We shall make a grand run."

It was a freshening night as the two harbour-lights of Honolulu faded away in the dusk.   The Halcyon sprang forward under the steady impulse of her straining sails, her sharp stem cutting the rolling waves and dashing the broken spray high over her quarter.   In oilskins and sou'wester Obed Lake faced the storm, and Olaf Jorgensen, a muffled brooding giant, towered at the foremast shrouds.

"Well off shore, and in for a clean home run.   Goodnight, Phil," murmured Goodloe, as he sought his state-room, leaving the young yachtsman thinking of one far away.

Above their heads two men, clinging to the swaying cordage, muttered, "It's for to-morrow, then, when we have them both on deck."   Their eyes sought each other in the excitement of final resolve. " I will give the signal from the cabin hatch," said Lake. " Don't lose a moment when they are both forward."

And no friendly angel of the night whispered a warning to the sleeping comrades.

The golden sun, leaping out of pearl-shaded skies, brought May and Goodloe on deck. There was not a sail in sight, and the wearied land-birds were dropping off in airy circles toward the west.

In the freshness of the early day the men were still busied washing decks. May's quick eye noted their work as he strolled to the forecastle. He made a wild leap forward as half a dozen sailors suddenly threw themselves on Goodloe, who was borne to the deck. May essayed to shout, but a darkness came over him, and when he opened his eyes, Obed Lake was critically examining his appearance. " Not badly hurt; only stunned," said the traitor, when Jorgensen neared the group around the captive. With an ungentle wrench of his arms the bewildered prisoner felt for the first time in his life the snap of handcuffs on his wrists. At the stem of the yacht, confused cries rose from the men struggling with the desperate Goodloe.

" What does this mean, you cowardly villain?" May cried.

" Take it easy, captain," Lake replied. " It means that you are going on a little cruise with me now. We've fooled around the ocean long enough with you. Now you had better be civil or it will go hard with you. I don't want to keep your boat; I only want one run on her. If you and your friend have any sense, you'll take your luck as it comes, and you may get your boat back. If there is any nonsense between you two, why,"—the scoundrel pointed to the green deep,—" overboard you both go. Now just lash him easily in the forward rigging, and one of you watch him while I attend to the other chap." And Obed Lake, now master of the Halcyon, stalked away.

May, raging in his wrath, realized that not a word was vouchsafed in answer by his stolid captors. Every man of them appeared half an hour later girdled with a belt and a heavy revolver. Goodloe had been forced below into the cabin.

May swept the pitiless ocean with his eyes : not a sign, not a vestige of man's dominion.

As he groaned in agony, his throbbing temples racked with pain, he recalled the hidden treasure. Had the mutineers discovered the golden bars in their leaden jacketing? No, for it would have been murder outright then. The pain in his wounded head became intolerable. The blow from behind had been all too effective. " Take him to the forecastle, and let one man watch him. I must put the boat about," said Lake. And as May, wounded and exhausted, closed his eyes in a sailor's bunk, his last thought was, "Silence, silence to the very death ! They may not know all yet."

CHAPTER XV.

GOVERNOR JOSÉ MARQUEZ stood on the red-tiled portico of the Presidio of Guaymas, glass in hand, following the last reflections of the lights of the retreating Ranger. It seemed as if the very spirit of love was hovering in the star-lit night, for with three ringing cheers the Yankee crew had decked the Ranger with all her ensigns, and manned the yards to show their appreciation of the hasty union of their dashing commander.

Gathered in a knot, at a respectful distance, the baffled tyrant's staff officers waited his orders.

José Marquez breathed curses loud and deep, as the Ranger turned the farthest point.

"She is lost, lost to me forever!" he growled. "And her father safely out of my clutches! The fiends of hell fight against me! I cannot even confiscate his lands and property. He has not been tried. The charges against him are not yet at the city of Mexico, and dare I explain the details of his escape! I must think! It might be dangerous to the future of my administration."

"General!" said a staff officer, approaching and breaking in on his reverie. "The troops are all embarked on the

Q

Democrata. She will have her water on board at daylight."

"Good!" answered the governor. He mused a moment. "Now for my revenge on these treacherous scoundrels! I will root out the whole tribe! No one shall dream of my real purpose!" Turning to the officer he sharply said, "Send me Major Villareal!"

There was a ferocious gleam in his eye as the officer neared him. Tricked out of the possession of the prisoner, his old family feud unsatisfied, and forced to see the Pearl of Guaymas borne away as the dashing commander's bride, his mood was wolfish. The guardsman saluted in silence.

"See here, Don Enrique!" briefly remarked the governor, whose cruel eyes flamed, "I have promoted you a grade. I have given you this expedition. The commander of the Democrata will land you, and then follow the course of this Yankee scoundrel who has carried away Dolores Pesquiera in triumph. I wish to know if she joins her father at Mazatlan."

He little dreamed that the Flying Halcyon was off shore, speeding towards the palm-fringed Sandwich Islands, with his deadly enemy.

"You will be reinforced by two companies from Mazatlan with a couple of guns to cover your landing. I have sent a chosen officer to lay out a work to cover your stores and protect your landing. The Democrata will leave you three of its largest boats with a swivel howitzer in each. You will cautiously advance up the river, skirmishing both banks, and allow my friend, the German engineer, to map and examine the whole river, as far as navigable. The

Yaquis will naturally retire beyond navigation for heavy boats. At the head of navigation form a strong camp,—stockade it. Guard well against surprise! I will send ample supplies in two weeks to maintain yourself. One of my staff officers will bring you detailed orders. The Democrata will cruise off and on Cape Haro and run down to Lobos Point. Her guns will support the work at the mouth of the river, to ensure the safety of your dépôt. I know you are brave ; I expect you to be wise."

Major Enrique Villareal bowed in silence.

" You will not be attacked by a strong force of those devils ! They will need the whole tribe elsewhere ! " finished Marquez, with a grim smile, for he nursed a magnificent strategic plan of his own.

The newly-made major noticed with surprise that the governor was in riding costume, his lithe sinewy form showing to advantage in the full trappings of a Mexican cavalry officer. José Marquez interpreted his glance of inquiry.

" Colonel Carbajal and myself leave for the interior as soon as it is dark. The Yaquis may have their spies here, even in Guaymas. I shall surprise them. I know their weak point." A sudden thought struck the anxious governor. " Are any of your officers ashore ? " he asked with a sinister smile.

" I kept three of them," answered the major ; " the other is with the detachment in command. I thought you might wish to explain your plan of campaign. They are all old Yaqui fighters."

" My plan is here ! " said Marquez, tapping his brow

impatiently. "Take them and go as quickly as you can to the prison. You are chief of a drum-head court. Carbajal, who is chief of staff, will give you the written order. Take that fool who allowed Pesquiera to escape, try him for cowardice, and shoot him in fifteen minutes. I shall not leave here till I here the volley. No mistake on your part, at your peril !"

Enrique Villareal's swarthy cheek was ashen as he hastened away to the deed of shame.

Marquez, with a satisfied grin, swiftly entered his council room.

"The bishop is in waiting, general. He craves a word with you. He leaves for Hermosillo to-morrow."

"Admit him !" cried Marquez, his brow darkening. He was waiting by the open casement to hear the volley at the prison ! "The smooth old hypocrite ! He aided this Yankee to bear away Dolores. If it were not for fear of the ignorant besotted dupes of the Church, I would have him waylaid on his way home."

"Ah ! your Eminence !" smiled the crafty governor. "I must speed him away. He might trifle with his proselytes, the Yaquis." And Marquez cordially greeted the man he fain would murder.

" You come from the wedding," said Marquez, for the harbour pilot had spread the details of the solemnity.

" I could not refuse, general," calmly said the bishop. " It was her father's last injunction to me, when he expected to go before the rifles every moment. And the maid herself agreed. I had no other course."

" Explain !" eagerly cried Marquez, his eyes lighting up.

"She was not in the prison! Have my officers dared—I will punish!" He sprang to his feet.

"They are innocent, your excellency. I knew not till I was in the cell that Dolores, on foot in the night, walked in disguise as an altar-boy, with my chaplain who brought the blessed elements. She was with her father to the last. She was hidden in his cell when you came."

"Ah! Dolores! Brave Dolores!" murmured Marquez in a sudden burst of manly admiration. "What an infamous scheme to steal her from me! I would have pardoned—I would have done all—for her sake."

"It is too late, your excellency; she is the commandante's bride," quietly replied Bishop Dominguez. "I am old and shaken. I would fain take leave!"

Marquez rose. "I will send a squadron of lancers to escort you to Hermosillo. The roads are dangerous. But, one word, when will you tell me the secrets of state, which Pesquiera claimed I should know?" The tyrant's voice was silken and coaxing.

"He is away on the high seas! I cannot gain his permission now, and he does not need to use them to save his life. The rules of my Church forbid me to speak now."

And the old churchman paced solemnly out of the chamber with a profound bow.

Marquez struck his brow with his clenched hand. "Fool! Tricked again! Ah!"

He smiled, as a crashing volley rang out on the still night air.

"One vengeance! Now for the Yaquis! Carbajal!" he shouted. "Order the horses! Send the lancers to picket the convent and escort the bishop homewards. Not a man to leave his party. Do you hear?"

The colonel bowed, as Villareal hastily entered, and saluting cried, "It is done."

Marquez suddenly faced them, as they stood gravely silent.

"Did either of you see this baby-faced renegade Mexican girl at the prison with the bishop that night? How did she get in?"

Their lives hung on a thread. With well-simulated astonishment, the officers looked blankly at each other. That secret of the gallant girl they guarded at the risk of their existence.

"It was fate," groaned Marquez. "But she is a brave one!"

Before the dawn La Democrata was rolling under her heavy load off the headlands, and Governor José Marquez sped out in the night to meet the Yaquis in battle.

Thoughts of beautiful defiant Dolores Pesquiera, lost to him for ever, goaded the fierce governor as he raced along through the defiles above Guaymas.

"We must be far away before the peons throng the trails for the early markets," Marquez cried to Carbajal. "Some of those scoundrels are half Yaqui in blood."

"Now we are safe!" said the governor, as he loosed his rein, and his splendid steed sniffed the fragrant forest breeze sweeping through a valley to the south-east of the

Ures road. "We are beyond all treachery now," Marquez said. "In an hour we will reach Domingo Garcia's ranch. I have a platoon of the lancers hidden there. These roads are dangerous by daylight. Jesus Maria! Quien vive?" cried the startled ruler, as his horse wildly plunged and reared.

Marquez dropped his useless pistol as Carbajal spurred to his side.

"Only a sleeping peccary! I heard him in the bushes. But I was startled. It is not too far from the line for a Yaqui spy."

As the riders clattered down the glen, a dark form rose from the thick grass and plunged down into the forest. A half-naked Indian runner brushed aside the bushes as he strode onward to the head of a great gorge leading to the river of the defiant hostiles.

"The road of the old gobernador, who has betrayed us," fearfully conjectured the watcher, who was a link in the chain of Yaqui pickets.

"Will the troops be here to hold the pass if we find it?" earnestly questioned Colonel Carbajal.

"By to-morrow night I will have fifteen hundred men ready to hold the defile. The detachments from Ures, Arispé, Hermosillo, and my road guards cannot fail me. If this fellow has only told the truth, then we have the key to their land. I will soon know. There is the smoke from the hacienda." And in the thin cool morning air the faint hinting of dawn showed the blue column ascending a mile away.

"Can you trust this information, general?" anxiously

asked Carbajal. A brave and experienced soldier, he was yet cautious. The past with its repeated butcheries of the Mexican troops weighed on his mind.

"Listen," said the governor. "I seized Pesquiera's rancho near Ures when I imprisoned him. I found the old intendente was still there. He was a foster-brother of the great governor, and was for years his major domo. Now, I learned from the priest at the Hacienda Pesquiera that the old fellow always conducted Mateo's father in his conferences with the wild Indians, and for years guided the columns who took the goods and supplies to the line. They were left on neutral ground, while he alone threaded the cañons and communicated with the Indians. I had this old fellow, who is quite rich, secretly arrested, and he is here at Garcia's closely guarded. Now, his only son has just been married. I have him, too, in the keeping of the lancers. I will make the old rascal inform his son of the secret pass Pesquiera used to us. He was a traitor, that great scoundrel! The Yaquis treated him like a king. The son shall guide us. If there is any deceit I will hang the grey-headed villain before his son's eyes, and then treat the son as the Yaquis treated our last prisoners—flay his feet, and make our lancers drive him back to Guaymas, where he will be shot as a traitor to Mexico."

"But will the Indians not defend the pass?" doubtfully replied Carbajal, as their tired horses pushed on to the now visible hacienda.

"No, colonel, I have tricked them. Villareal will be ascending the river from the sea. They will descend to oppose him. This cañon in the Sierra de Bocatel once held by us, they are cut off between our fires here and his below. They cannot get out of the valley. Our boats on the river will sink their canoes with the swivels. At the mouth of this cañon one strong post, with a guard station on the hills, will control their whole land. The principal chiefs I will take back to Guaymas, and make them disclose their hidden mines. If they do not, then the first tree and a lariat will bring them to their senses. I forced this old intendente to admit that Pesquiera got gold in plenty from this region, but the mines are hidden. I had to threaten the sly old miser with hanging him myself. He is too old to make the trip, too feeble ; but his son knows. The priest tells me they have had secret dealings for years with these fellows."

"How long is this cañon, general ? " ruefully asked his chief of staff.

" It is six or eight miles long, and very dark ; but where Pesquiera's pack-mules went, I can lead my troops," confidently replied Marquez. " By to-morrow night all my men will be up. Villareal will be at least fifty miles from the mouth of the Rio Yaqui. I shall rest the men all next day, and at midnight mass them around the pass. As day dawns we will push in."

" It is a fearful risk," thought gallant Carbajal, "and Marquez may not know the longer the column the more helpless in ambush." But he sprang off and aided his chief to alight as the nimble lancers crowded out to greet their general.

When the moon sailed over the great sierras to the east next night, the glens around Garcia's ranch were peopled with dark moving knots of hardy soldiers. On three different trails they trooped, in, and took the positions assigned by Carbajal, with the aid of Garcia's vaqueros.

In the gray of dawn, José Marquez sprang upon his horse, and the command moved down into the valley drained by the Yaqui River. Guarded by four picked sergeants, the guide, unarmed, led the way. With Carbajal at his side, Governor Marquez boldly crossed the line, whence no victorious Mexican column had ever returned. Save the occasional neigh of a steed, the rattle of a carbine, or a smothered exclamation as a wild charger plunged in fright at the narrowing forest tangles, all was still.

"Remember," sternly said Marquez to the unwilling guide, "another life than yours hangs on your faith. Your wife shall rot in prison if you lead us astray."

In advance a dozen mountaineers, armed only with the machête, sprang down the glen on foot, as advance skirmishers. It was the clear hush of the sunrise hour, and not a bird twittered in the unbroken silence, as the path led down into a narrow chasm, which turning and twisting, sank abruptly towards the far Yaqui.

José Marquez, bold as he was, shivered slightly as the guide, his pale face gleaming ghastly with fright, turned his head and pointed into the deepening gloom.

"The Cañon de Bocatel," he simply said. "But only two abreast."

The sun's bright lances splintered on the dark masses of boulders, gray with the mosses of ages above them, as the bronzed horsemen pricked their rebellious steeds down the slipping trail. By dint of urging, Carbajal had succeeded in detaching a picked band of fifty riflemen to explore the silent gorge. They were swallowed up in the gloomy depths, and with grave faces and anxious eyes the guerilla levies of Marquez threaded the silent defiles. No word of command sounded in the air, no martial bugle broke the haunting stillness. For an hour the column toiled, until it was spread out in a line of a half league.

"We must be half way to the river, colonel," said the triumphant governor, as he forced his steed to the side of Carbajal. "And there is not a Yaqui in the gorge!"

It was a seeming truth, for far in advance the nimble riflemen climbed the jutting points, and above them the walls rose almost precipitous for hundreds of feet. Men and horses nearing exhaustion, the governor signalled a halt, and in a half-hour the toilsome march was resumed. Finally, the narrow path wound around a bluff, from which, on either side, the walls rose for fifteen hundred feet above, and a torrent dashed down through a cleft, losing itself in the gloom below.

The governor's brow lightened with a conqueror's pride, as the last great alley in the huge rifted basalt cliffs showed a distant glimpse of green slopes, and the broad river sweeping away in a graceful curve.

Fancifully piled masses of detached rock, in fantastic form, lay at the distant mouth of the cañon, as if scattered in one last throe of nature's creative agony.

"There, colonel, I will build the fort!" joyously cried

Marquez, as he urged his tired steed. " It has been a wonderful march ! "

Carbajal turned in his saddle, as he said, slowly, " We are not safe yet, general. It will take another hour to——"

There was a wild storm of hideous yells drowning the speaker's voice before Marquez could draw his useless sword. From scrubby bush, dark cleft, and ragged boulders on each side of the gorge, a rain of bullets was showered upon the startled Mexicans. In vain fury, the soldiers, entangled with their falling steeds, fired at every spot within reach. But the balls glanced off the cliffs, from whence, with a mighty crushing sound, an avalanche of loosened boulders and huge rocks swept down upon the entangled Mexicans. Yells of pain, the snort of the crazed animals, the groans of the dying rose on the air, now vibrating to the hideous war-cries of the dark foemen who peopled the cliffs above them. In vain did the dauntless rancheros strive to clamber into places from whence their fire could be effective. The narrow defile was filled with the dead and dying, and frightened steeds dashed down the cañon, hurling the dismayed troopers into the dashing stream below.

" Cut our way through ! Forward, forward ! " bravely cried Marquez, but the exhausted soldiers, with wild cries, abandoned their floundering steeds and hid in the straggling bushes from the fire of the pitiless Yaquis, leaping down the heights to rifle the richly caparisoned steeds of the mountain riders. In vain Carbajal forced his buglers to sound the " Forward " and the " Rally." The weird notes wailed through the gorge where death revelled, and the column was cut in twain. A few score of men, bruised, bleeding and exhausted, finally reached the opening of the gorge, Carbajal at their head. He had lost sight of the governor, who fought with the desperate courage of the Mexican at bay. The main body of the troops were in full retreat towards Garcia's, and though momentarily suffering, finally by sharp volleys checked the Indians, now sated with blood. Darting under overhanging cliffs, hiding in angles where the huge boulders thundering down could not reach them, the fugitives by sundown began to struggle back to Garcia's hacienda, where the rear guard hastened to cover their flight.

When the sun set on the scene of slaughter, the signal fires of the Yaquis lit up the grim gorge. The boom of the night owl resounded mournfully, and the mountain wolves stole down upon the scattered corpses of four hundred of the soldiers who followed their stern chief into the mantrap of the wily natives.

As the sun's last rays glittered in the western skies, by the strand of the lonely Yaqui River, a wounded, defeated man strove in his impotent rage to burst the bonds which tightly confined his swollen wrists. Pesquiera was avenged, for with no gentle hand, Marquez was roughly pushed into a canoe manned by eight hideously-painted warriors.

With wild shouts of triumph, they paddled a mile down the rushing stream, to a bend where a hundred thatched huts were crowded with the wives and children of the strange tribe.

The yells and shouts of triumph from the gorge told the

defeated leader of the grim work of pillage and torture. As the frail canoe whirled in the strong eddies, Marquez groaned, "Who will rule Sonora now? Who will lead my poor followers out of the devil's trap?" And a thought of Carbajal entered his mind. Was he dead?

But wonder filled his mind as he was dragged from the light bark, for with a mighty shout of triumph a flotilla of a hundred canoes pushed off from the strand of the Indian village, and were swept downward in the swift current toward the mouth of the stream.

"They go to attack Villareal! They will overwhelm him! I have been betrayed. But who fathomed all my plans? No one knew but Carbajal!"

Expecting only a miserable death by torture, the governor, now the prisoner of relentless savages, was haled to a huge dome-thatched council-house.

Tears of impotent rage filled his eyes, as between two old savage priests, and surrounded by war chiefs, their machêtes reeking with the blood of his followers, stood Andrès Vargas.

"You here!" stammered Marquez, and the tyrant knew the cause of his complete defeat.

"Traitor!" he cried. "You lead these devils against your countrymen. You—a Castilian!"

"Marquez, you lie!" sternly said the returned messenger. "I rode from Vera Cruz over the Cordilleras, only to free Sonora from your iron grasp; to save my benefactor, whom you would have murdered. But he is far out of your reach. You are governor of Sonora no more. And I have not lifted a hand against my brothers. The war chiefs knew of your plans through Pesquiera's friends, it is true! I shall hold you as a hostage. And your estates, your stolen wealth, shall be divided among the families of your unfortunate troops. Fear not for your life. A living hell of remorse is a greater punishment than death to you. Pesquiera shall rule in his old domain. And you—a hunted fugitive—may seek the wilds of Yucatan. I care not!"

Marquez thought of Dolores, now perhaps in the arms of her husband.

" All is lost, kill me !" he cried. " I ask but that."

"You shall live ! " coldly answered Vargas. " I would to God I could save your brave men at the mouth of the river. They must be driven off, for as long as these rocks stand, the Yaquis have sworn to defend their land. You will be proscribed by the national government for the ruin of the army of Sonora !"

" Tell me ! " he questioned, " what of Carbajal ? "

"I know nothing," doggedly said the sullen prisoner. " He was fighting like a man when I saw him last.

" I would save him. I have ordered the carnage to be stopped !" replied Vargas; " I only sought to free Pesquiera !

" You hunted me out of Sonora, and I came back to measure swords with you in a fair field ! But the Yaquis have avenged me and freed Mateo !"

Giving some brief directions for the prisoner's treatment, Captain Vargas strode out to order a search for the gallant Carbajal. " He was my playfellow ! I must save him."

But the stars swept over the cañon 'de los Muertes,' and Carbajal was not found. Andrès Vargas sought his couch, when the last swift canoe had brought a runner, who reported that the Mexicans had been driven out of the gorge, and that hundreds of trees had been rolled into it, blocking its way to all approach. The gateway had only been left open to draw Marquez into a fatal ambush.

"He may have escaped," mused Vargas, as his heavy eyes closed. "But he was fighting at the front!"

While the livelong night, the sounds of feasting and triumph resounded in the Yaqui village, far below, clinging to a frail canoe, a despairing fugitive strove with his last energies to keep the light bark in the middle thread of the strong current.

It was Carbajal, who thought, wounded and spent as he was, only of the doomed column slowly ascending the river. "If I can reach them, can warn them, I may save a frightful massacre!"

When his ammunition was exhausted, he had cut his way through a string of natives, closing in on the head of the column, and gaining the chapparal, had loosed a stray canoe and floated away unobserved.

"If I can only keep awake!" thought the messenger of dark tidings. "It is only eighty miles, at daybreak I may meet Villareal's picket boats!" But the flotilla of canoes at the village had not escaped his eye, as he drifted by, lying down in the light skiff. "They will swarm down as soon as they have glutted their vengeance!" And he called on the Blessed Virgin to aid him in his hour of need.

The sun was shining on the forest-fringed banks of the tidal river when Carbajal slowly regained consciousness. His canoe, caught by projecting branches, had stranded, for the paddle was gone. His nerveless hands had failed him. The sound of distant shouts aroused him. Gazing up the river he saw a cloud of canoes filled with warriors, in two columns slowly drifting down around a bend, a mile away. "I must hasten! They cannot be far off now!" He sprang on shore and wrenching off a limb began to pole his bark out into the stream. It gathered headway. A ray of hope entered his despairing soul. "They will think I am one of their fishermen!" He recognized the peaks and serrated ridges around him. "Where is Villareal?" he muttered. "Three hours more would bring me to the sea," and with desperate energy, sore and stiff with his wounds, he kept on his downward course.

Suddenly, as the semi-controlled canoe swept around a bend, he saw the Mexican flag fluttering on three heavy barges moored to the strand. The smoke of camp fires ascended on either side of the river. He strove with his failing energies to hasten the course of his boat, poling along near the shore. "All seems quiet, the enemy are not here yet!" He sprang up and waved his hands wildly to attract attention. Five minutes more and he would arouse the camp.

There was a rustling of leaves, a quick springing up of dark forms, as the boat swept inward to the dark forest fringing the banks. A score of arrows whistled in the cool morning air, and before the canoe, bearing the dead body of the gallant soldier, stranded on the silver sand of the encampment, the Yaquis were pouring out from the forest on either side, leaping like tigers on their defenceless foe. When Villareal's decimated forces reached the cover of the guns of the Democrata, they knew not of the defeat and capture of Marquez, for the last drops of the messenger's life blood were useless. Carbajal had died in vain !

CHAPTER XVI.

THE TAI-FUN.

WHEN PHILIP MAY opened his eyes, first as a prisoner, after the feverish sleep of exhaustion, he at once recognized the mate's state-room. It was dark and no friendly light streamed in from the three heavy plate-glass dead lights. From the oil safety lamp, swinging smartly in its gimbals, he only learned that he was alone, and that the Halcyon was flying swiftly on.

"I must have lain a long while," he vacantly muttered, as he strove to leap from his bunk and dash at the door swinging partly open. He fell back, in a fainting spell, for flashes of fire darted across his swimming eyes. When he regained consciousness, two men were bending over him, and the coolness of an aromatic application to his head aided to settle his mind.

Obed Lake spoke roughly. "See here, my friend, you are no fool. If you wish to keep the inflammation out of your head, you will keep cool. Now, this Chinaman will serve you anything you need. You can spare yourself the trouble of pumping him. Ah Sam knows the big shark who travels under our lee, and he would just fit that fellow's maw. I have put loose chains and double padlocks on your door. You can call when you wish anything, for an

armed sentinel will occupy the old captain's room opposite.
As you have turned Jorgensen out of his room, we have
moved aft ! "

The cool villain grinned as Ah Sam, in fearful dumb
show, offered May the varied solace of an amply filled tray.
His yellow face was blanched with fear, but his eyes spoke
volumes. The Mongolian's lips seemed to frame the
syllables " By-an'-by."

May's naturally high temper overcame his prudent
thoughts of the leaden ballast and its yellow cores of golden
bars. " You infernal scoundrel ! You will be hung as a
pirate ! " he snarled, as Lake leisurely surveyed the surroundings.

" Nonsense ! " sharply answered Lake. " The yacht
is free of customs examinations, and I find the papers
in regular order, for a trading cruise in the Pacific, as
well, and made out in the name of the schooner Constance.
So, we are all right ! I watched you closely when you fixed
her up for your hide-and-seek game in Mexico. Now, you
got away with the old Don, and we got away with you—
that's all ! "

Lake chuckled as he added, " You can have any of your
things you want. Just be civil ! Now, see what I have
done for you ! I've brought you the pretty widow to keep
you company. You would not get her name involved in
any scandal. I found this in your berth ! "

May's eyes blazed as the robust villain daintily affixed the
picture of sweet Constance Lee to the framed mirror.

" As for us getting into trouble—Lord ! our friends on the
coast are up in the thirty-third degree, Captain May ! We

have our private signal for every harbour from Kodiak to San Diego!"

"You are lying to me!" raged May. "You have been led away by some mad freak to this devilish business! See here, Lake! If you will come to your senses, I pledge you my word as an officer and gentleman, we will run the boat straight home, and give you all six months' pay and allowances! Be a man! I've always treated you decently!"

"Oh! I can do better! I am operating on private account!" confidently replied Lake, as he turned to go. "Don't forget it! You will be well treated—but cut up any monkey shines, and—by God!—over you go, and Goodloe too! Mr. Ah Sam first! I am apt to make sure of my work!" He tapped his revolver butt significantly.

"But, you'll be reasonable! I am a good navigator, and you will come out all right! Don't stand in your own light! I made up my mind those moonlight nights off Monterey, that the Nevada queen was thinking of ordering a new wedding outfit of running gear! I should hate to see her change those racing sails for a dead-black suit. You'll have a good run, and the lady shall have her boat back, and you shall make the Del Monte run again, when you are spliced for life!"

"I'll follow yer pious example!" leered Lake, as he cut a substantial quid. "I'll lay this boat plum in the Arctic ice, nipped flat, but I'll take a fortune out of the run! Don't you fret! You had better send word by Sam to your chum not to tease Jorgensen to death. Ac-ci-dentally, that Swede's got an ugly temper; your friend is a tongue-lashing

him, and he might crack him one with a marlin spike. For
he's on a home run, to a big limber-waisted blue-eyed gal
a-waitin' in the Baltic.

" As we retire, we want some money, but, Lord bless you,
the 'gang' will see us safe in. You're pretty green in
'Frisco, or you'd a suspected how old Warner has made his
fortune. He's a slick one—the old boy, and is free of the
coast.

" Now, cool down. Sam can bring your books in, and
I'll look in on you."

With a malicious grin, Lake saw Ah Sam depart first, a
ceremonial politeness which became a rule.

" These fellows know their own mind," bitterly mused
May, as daylight brought him fresh counsel. It was easy
for him to divine that the yacht was driving westward like
a greyhound of the seas. Splendidly ballasted, and fresh
from dock, she sped along superbly handled. " It is clear
that their plan was thought of in San Francisco, perhaps
matured in Mexican waters or at Honolulu. They would
not dare to sell her. No ! The Halcyon would be recognised. And our hidden treasure ! It seems that I can do
nothing. If Sam would only talk ! If I could in any way
communicate with Goodloe !" But as the hours ran into
days, and two weeks crawled away, Philip May relapsed
into dreams of the future, or sat studying the sweet silent
eyes of beautiful Constance Lee. As the yacht ran out of
the warm latitudes, and the sea freshened, May realised
that the boat was skilfully headed for China or Japan. His
wound gave him no further trouble, and his personal freedom was less restrained.

Guarded by the sentinel, lolling easily on duty, he was allowed occasional exercise on deck at night, never being allowed abaft the foremast. He was permitted the free use of the crew's quarters forward under surveillance.

"I am glad to see you have such a sensible spirit, captain," said Lake, who visited him on every ·watch. "Now, your friend is a very moody irritable nature, and Jorgensen has had the irons on him once for a few hours. You would not give me that trouble, I am sure," said Lake significantly, "for I am a serious man and I will stand no boy play nonsense. I fancy the young lady from Paris will have trouble with his cussed temper. It's a bad thing for a family man." The pirate skipper was so frankly serious that May burst out laughing.

"So, you are marrying Mr. Goodloe off too, Lake?" curiously remarked Phil.

"Yes! and I'm sorry for the girl;" with unmoved gravity the freebooter's answer came, "for he is an ugly customer."

"I dare say you are right, and you should give him a wide berth if you ever see him again," May continued.

"I am not likely to—nor you, either—captain!" was the parting shot of the defiant law-breaker. "But I wouldn't mind going to your wedding. Why, that woman's smile is as cheering as a moon breaking out on a black stormy night. She is a regular out-an'-outer, like her boat— the queen of the Pacific!" And, carefully inspecting his sentinels, Obed Lake guided the flying yacht westward to the distant shores of Cathay. May was perfectly assured of Goodloe's daily welfare by occasional notes inspected by

Lake, who resolutely guarded every secret of the voyage. One or two attempts to open communication by the use of marked books were detected by the sharp mutineer, who said simply, " No go ! Mr. May, I am up to all these dodges. I have done time myself, and know too much. I hate to lose a good cook, but I give you fair warning. Overboard he goes the next time." And Lake gave Ah Sam a few rude object lessons in discipline.

" What did you get in trouble about, Lake ? " said Philip, one day, shortly after this burst of confidence.

" The same thing that worries you and your high-spirited friend. A woman too good looking to be left long alone ! It was a little too hard on the other fellow. I had been away on a cruise ; I was young and hot tempered." He made the significant motion of a knife thrust, then slowly added : " In seven years, I was another man. When I was turned loose I found only one thing lasts longer than the love of woman." The pirate's voice grew hard and stern.

" And that is ? " Philip queried.

" The love of money—the good yellow stuff," stoutly answered the bluff rogue. " Money is the one cure for all. It brings woman's white arms clinging fondly to your neck, and man to your side. The best friend to a lonely man is a long purse. Friends cling to you like a sou'-wester, as long as they can hear the yellow stuff rattle."

" You are a bit of a cynic, " mused Philip May, thinking of the wretch in his lonely cell, dreaming of the woman who had found a new mate, perhaps before the prison clothes were fitted on her last lover.

" I know I'm out for the gold—the clean stuff—on this

cruise," was the clean-cut announcement of Captain Obed Lake, of the now anxiously-awaited Halcyon.

Philip May, as the days ran by, doubted not of a settled purpose and definite object of the mutineers. The discipline of the boat was excellent. His own health began to suffer from the enforced confinement. It was vain to read, to frame a thousand theories of the future, and his room was now haunted by the shadowy presence of the woman he adored.

Spite of wayward fortune, of adverse fates, of mocking distance, and the cold lapse of time, the old old fashion of Love rules under the stars to-day. The thrilling human heart, a lyre of widest range, answers to the spirit touch of Memory, under the call of the arch-magician Love. Victorious over time and space, defying Fortune's frown, in stead fast constancy baffling Death itself, the lover's heart turns like the magnet to the pole. For all the love that ever thrilled in the pleading passionate bosoms now stilled for ever, whether eager man or white-bosomed maid, now in its tender impulse of unrest, quivers in the bosom of humanity ; ruled, swayed, and touched with an infinite tenderness by the throbbing waves of the living sea of Love. The lonely Scottish soldier in the Low Countries, seeing far Maxwelton's braes, the hardy sailor in his midnight watch, the prisoner of the Neva, weary eyed watching the slanting sunlight die in a prison floor, the sick pilgrim in far lands ; Trenck dreaming of the proud patrician face of his princess, in seventeen years of grim solitary durance; the soldier at midnight straining his eyes towards the mysterious darkness which embosoms the foe. Wherever humanity longs, waits, lingers and sighs, the minor chords of passionate unsatisfied love sweep the life paths of our kind in resistless currents. Death cannot conquer, time cannot weaken, danger cannot appal, suffering and years cannot blight, the Love for which we live, with which we die. For it is the invisible ether of this quickened atmosphere of the humanity which fences us in, this same impalpable and eternal Love !

Before her picture, standing with folded hands, rapt in his dreams of a beauty which the picture did not bring him, Philip May, with the artist hand of glowing tint and tender shade, recalled the picture in his heart, deeply graven. Constance Lee, a sweet and graceful memory now, a shadowy presence which came to him in the long silent nights, when the winds freshened and the frail yacht raced into the billowy grasp of giant seas, was the witch of the Halcyon. For, in uneasy dreams, his passionate heart beating for her alone, he looked through the clouds of his strange captivity to the glow of a future wherein there should be no shadows of parting.

" This cannot last for ever. We must be nearing Japan," thought May, as the dainty Halcyon lay suddenly becalmed on the twenty-fifth day from their seizure. From his windows the floating sea-weed and drift-wood, the occasional flight of birds, told the ex-sailor of the proximity of land.

He lay in his berth, moodily musing, as the coppery sun angrily burned in the west. A strange stillness seemed to oppress the prisoner. The sails flapped idly, and the creak of the booms alone was heard as the graceful boat swam heavily in the sullen oily flood.

" They may run her ashore, the stubborn fools, and

lose a fortune for the Delmars, as well as wreck us all!"
May groaned in impotent rage, for he had even tempted
Lake with a great bribe to return to his duty. The effort
had failed utterly.

"It's a fair proposition—a good one, Mr. May!" frankly
said the mutineer, "but I am powerless. I wouldn't mind,
—there's enough for me and Jorgensen—but, you see,
the men are all in on this run, and they'd kill us in a
minute!"

The haggard lover's eyes sought the one sweet face,
which shining on him brought the light of a future love to
these dark days. "Constance, Constance, if it were not
to meet you again, face to face, I bear these weary days in
patience, I would end it all!" He paced the narrow
officer's room like a chained tiger. Suddenly he sprang to
the padlocked door and shook its chains with useless
frenzy, for a great commotion on the deck had aroused him.
"Can it be a tragedy?" His heart sank as he thought
of the half-crazed Goodloe, perhaps being murdered
by the angry ruffians. The shouts of command, and
a quick trampling of feet came from the deck.
Suddenly the yacht took a great plunge, as if some great
impulse had buried her deep in the blackening waters.
May sprang to the port-holes. A darkening gloom was
coming from the west. The water was churned and broken
far in front, and the sails ominously rattled. The frightened
voice of Ah Sam was now audible, as he called the sentinel
who had harshly threatened the prisoner at his chained
door.

"Sam, Sam!" called Philip, as the sails came rattling

down, and the shouts and yells on deck continued. It was the mariner's note of alarm. The Chinese cook's face peered through the door in answer to May's appeal.

"What is wrong?" cried Philip. The roar of angry waters, the hissing of a sudden squall, was the accompaniment of Ah Sam's reply, as he clung to the narrow companion way for support.

"Tai-fun, him come—Big wind—bimeby storm like hell!" and the stout Mongolian answered a call, which took him to the aid of the busy men on deck. A mighty hand seemed have seized the yacht, but now dreaming idly on the waters, and thrust her into the boiling maelstrom of a sudden cyclone.

"We shall see what sort of a sailor Lake is." was May's first thought, as with a crash the yacht nearly went on her beam-ends, when the force of the howling storm struck her. Typhoon is the loosened demon of the angry winds, named by the Chinese Tai-Fun. Blown by fleets far out to sea from the Chinese and Japanese shores, the fatalistic Mongolians in despair have, with folded hands, faced death for scores of years when the Storm King has twisted their frail junks into confused masses of wreckage.

With appalling rapidity the black storm was upon them, and flashes of lightning, with roaring ominous thunder, broke upon the awful waiting hour before the storm. Under angry skies, the huge gray-green billows united to great black masses, striking the strong yacht in angry savagery, and making her reel and quiver from keelson to deck.

The dashing about of loose articles below increased the clamour, and the breaking of huge waves above, rolling clean over the decks, added to the din; above all, the shrill singing storm notes of the rising wind, howling in the steel wire rigging, rose in a wild menace. May raged in his pent-up confinement. His strong soul stirred within him. " My God ! To play a man's part, to be allowed to fight for my life ! But here, penned up like a dog, I must perhaps go down to-night ! "

For with frightened, maddened plunges the yacht rose and fell from sickening gulf to the dizzy summit of the awful forty-foot waves of the Pacific, under the lash of the storm-fiend. May yelled, clamoured and dashed again at his door. With bruised and bleeding fingers he gave over his useless task.

And then he threw himself into his bunk, for it was impossible to keep his feet longer, and clutching the storm bands, his spirit loosened its maledictions upon the faithless wretches who had turned the graceful Halcyon far west into this seething hell of waters, lashed by the flail of the giant demon sweeping from icy Mongolia. The unequal battle of the beautiful waterwitch, and the waning storm-spirit, tried every tough rib in her stout sides, and wrenched at the copper-bolt riveting in her graceful symmetry. The water found its way into the forecastle, and the dashing about of the stray flood added to May's discomfort. With short, frantic, staggering leaps the yacht was hurled to and fro on the crests of the hungry waves. An unusual wrench put the swinging light out, and the prisoned lover could no longer see the sweet face of Constance Lee, her spirit eyes shining steadily on him in the wild unrest of the awful night. As Philip clung to his couch, he muttered in despair, " It is now a battle to the death ! She's the rarest thing that ever floated, if she fights

her way through this !" for he remembered the ghastly
havoc of the great typhoon, which drowned seven thousand
Chinese and Japanese fishermen, and landed a foreign fleet
high up the market-place of a coast town, with one or two
vessels overturned on their anchors, as ghastly floating
coffins for the helpless crew.

The prisoner's spirit burned within him, as in helpless
confinement he heard, in the lulls of the storm, the yells
of the excited crew battling for their lives. Deep in his
heart he swore a mighty oath of vengeance, and clenched
his fists in helpless rage as he vowed to track out and
punish the miscreants who had marooned the lovely yacht.

"If this blows the masts out of her, we may float
helplessly for days, a mere wreck upon a waste of waters,
without a sail !" and then, in the grim chaos of the night,
came awful, unshapen thoughts to May. Stray leaves
snatched from the dark book of human suffering : "The supplies must be running short. Food and water may lack us, and
if we drifted dismasted, our decks swept clean, upon this
watery desert, the great Japanese current might bear us a
mere water-logged wreck under the sweltering skies, to drift
till famine and thirst turned human natures into ravening
wolves !" There were ghastly wrecks which he had seen
drift by, wave-washed and covered with green slime, whose
voiceless witness of suggested tragedy was awful in its pathos ;
and, as the sea of life is covered with the wrecks which float
and tell no tale, so the great bosom of the merciless ocean
bears the awful mementoes of deaths, wrapped in the mantle
of a horrible silence.

In a frenzy of exaltation, haunted by ghoul-like thoughts

creeping out of the dark caves of memory, Philip May
passed the terrible night, until a sickly straggling daylight
showed the wrinkled face of man's unconquered enemy,
the ocean! For in its resistless storm-swept rage, its cruel
spirit roused in wrath, old ocean's horrible set face, is that
of an eternal Death, ravening for its prey.

Drenched, staggering, his stern eyes wild in hopeless
inquiry, Obed Lake came to the den where Philip May was
chafing like a lion in the net. "I've done all I could," he
doggedly cried. "The vessel is labouring terribly! Can
you not help me? She is swept around, and hurled backward. I've managed to keep her head to the storm. If
the steering-gear gives out, we'll all go together!" In his
hour of need, the practical sailor had the implicit reliance
on May's superior culture and implied powers, which marks
the limit of the inferior.

"Where's Goodloe?" shouted May, his sailor spirit
rising as he tried to crawl safely out of the little cabin.

"He is lashed in his berth with three ribs broken!"
gloomily responded the sullen mutineer. "Come on,
you are our only hope now. If you can't pick up some
man-o'-war's trick, I am afraid we are lost! If she ever
gets in the trough of the sea, goodbye to the Halcyon!"

And the rebel spoke, even in his hour of ultimate danger,
almost lovingly of the gallant craft which had through the
horrible night tossed aloft her quivering spars in gallant
defiance, and sent the rays of her masthead light out in
man's acceptance of a challenge from the angry spirit of
the waters.

Clinging to the life-lines, the strangely assorted pair

reached the men at the wheel, for two of the crew stubbornly held to the spokes, and exchanged mute glances, for they were, too, lashed for safety. A single rag of a half-reefed jib was the only canvas on the boat, and the decks were swept clean of all her furnishings.

One glance told May of the havoc of the night. He turned to Lake with a sinking heart, " The boats ? "

" All gone—everything ! " was the despairing reply.

" The water butts ! " May screamed, as the storm shrilled through the taut wires.

" Everything clean as you see it, but I have two casks of water below," the pirate humbly answered.

Phil May cast a glance over the seething waters. Holding hard, the deep delicious draughts of the magnetized ocean air restored his mental dash. A defiant recklessness surged through his veins ! " Let us all go to hell together," he shouted, "unless you tell me where we are ! "

" Two hundred miles from Nagasaki, when the storm broke ! " shouted Lake, using his closed hand as a trumpet.

There, in the wild flying storm wreck, the sailor lover seemed to see a gleam of hope, as if one glance from Constance Lee's eyes had gilded the gray clouds driving down on them. By dumb show, and stern brief commands, May imparted to Lake his proposed measures. The mutineer edged towards him, and with grateful eyes, shouted, " I'll put you with Goodloe, if you save us ; and I'll drop you nearer home than you think." In a tacit truce, May directed the spray-drenched wretches at the wheel, while Lake, fearless and energetic, groped his way forward. The clinging crew followed him one by one as

the gallant boat lifted herself over the huge seas. But as
she rose, she was bodily driven backwards, and fell off,
threatening to roll into the trough of the terrific sea. The
bronzed, angry face of the sun broke through the clouds.

As the men gathered on the forecastle, Philip May cast
his eyes toward the tightly battened cabin-hatch.

He gave up all idea of asserting authority. " Basil
disabled—without arms—the boat in jeopardy! I would
be a madman!" Keenly watching the rollers, he thought
of Pauline Delmar's trust of honour—the concealed golden
ingots!

In half an hour, with infinite toil, the Halcyon was straining at twenty fathoms of chain from each hawse-hole, with
a spare anchor dragging on each.

Groping back, Obed Lake, wearied and exhausted, neared
May, who admired the old sea-dog's nerve and vigour.
" Jorgensen is rigging the sea anchor, and will have it out
in a jiffy! I've sent half the men below to roll forward a
couple of barrels of the palm oil. Will you follow me and
boss the job ? "

Attached to Lake's lifeline, the strange partners reached
the forward companion-way, and, by the aid of half the
crew, quickly-fashioned oil bags were improvised from the
men's kits.

One by one, at the risk of a man's life, the loosely-
punctured oil bags were slung from the bow, and the effect
became apparent in the easier riding of the labouring yacht.
May blessed the lucky chance which caused him to good-
humouredly allow the men to take on board twenty casks at
Honolulu as a trading venture. The triangular-bellied

sail drag, paid out on a double hawser, eased the working
of the dainty boat. As Ah Sam crept along with cans of
coffee and a grog ration for the men, May cried to Obed
Lake, "You can waste a hogshead now, thrown off in single
bucketfuls!"

There was an easement in the vessel's motion which
astonished even the disheartened crew.

When the oil had been thrown out with infinite difficulty,
Philip May crawled on deck, to see a clearly-defined floating
area of smoother water clinging to the yacht's oil-soaked
bows.

The wind had insensibly lessened its force, but the huge
rolling seas still made the Halcyon shiver in every timber.
Half hidden in the forward hatch, wedged in with a couple
of mattresses, May aided the partners in crime, Lake and
Jorgensen, in the awful ordeal of the typhoon's second day.
Towards sundown, the Swede, his defiant blue eyes averted,
roared out with the voice of a clarion, "Glass better.
Twenty-nine now; was twenty-eight, thirty last night. We
will see it through now!"

And as the moonlight broke over the sharply-shivered
masses of the sea still running mountain high, May in his
drenched couch lay dreaming of one who was far away.
For the Flying Halcyon was steadily rising in even strain
over the heavy blows of the sea. May was sore and bruised
next morning as he awoke, but the regular motion of the
boat proved her to be under sail. He gazed blankly at
Lake, who stood by his couch, with a stern face greatly
softened.

"She's running under jib and close-reefed mainsail.

I'll take you in to join Captain Goodloe to-night. You
have saved the boat ! "

" And then ? " queried Phil, as he eagerly grasped the
coffee Ah Sam held out—

" I'll lay off Nagasaki—send in word and refit at an
island near there ! I pledge you my word, I would land
you both if I dared, but the men would kill me ! I must
make this run ! "

" Who are your mysterious associates ? What is your
desperate game ? "

" You'll know by-and-bye ! I'll only watch you—and
the little widow shall see the Halcyon ship-shape yet, with
both of you aboard ! "

Obed Lake was gone ; and May, with darkening brows,
felt that he was again under guard.

As the sun sank on a steel-bronze mass of broken, heaving
currents, lashed over the ridges of sub-oceanic mountains, a
faint blue ridge to the North showed the first sign of the
Eastern world to May, as he sullenly followed Lake along
the deck to the cabin where Goodloe lay, in fever, under
the rough surgery of the mutineers. " It has been a hard
old typhoon," said Obed Lake. " We passed seven water-
logged or dismasted junks this afternoon, and wreckage
enough for a whole fleet ! This has drowned hundreds of
Japs." The crew busied in getting the staunch boat to
rights guarded their menacing silent hostility, and as Philip
May gazed into the open door of the cabin, opposite Goodloe's sick bay, a determined man faced him, through the
open door, holding a rifle ready across his knees. Philip's
thoughts were only of his suffering friend, but as he gazed

s 2

into the cabin, from whence he had been tricked to his capture, Constance Lee's handkerchief, delicate and filmy, fluttering from the lamp standard, spoke to him of the happy hour when she had wreathed it there, laughingly crying "Sailor's Luck and a Happy Cruise!"

In another moment, May, with a swelling heart, was kneeling by the side of Goodloe, who was mentally wandering far away. The sick man was roughly bandaged and strapped in his berth with padded bands, stayed with pillows and blankets.

Ah Sam, frightened, and with an eager sympathy in his almond-shaped eyes, was murmuring in Chinese stubborn objurgations upon the malevolent new Commander. Goodloe's sunken cheeks and haggard air told of the useless struggles of his indomitable heart! May leaned over him, "Basil! Do you know me?" he eagerly cried. "Cheer up, old man! Land in sight!" But the glassy staring eyes, the quick disjointed utterances, the flushed feverish cheeks, told of the ravaging fires within! His comrade's voice roused his failing mental control. He struggled to free himself, and shouted, "I tell you, we are lost,—all is lost! There is no harbour for us! Gone—all gone! Anita —May—Harry—all gone—all dead! Life—life is a lie! We are all drifting! Life's a long cruise, Phil!" He clasped his friend's hands in frenzy. His voice rang out mournfully. "Life! Only a cruise on a rudderless ship— driving along, all sails set. We have no chart, Harry, no stars to guide. Nothing! all is dark! There are no buoys on the channels of our dark fortunes, the currents swing around us madly. I tell you," he shouted, "I see the rocks of ruin ! We are driving along—all of us—to the reefs of human woe ! Lost—lost ! "

Phil May's bitter tears fell on the hands of his helpless comrade, and in deep dejection he sat long, soothing the excited sick man, till through the port-hole he saw the star of Love, following the moon climbing through the brightening heavens.

Tired and weary, he threw himself on a rug and slept, while the beautiful boat, her white wings loosened all, sped along into the cloudless glow of the Eastern skies.

CHAPTER XVII.

IT was four bells when Philip May awoke, with a sense of having passed out of the heart of the storm into the wooing breezes of the Lotos land! Struggling to his feet, he forgot his bruised and stiffened frame, as the cool splash of the waves singing by the quarter told him of ocean's dreaming, tiger-like, restful mood! The clinging warmth of the air spoke of tropic shores, and he signed to his guard that he would go on deck. Stealing a glance at Goodloe, lying in the dreamless trance of exhaustion, May nodded kindly to Ah Sam, whose broad Mongolian face lit up with a re-assuring smile.

Conducted to the deck, May's eyes rested upon the rugged outlines of the southern extremity of the Japanese archipelago! The old man-o'-war days told him of his surroundings. For, as the Halcyon bounded along under every stitch of canvas, the panorama of wooded slope, temple, crowned hills, and nestling villages glided by. Far in shore, the storm-scattered junks were beginning to hoist their square parti-coloured single sails, and brave again the dangers of the treacherous Japanese sea. Under a cloud of canvas the yacht drove along, spurning the greasy rolling waves, which in black masses had hurled themselves over her, in the hopeless struggle of the typhoon. Clouds of little fishing-boats, skimming the deepening blue, timidly flecked the inshore waters with winged pinions of flitting white.

"It's a clean run for Nagasaki, now," thought May, his repressed anger mastering him, as he noted burly Jorgensen, his revolver at his belt, pacing the dead line between him and the helmsman. "Sixty degrees of longitude, and twenty of latitude : a bold sweep for these scoundrels !" mused Philip. "How will they refit at Nagasaki ! If I could only communicate ! The pilot ! For there are always foreign fleets at Nagasaki. Oh ! for a launch, and a dozen of the 'Swatara's' old crew ! I would sweep this scum into the sea ! "

But he sighed heavily as he thought of helpless Goodloe, burning in fever below. "They would knife him, and toss me overboard ! I must wait. Their plan must soon unfold now. If it were not for the fatal hidden treasure, I would try a dash for liberty at the first chance !" He wearily turned his eyes to the East, where the gray of early dawn lightened to amethyst and rose, and flushes of gold broke through, gilding the crests of the mountains, faintly pencilled against the green tinge of the morning skies. The fluttering breeze strengthened, and the exquisite racer, tossing her dainty prow in eager reaches, quivered with a thrilling yearning toward the nearing shores.

In glory and splendour, crimson, rose and gold, the sun leaped up from the wreck-strewn watery waste behind; and forgetting his sorrows, his mind drifting back to happier days of manly adventure, Philip May felt the life blood coursing strong within his veins. From her golden hills, by the brown-cliffed Californian shores, a message of hope and peace and undying love was borne in the golden radiance of the triumphant day! There was a hovering spirit of love, ever lingering near, to cheer and bless the yearning prisoner, which spoke of one fair woman, waiting far away to see the silver gleam of the Halcyon's sails!

As the crisp waves broke and sparkled in the glittering sun, and graceful sea birds wheeled their airy flight, in welcome to the peerless princess of the storm, May leaning against the rail listened to the song of the waves rippling by. Thackeray's tender lines returned as he rejoiced in the growing day—

> "And when the storm had ended,
> Its harmless force expended,
> And as the sunrise splendid
> Came blushing o'er the sea."

An infinite promise of the golden future stole into the wearied prisoner's soul, for behind the glowing golden eastern clouds, he saw the future—a happy future: Life and Love! A noble life lit with a golden love; and in the gateway where Hope, the prisoner's guardian angel, with folded white wings, waited—he saw the tender face, the outstretched arms of Constance Lee, her exquisite face bent toward him, with earnest eyes of womanly tenderness shining on him from afar!

The day wore on, and under his ministrations, Basil Goodloe's repose was that of a man slowly emerging from the haunting dreams of Shadowland.

It was evening when the yacht ran up under Nagasaki Point; the darkened seas were far lit up with the dancing single lights of the little fisher-boats. A long and earnest conference between Lake and Jorgensen had busied the two sturdy rebels in the afternoon hours, while Goodloe slept, guarded by the Chinese steward, and May was guarded amidships in plain sight of his captors.

Finally, Lake with rough directness accosted May, whose soul burned in an eager anxiety.

"Captain May, you are a true sailor!" the adventurer began. "I would be a brute if I was not grateful for you saving this beauty. Now, I won't mince words. I shall stand off-and-on here, and signal a pilot. I will send in word, and get a deck outfit, some whale-boats and my supplies, and run into an island harbour I know here. Your friend is sick: he shall have the best Japanese doctors, and I will treat you well. I will land you both if you will promise me, on your honour, you will not try to escape."

Lake gazed steadily in May's eyes.

"And if I do not?" hotly broke in the outraged officer

"Then, he takes his chances ashore, alone, while I refit; and you—well—it's rather hot to be cooped up in the Yellow Sea, a week in a close cabin. I am not afraid of him," the pirate lightly said, "but for this cruise I must keep my particular eye on you!" He grinned in compliment to Phil's steady courage. "It's for your friend's welfare, not your own. You'll come out of many a tight squeeze yet. You are a born sailor Jack."

"I'll give you my answer when you make the island. Where is it?" said May, doubtfully, in reply.

" That's my business ! " roughly answered Lake, as his face darkened, and he bade the guard take May below.

With a soul burning in rage, Philip glared at his guard behind closed doors, as from the cabin ports he could see the heavy forts and turreted lights of Nagasaki Inlet.   Even the white flag with its crimson ball mocked him, as the light pilot junk swept near.   The chattering of friendly voices, the glimpses of a flitting sampan, as lightly resting on the starlit waves as a drifted feather, and the knowledge of his helplessness stirred his very soul.   He meditated a spring upon the stolid guard, and a wild rush.   A dozen strokes for liberty, and he might reach the pilot's shallop, drifting near, while Lake effected his shore communication.   But the revolver was at full cock which faced him as he half rose, and a growl from the guard recalled him from the mad impulse.

" Pauline Delmar's half-million—and—" his eyes rested on the signal kerchief—" Constance Lee."

So, hiding his feelings behind half-closed eyes, he dreamed, as the Halcyon gathered headway, of the sweet and gracious presence of the woman he loved with all the fresh fervour of his manly youth.   "Some old pirate haunt in the Yellow Sea will hide us, and then—?" May was yet ignorant of the purposes of the runaways.   He little dreamed of the far-reaching schemes of the banded associates, whose members embraced, in strange companionship, smug politician, smooth merchant, greedy official, and desperate adventurer, backed by a vile riff-raff in the Orient, as well as on the Pacific shores of the United States.   For gold, the lust of gold, brings strange schemes to the hidden

backers of crime on land, and turns many a prow on strangely
romantic guests.   The dark adventurers of the waters of the
Orient are never pictured in the mind of a public syste-
matically hoodwinked as to the chronicles of the ocean.
" Water leaves no trail," and the sea breeze bears away
secrets unheard, out upon the limitless expanse of the
ocean.

It was morning when the rattling ot the dropping anchor
roused May, who sprang from his couch.   A sudden
reminder of his position was the loosely-chained door from
before which his guard demanded his wishes.

Hastily dressing, when he reached the deck May found
the restless Halcyon securely swinging from both anchors in
the tranquil reaches of an exquisite bay.   As Obed Lake
strode toward him, with one glance at the towering wooded
mountain ridge of the island, the old temples gleaming from
jutting points, and the bluff headlands faintly drawn on the
eastern side of the channel, the prisoner cried : "Tchusima !"
For well he knew the old stepping-stone of the Chinese and
Tartar invaders of prehistoric Japan.   There it lay, its
varied and romantic shores fringed with the silent forests of
antiquity, where no woodman's axe rung out a knell.   The
pirate spoke at once :—

"Have you made up your mind, Captain?   I will give
you one chance to decide.   I shall land your friend at once.
I must refit this boat, and clear out of here."

Philip May did not know that the heavy masts and fluttering star flag of the Lancaster startled the rebel commander
on the evening before, as the flag-ship of the American-
Asiatic squadron swept by into Nagasaki Harbour with her

men at the open ports, called to quarters, ready to give and
return the quick salute of port courtesy. The mutineers
felt an instinctive thrill, as of a yard-arm rope tightening on
each neck, as the Yankee frigate passed within hail. Even
daredevil Obed Lake dare not laugh, as he dipped the
American flag in passing courtesy. He well knew that the
naval officers of the fleets made frequent shooting visits to
the lonely island whose possession Corea and Japan have
debated for years. Russia, England and China, covet the
superb home of old tradition. Sleeping like a flashing jewel
on the bosom of the Corean channel, Tchusima's vales and
fragrant copses are thronged with rich-plumaged pheasants,
and its hills shelter the quaint beasts of the Asiatic jungle.
Around its shores, where myriads of strange fishes swarm in
the crystal waters, the simple-minded Japanese fishermen
and maids gaze reverently on the silent temples of a faith
that has faded and passed from the minds of men. Only
grey tombs, mossy tablets in a strange, forgotten tongue, tell
of the human hearts whose theatre of action was the en-
chanted island, lost in its dreaming seas, and breathing
in its perfumed zephyrs to-day only the romance of old !

May bowed his head in a submission which galled him ;
and was only comforted when, as they neared the shore, two
hours later, Basil Goodloe lifted his eyes toward him, in
returning reason and murmured, " Phil, where are we ? "

That night the prisoners, guarded by four sailors, slept in
a Japanese cottage nestling at the foot of the ruins of a great
temple. Ah Sam was busied in his simple craft, and when
Goodloe's weary eyes were closed in sleep, Philip May gazed
on the moonlight breaking in upon the silent shadows of the

roofless fane. Its great stairway, massive walls and huge
pillars gleamed in the silver flood of pale beams. Far away
over the strand twinkled a lighthouse, and below the temple
point, a great white ocean bird, the Halcyon, rocked in
welcome rest, her masthead-light scarce trembling to the
rippling wave.

Near him his watchful guard hovered, with ready weapon ;
and in the evening hush, the impassioned voice of a
Japanese girl rose in the songs of the Samauri and the
Ronin.

"It is a strange quest—an ocean mystery," thought
Philip May, as he laid his tired brow on a simple couch and
drifted out upon the sea of uneasy dreams. A week later,
the Halcyon was ready for sea. But two things galled
May. It was his separation from the now-restored Goodloe,
who though weak, was still mending rapidly, under the care
of an old Japanese native Doctor.

"I hate to do this," was Obed Lake's comment, as May
was conducted to a lonely point a league away. In a
Japanese fisher-hut, he was watched by a boat's crew of the
rebels. "Your friend is too devilishly rebellious, and if I left
you alone, he would counsel you to some mad attempt,
which would cost you both your lives. It is for your own
good I do this."

And thereafter, Philip May bitterly communed in silence.
For the fruitless councils of the two officers were vain as to
their destination,—the real objects of the seizing of the
yacht—and their own immediate future. It was only
apparent that Obed Lake was the agent of a powerful
association, for a plentiful outfit was being supplied to the

captured yacht from a fleet of queer Japanese junks, through whose agency the whale-boats, missing gear, and provisions were transported. "We will revenge ourselves on these brutes, Phil," had cried Goodloe, whose fiery soul burned to follow the fortunes of Pauline Delmar, and the woman whose arms first closed round him in the mistral-lashed waters of the Mediterranean. "Ah, Basil, there is some strong influence behind these malefactors," rejoined the cooler May. "They have partners and associates who will turn our bolts aside. Beware, lest your anger provoke a brutal and a final visitation on our heads. We must wait. Like countless others, walking in innocence, we may be forced to forego a return of these wrongs."

So, in his solitary separation, May passed the waiting days in peace. To prevent hidden communication through the too-friendly Ah Sam, Philip May's few commissions at the yacht and the temple prison of the now-vigorously rebellious Goodloe, were entrusted to the fisher's daughter, a Japanese maiden of sixteen. Standing in the stern of the sampan skiff, a heavy scull in her slender hand, the dark-eyed girl was a dream of graceful energy. Her supple back willowed under the swaying motions of her rounded youthful body, lithe as a deer in its spring. Nude in torso, a dark blue robe sweeping around her swelling loins, the barefooted fisher-girl was the sculptor's ideal of form.

Soft in voice, with a gentle caressing manner, and lustrous eyes black as the sloe, the island maiden was a creature of the wooing winds and murmuring waves. Seated at his feet in the attitude of submission, her delicate features kindled in curiosity, the fisher-girl, with bended head, sat with folded hands, while May indited the few words he was permitted to exchange with Goodloe. Gazing at her simple, youthful face, the blue-black masses of her hair caught in a graceful knot, the rounded Hebe shoulders, the artless freedom of her trusting nature, the sailor mourned that so much of the flush and dainty beauty of a spring-time life should be wasted on the toilsome oar. Watching her eager, ready smile, as springing to the oar she propelled her dainty craft afar with the nervous thrusts of her agile young arms, he envied her the freedom of a beggar peasant girl upon the mimosa-fringed shores of lost Tchusima.

"What matters it, bond or free ?" bitterly mused May, as he turned away to pace the strand alone. "We are all bond in this world ! Slaves to sorrow, sickness, distance, disappointment, and the ultimate prey of death. The wearer of the kingly crown, in failing age would gladly change with yon fisher-girl the bronzed outline of an unspent royal youth, and, sorrow seeks the hut as well as the palace. For, life's saddest truth is—that while pleasures flit on before, while joys fade and vanish, there is the whole world's agonies in the capacity for suffering of even the humblest human heart. But rarely do the loud pæans of joy ring out in singing, soaring treble to drown the minor chords of the flowing tide of human misery. The eternity of sorrow has wrapped the brief space of human existence in its vast folds, for darkness, night, sorrow's pall and death, are the ministers of our Lady of Pain. The world's last wreck will be but one universal parting." And the young lover set his face to the shadows, mindful only of Time and Distance,—of the drifting away of clinging lips—of the dying echoes of loving voices. The silent, speechless agony with which loving arms unwind for the last time, when hearts are torn asunder, is the last seal of human sorrow !

It was in a desperate defiant mood that May, rudely awakened at midnight, followed his stern guard to the strand where the yacht's whale-boat waited him.

"We sail at once !" was Lake's rude exclamation, as May was half led, half dragged, to his old quarters forward.

Then, with rough alacrity, the eager crew toiled at the anchors, aided by a crowd of eager Japanese, who had seemingly brought tidings in a swift-sailing junk. Among the throng, the discordant voices of Coreans, Lascars and Chinese mingled with the island dialect. A slowly gathering headway followed the hoisting of the sails, the swelling canvas caught the stiff night breeze ; the chattering cries died away far behind, and with a mighty rush of her huge white wings, the Halcyon swept out into the night.

A strange voyage on an unknown sea ! Whither? The disheartened captive knew not, and blank despair took hold upon his mind. He realised that some occurrence had produced a temporary severity, and it was hidden from him sedulously that Goodloe, rash and unmindful of their joint interest, had been recaptured miles off the lonely shores, in a stray sampan, vainly trying to cross the Corean Strait alone, with the aid of his single nerveless arm. Out into the silent mystery of the night, dashing the spray haughtily from her glancing cutwater, the Halcyon drove along, sweeping through storm and sea, like an arrow to its mark. And restless and wearied as the two prisoners were in their cabined helplessness, there was a keener bitterness far away thrilling the hearts of the women who watched, in wondering sadness by the Golden Gate for the gliding vision of the spectral Halcyon, stealing along the waves in her silvery fleecy robes of white above the spotless symmetry of her curved outlines! For no breeze bore in from sea the precious golden freight, no favouring gale brought home the wanderers for whom three loving women knelt at night in prayer to the God of storms.

The increasing heat, occasional calms and the hue of the shallowing waters, with an occasional glimpse of a passing junk or distant steamer, told Philip May, whose spirit began to fail, that the Halcyon was daily farther hidden in the Yellow Sea. Denied now his usual exercise, his meals handed in by the mute sailor guard, May could form no conclusion as to the schooner's position. But the sound of working parties in the hold indicated that some plan was being arranged for the use of the vessel.

"Can they be intending to join the smugglers around Shanghai? Will they join the semi-piratical white castaways of the Chinese coast?" The sickening captive tortured his mind in useless conjectures. A dazed, excited restless fever centred in his very soul, and his self-control began to fail. He became uncertain of himself, and voices seemed to break in upon his slumbers! His eyesight swam and the shadows of the swinging night lamp took on grotesque forms. Obed Lake came not to his room, in these days, though his eager commands were heard as he directed the workers in the hold.

"My God! If they should discover the treasure, or throw it overboard. Perhaps trade is off in some native port!"

the captive thought.   And, worn and wearied, he pondered
if he might not bribe Lake with a part of the treasure to
land his comrade and himself at a Chinese port.   " Fool I
am ! " thought the sailor lover.   " He would take all, and
our doom would be sealed ! "   The young man suddenly
reflected that since seven days the lonely island of Tchusima
had faded behind them, and not a token had reached him
from Goodloe.   " He is dead ! " thought May, in a sudden
panic of alarm.   " And they only keep me, in case of need
to force me to help navigate the schooner ! "   And this
horrible fear took possession of May.   It was not lightened
by the morose silence of Jorgensen, who now, armed to the
teeth, made frequent visits of inspection.

From his window, Philip May divined the reasons of this
change of masters.   The low bluffs and rude forbidding
shores of the Chinese coast were a few miles to the larboard.
Before one or two squalid-looking villages, fleets of fishing
junks lumbered up and down in the muddy sea.   Their
distinctive Chinese rig and the trend of the coast confirmed
the story of their destination.   There was a break in the
awful monotony of the prisoner's bondage, when the weary
morning came to prove to May that the schooner was
riding at anchor in the shallow roadstead off Tungchow.

May rubbed his eyes, as in a dream, when he recognised
the mud-walled city he had seen years before.   " There is
some scoundrelly business preparing now ! " he thought, as
he tried to gather his scattered thoughts.   " Tung-chow is
the resort of every desperate character of the Yellow Sea."
And he strained every nerve to catch the import of each
unusual movement or every passing footstep.

He was rewarded after hours of waiting by a passing glimpse of the stern-faced Lake, departing for the shore, in a whale-boat evidently fitted out for a river voyage. The crew were roughly accoutred as if armed for their chief's protection. They passed on and swept out of sight, while dreary hours were only marked by the tread of the sailors overhead and the monotonous clang of the bell ringing the crawling hours.

As night fell, and May for the hundredth time turned away from the port-holes of his cabin, Obed Lake, the mutineer, sat comfortably at dinner in a Chinese villa house twenty miles up the river, flowing into the Yellow Sea, near the stolen schooner's anchorage. Lake's host was a heavy, middle-aged Chinese merchant, whose round face was a study of blended energy and repose. The crafty eyes read every thought of the bluff sailor desperado, while the smooth oily tongue and placid unruffled demeanour marked the able Mongolian "Comprador." Around them were gathered several Portuguese refugees, and a sleek scribe. In a corner, two of Lake's armed sailors enjoyed the plentiful liquors and cigars, while the mutineer and the Chinese magnate conversed in low tones.

The room was furnished with a mingling of Chinese splendour and easy European comfort, for Hop Wo had learned sybaritic lessons while serving his apprenticeship at deviltry in Shanghai. Beginning as a packer of Mexican dollars, his ready mastery of English gave him a subordinate bank clerkship. From this, a varied service with the different steamship lines led him into an easy association with the wealthy band of scoundrels who centred in San Fran-

cisco. Japan, the Sandwich Islands, Alaska, British
Columbia, China and the coast of Oregon and California
were all branch stations of this circle of white and brown
thieves. Rich and powerful, Hop Wo was a master mind
in this international conspiracy which for years has sapped
the customs' receipts of the easy-going American nation.
With a cable code cipher, with agents on every steamer
crossing the Pacific, the gigantic operations of the silk and
opium smuggling ring were aided by bankers and officials.
But, whether greedy American politician, sly Chinese
capitalist or pliant adventurer, the masters of the coolie
slave trade, the opium and silk ring, had no more powerful
ally than Hop Wo. His easy-going cosmopolitan vices
were picked up in serving the secret conspiracy in Hong
Kong, Honolulu, Yokohama, Victoria, and San Francisco.
A daring gambler, he disdained not the silver-necked flagons
of coquettish Veuve Cliquot, and the bright-eyed, hard-
hearted women spies of the "Ring," knew well his princely
hospitalities at the "Chinese Restaurant" at San Francisco,
and the luxuriant retirement of his Shanghai villa.

"You have never had a cargo before under your own
charge," said Hop Wo to Lake, as he thoughtfully studied a
letter from Wong Lee, the Honolulu Chinese Rothschild.

"True," replied Lake, filling his glass, "but I sailed
second with "——, and he lowered his voice as he glanced
at his sailors.

"Then you should be able for this run, but it is a great
risk. I am not afraid of your boat. I know your devotion.
Can you make a safe land fall? This will be the richest
cargo we have risked for three years! Where would you try

to run it in ?" and the crafty Chinese villain filled and
refilled Lake's glass, as he explored every corner of the
mariner's fertile brain. The conference was a long one, and
lasted after Lake's attendant guard were stretched snoring
on two benches in the open court.

"I will think it all over, Lake," finally decided the prince
of thieves. "I know I can trust you, but I wish you were
not loaded down with these two fellows ! Why don't you
cut their throats, and throw them overboard ?"

Hop Wo spoke as gently as if he were bidding the
languishing prisoners to a feast at his board.

Lake turned, with a sudden burst of manly feeling. "I
would sooner run her home empty," he cried, rising. "First,
this young May is a man all over, and saved the boat in that
cursed typhoon. It was a hell of a blow !" he drained his
glass, and thoughtfully added, "They are both gentlemen.
I have had to watch the other one like a caged eagle. He
tried to paddle the Corean Strait at night. Now, they are
naval officers ! If they should meet with harm, we
would be hunted all along the line ! I know this
rich young widow who owns the boat we stole. She is a
devil for spirit and gameness. Why, Hop Wo, she loves
this man, and she would back the search for them
with her millions. They have had a rough time ! Now
each of them has a faithful woman waiting at home for
him." The pirate's voice softened in an involuntary tremor.
"They will be so overjoyed to be turned loose safely, that
we will not be chased down. She and her friends are
powerful ! They will smooth things over, for they don't

care to have the customs authorities get hold of their operations with the old Mexican we ran off! I will answer for
them, but I will not hurt a hair of their heads!"

"You may be right! They will all be grateful for their
escape! I will think it over! I can only give you a half
cargo here down at Yellow Point. I have a reserve at
Nagasaki. I intended to send it over packed in fish barrels
by the Alaska route. You might take this on and run over
to Nagasaki and get the rest."

"Hop Wo! I am afraid of the cursed navy vessels!"
uneasily said the marooner. "You know there is a cable
to Nagasaki. Now this navy fellow, Goodloe, is on leave,
the other is retired. These women might make a fuss
about the boat and cable over to have the missing schooner
looked for."

"I can easily fix that," smiled Hop Wo. "All the
Nagasaki pilots will be on the look-out for you. My
trading steamer leaves to-morrow, and if there should be
inquiry there you can run around to Hakodadi and finish
your load there. You know our whalers always run in
easily from there. I wish you to go out by the Kuriles,
and sweep over to Victoria and the Oregon coast! I
think I can trust you. Will you go down the river to-night?"

"Yes," answered Lake, uneasily. "I can only trust
Jorgensen. He is a courageous devil, but if these two
fellows should get loose, they might retake the boat. I have
a heavy outfit of rifles and ammunition we took for the
Mexican trip!"

"Well, I am glad of that," answered Hop Wo. "You

will be able to defend your cargo. I will come down in the steam launch to-morrow and make the final arrangements. I will give you twenty or thirty of my fellows here. You say you have arms for them. There are some ugly pirate junks here in the Yellow Sea. Now, you can keep these fellows below out of sight. It might attract the attention of any Chinese gunboat! They can hasten your loading, and you can leave them at Nagasaki. They can come over on my trading boat. Look sharp in the Yellow Sea. You are never safe till you have passed Simoneseki Strait. Lake, if you make this run you will have all the money you ever want. So look sharp! I'll come down to you to-morrow. You shall have your load if nothing happens."

Rousing his boat's crew, Obed Lake sped away down the river, eight oars aiding the swift current. The would-be smuggler king gazed at the stars as he was driven along And thinking of the ill-gotten gold, soon to give him a sense of delicious power, his hardened heart softened as he thought of the woman for whose guilty love he slaved seven years in prison garb. " I would give it all to see her face but once again," he muttered, as the boat drove on to the river's mouth.

CHAPTER XVIII.

OBED LAKE sprang on board the Halcyon with a sense of intense anxiety. His personal triumph could now only be marred by some awkward event in his absence.

"All right," growled Jorgensen. "Goodloe is asleep, but the other young fellow is getting nervous. He has not slept yet, and the light is still burning in his cabin. But he's there fast enough."

"Good!" cried Lake. "I'll just take one look at him before I turn in." It was two o'clock, and the white glittering stars hung wearily over the dreary-looking Chinese hills to the west, as the mutineer descended to face the man whose life had been so lately in debate between the plotting scoundrels. Philip May heard not the loosening of the chains of his door. He sat with his wearied head buried upon his hands, for he had fallen asleep, while his yearning heart was fixed upon the pictured face of the loving woman far away beyond the tossing breakers of the Farallones, whose mute influence had saved the lives of the imprisoned officers that lonely night in the Yellow Sea !

"I'll not disturb him," thought the anxious adventurer. "We will clear out of here to-morrow, and the home run

will brighten him up!" Lake cast one glance with averted
eyes at the picture of Constance Lee, for her steadfast
womanly glance seemed to follow him the notorious schemer
even in his hour of joy. "Poor little woman," Lake murmured. "She is wondering perhaps where the Halcyon is
to-night."

Blurred and confused lying before the sleeping prisoner
were the words in which his heart strove to reach that
gentle one far away from the yellow shores of Tungchow
headland. His hand had failed before his task was finished.

> Your face is with me in the night
>   Out on the sea,
> And all I dreamed of heaven bright—
>   It brings to me,
> A star to guide, a hope to bless,
> A mystery of loveliness!
>
> Your love has sealed our souls for aye,
>   Dear one, afar,
> My heart, unswerving, turns each day
>   To where you are,
> That other soul my being knows,
> And seeks within your breast repose!
>
> Your voice, your hand, are near me now,
>   With passion's thrill.
> Love's fadeless light upon your brow,
>   You hold me, still,
> In bonds whose sway, I now confess,
> Love's magic charm of tenderness!
>
> Some day ——

Philip May was aroused in the cold gray dawn by the
throbbing screw of a smart steam-launch which swept past his
sight as he sprang to the port-holes with an instinct born

of his old days as a watch officer on a steam frigate. Realising his helplessness, he cast a glance at his confining bulkhead walls, and threw himself on his couch.

"Some devilish plan of scoundrelism! They must have backers among the adventurers here!" He forgot his surprise in the mental and physical weariness of his vigil.

Long before the captive officer realised that a definite shape had been given to the mutineer's projects, Hop Wo had finished his last conferences with Lake. The cool Mongolian examined and admired every point of the white-winged beauty which had baffled the typhoon's wildest rage!

"If your log-book does not lie, Captain Lake, she is an ocean wonder. You can laugh at Uncle Sam's revenue cutters with this water-witch under you!"

The two villains, knitted together by the hope of sharing ill gotten gains, stood face to face on the Halcyon's deck.

Lake's heart beat like a trip hammer, as he watched the play of feeling on the wily Chinese scoundrel's crafty face. Hop Wo scanned the faces of the crew, and a few earnest sentences apart with Jorgensen aroused a dull feeling of jealousy in Obed Lake's bitter heart!

His hand instinctively sought his knife-hilt,—the sailor cross blood of the criminal was flooding his heated brain. "If they should try to take the command away from me,—Jorgensen wants these two men killed. He hates Goodloe! Hop Wo is as merciless as a tiger. What would become of me? By God! I'll cut his heart-strings out, if he raises a hand in my sight. I will run the Halcyon in, or die on her deck,—and May shall live! I swear it!" The moody

rebel was soon undeceived, for a flying junk skimmed alongside, with a bronzed gang of bold-looking Tartar Chinese.
They leaped on board at a signal from Hop Wo, and
huddled around a brazier passed over to the forecastle,
where in five minutes the opium pipes were scenting the
breeze. Cold, hard-faced, desperate fatalists, these men
were only pawns in the game played on life's chess board
by Hop Wo. His nervous sinewy fingers, on which an
immense diamond shone, trifled with his cheroot as he
sharply drew Lake aside.

"Now, Captain! Get under way at once! I have sent a
swift runner to the nearest telegraph station, with my cipher
dispatch. My junks will come down to Yellow Point,
within four days with every ounce I have in the go downs.
I am satisfied to trust you! I find Jorgensen knows the
whole coast, and I only spoke to him to find out if he was
competent, in case anything should happen to you!"

Lake started, and a queer cold chill made his teeth
chatter!

"What do you mean?" he sharply cried, as he wheeled
and faced Hop Wo.

The cool Chinese type of an under-estimated race met
his angry gaze unflinchingly.

"Don't be a fool, Lake! You are in the Yellow Sea,
and you know the devil and his imps haunt the Chinese
coast! Keep your eyes open! Watch for rebel pirates, the
cursed customs and the English gunboats. As for your
own countrymen, "he laughed," you will find them dancing
or drinking at Shanghai. The Americans boast a tied up
navy!"

"Here! Ah Kee!" Hop Wo signalled a burly Chinese, evidently the leader of his longshoremen, "Captain Lake, Kee is a pilot for every port from Macao to Hakodadi. He's a devil to fight, and game enough, only, if you find him opium drunk, you can have him tied up in the rigging, and give him twenty buckets of cold water, with fifty good lashes. Do you hear, Kee?" The repulsive-looking Mongolian grinned and showed his opium-blackened straggling teeth. It was the smile of a hungry tiger.

"He is a useful fellow. I saved him from a pirate execution five years ago. He is devoted to me, as he is the last one of twenty-eight, who knelt tied in two rows, with an executioner springing from stake to stake. I saved this fellow when the two-handed sword swung over his nearest comrade's neck. Stand off-and-on Yellow Point till you see my private signal flying. Here!" Hop Wo signed for the steersman of his launch to pass the flag on board, fluttering at the stern of his dainty little steamer. "Now, my clerk goes down as supercargo on the launch to-night. He will have letters. Take him over to Nagasaki, and leave him there. He will attend to all. Take a good look out, and run below Yellow Point, and stand back. It will be safer, for the customs boats hug the shore. With the men I have given you, you are safe ; but, keep your eyes open !"

Lake concealed his joy at Hop Wo's frank trust in his devotion to the "hidden circle," by calling all hands to weigh anchor. The sturdy iron-muscled Chinese sprang to the windlass, and the white crew, marshalled by Jorgensen, loosed the white sails of the restless ocean rover.

A breeze of morning moved as Hop Wo, casting his eyes

lazily around to see no customs boat in the offing, stepped down the companion-way to his launch. "I'll leave you, now, Lake, for I am not the best of recommendations if a gunboat should happen to run along the shore!" With a last warning command: "Remember, don't be caught napping!" the adroit scoundrel folded his mandarin fur cloak around him and signalled "Go ahead!"

When Philip May awoke, the bleak shores of Tungchow were far astern, and the yacht was driving merrily along before a stiff ten-knot breeze. The chattering of the Chinese labourers near him filled him with astonishment, and he could not refrain from another attempt to interrogate Ah Sam, who visited him with his repast.

"Soon go home!" was all the frightened steward dared whisper, as the door swung a moment in a lively swing of the dancing yacht.

" Mr. Goodloe, he very well—all right!" whispered the steward, as the guard strode into the room.

The next night, the Halcyon was far out toward the Corean coast, and May, wondering at Obed Lake's absence, and at the yacht's increase of population, only knew by his astonished eyes that the Yellow Sea had been traversed, where the schooner glided into a land-locked bay, under the lee of Yellow Point.

"I have been hoodwinked for some reason," mused May. "I suppose the Halcyon changed course a dozen times since we left Tungchow!" The surroundings of the lovely bay were strange to him, and only a crumbling old Tartar watch-tower, on a bleak hill, spoke of the presence of man ! But a broad river flowed into the bay, and as the yacht swung idly at her anchors with the tide, May divined some purpose in waiting. The bay was sheltered, the holding ground good. " What do we wait here for ? " grumbled the prisoner. " The game is made, whatever it is ! "

The wind died away and an intense heat made the two next days of Philip May's drawn-out captivity almost intolerable. His eyes roved over the headlands and the silent shore in vain inquiry, as the slumbering oily shallows glowed under the intense heat of the sun of a Chinese summer.

The crowded forecastle was another source of discomfort, or the shouts of the lazy Chinese playing fan-tan oppressed his weary loneliness, and the sickening penetrating odour of the opium began to affect his weakened nerves !

Ah Sam came no more, for the guard had evidently detected the steward's furtive conversation. Thoroughly reckless, May endeavoured to provoke the varying guards out of the sullen silence they maintained by taunt and gibe. He was prepared for the worst, when Obed Lake strode angrily into his cabin. Philip had caught sight of a strange signal flag flying on the old Tartar town, and his old signal practice told him it was the same which fluttered at the stern of Hop Wo's natty steam launch.

" Captain May ! I do not wish to iron you ! We will be here but a day or so now. Do not force me to use the roughness I have effectually applied to your half-crazy comrade. Now, I will send you on deck at night for air and exercise. I shall be busy here loading the boat. From two o'clock till daybreak you can have the deck for sleep or exercise. But, mark me, youngster, I draw the dead line at the mainmast. If you attempt to sneak aft of the mainmast you'll go where Hop Wo advised me to send you, overboard with a ball in your brain. That's all ! You are in peril of your life if you taunt my sentinels again. I propose to run this cruise to suit myself. Now, you are warned !"

Lake, who was, under the chafing restraint of some hidden excitement, left the room without another word to him, but his stern order to the guard gave the captain a last warning : " Don't fool with him any more, Pete. Call me, and I'll shoot him myself ! He can take the other fellow with him. The sharks won't mind two !"

Philip May glanced in the maddening frenzy of helpless rage as the brute cast a last glance at him.

Two hours later the whistle of a steam launch brought May to his cabin windows. There was the Tungchow visitor again, and displaying the signal now floating on the old tower. Four heavy barges, dreaming down the river current lazily, their high sterns rising in uncouth shape, swept around the river bend, propelled by single sails of matting.

Late into the night the shouts of the excited coolies, the harsh voice of command, the rattle of tackle, and the confused tramping of feet proved that all hands were hard at work.

" I will know something of this later," mused May, whose self-control had returned. " They are loading in a regular cargo." The crash and thud of heavy hands, the sounds of the stowing gangs told him that the Flying Halcyon was now being made ready for her final cruise.

" And whither?" The wearied prisoner laid his throbbing brow upon his couch to seek relief from vain questions. " I will know to-night. For I shall yield to this determined scoundrel's will. If it were not for her," and he cast a glance at Constance Lee's wistful face, " I would strangle myself with this curtain cord!" And again the hidden treasure came to his remembrance. " I must be cool—for alas! my rebellion would mean Goodloe's instant death!"

When the yacht's bell tapped musically four times when midnight had passed, and the tired coolies lay around the forecastle in heaps, the prisoner was led on deck by the sentinel. Around him all was silence.

The guard signed to the forward watch to guard the hatchway, and leading May to the foremast said, " My orders! Here, to there!" he gruffly concluded, as he pointed to the companion-way they had left and indicated the mainmast.

" Your life is in your own hands !" The guard sat down within half pistol range, his repeating rifle across his knees !

Philip nodded, and baring his breast to the welcome air of night, watched the sickly yellow heat mist rising in fantastic shapes from the waters yet under the impulse of the blazing sun. As the beautiful yacht swung lightly at her double chains, only the plash of a leaping fish was heard, or the long-drawn breathing of some sailor sleeping on deck.

At the stern, one of the watch paced from side to side, peering into the stillness of the night, and a half-dozen of the sturdy mutineers lay around on the cabin house. It was easy to see that the watch was armed, for he bore his Winchester rifle at a ready !

" Fool ! " thought May. " Fool I was to insist that we should be well armed for a brush with the Mexicans. These villains are turning our own weapons to our breasts ! What madness to take a crew without knowing its character ! If Warner had been more careful—" he stopped, and smote his brow with his clenched fist. " Dolt that I am ! I see the secret of the old fellow's riches. He is a protected agent of these wretches ! They need his skill, his services on shore, the easy retreat of his shipyard, his powerful influence along the city front and with the customs officials. Ah, yes ! This is indeed a Golden Circle ! The Forty Thieves ! For there are friends and trusted agents in every port."

As the few stars visible glimmered weakly white in the zenith, through the sickly yellow mist clouds pushed along, as the impatient yacht whipped its tall spars, a gleam of comfort stole into the prisoner's darkened mind. " They will probably not kill us ; it might provoke dangerous inquiry. But they will probably turn us ashore on some lonely island to be picked up by a passing trader or whaler. It would not pay to butcher us. They could have easily finished that off at once when they seized us ! Do they wish to keep our navigating ability ready in case of accident ? What matters it," he bitterly ended, " if our lives are spared,

U

when they run away with the yacht and the lead-cased golden bars ? "

A thousand times he had pictured the unavailing distress of Pauline Delmar and the spirited Anita ; their agony of suspense, waiting for the brave man who had aided to regain a part of their fortune. He wondered if gentle Dolores still turned her dark passionate eyes in sorrow from the convent windows, her hands clasped on a bosom anxious for a father's love. For he knew not that the seal of a life's love had been pressed on her rosy lips by the daring commander of the Ranger. " Wainwright must think we have let her go down in a squall, like two amateur land-lubber yachtsmen ! " Promptly at the streakings of daylight, the guard significantly marshalled May to his day prison, with the extended muzzle of a loaded rifle.

On the third day after the arrival of the mysterious cargo, Philip May noted the cessation of the work of loading. On each night, he had noted the vessel's increasing draught, and murmured, " She will sail like a bird when she sits a little deeper in the water ! " But it seemed strange to him, that the hatches were closed and battened, and the deck tackle cleared away, as if the boat were ready to sail. It was the mysterious hour before the dawn of the fourth day at Yellow Point, when May, leaning on the rail, gazed out into the murky night ! The mists rose thickly over the stagnant waters of the lonely bay, and the sailor watch at bow and stern listlessly gasped in the clammy over-heated night ! May's guard reclined against the foremast, his rifle lying in his folded arms, and only the gentle murmur of the

slight current lapping the vessel's side was heard. All
nature seemed relaxed, and the loose cordage of the rigging
limply hung as the vessel merely twisted on her cable.
There is something weird and uncanny in the hour before
dawn! It is the dead point of the human nerve system,
and the unfreshened blood clogs the tired brain-cells with
congested dreams of misshapen, uncanny things! May had
been lost in wonder as to the nature of the mysterious cargo!
" Can it be rum or brandy ? " he thought. " Do these fellows
dream of a trading tour among the South Sea Islands, where
the dark-skinned native girls, crowned with flowers, dance
on the pearl shell-strewn strands? Will Lake become the
chief of a band of daring rascals, trading in slaves, and
running among the islets of the South Pacific Archipelago,
where the Southern Cross gleams? It must be that ; they
will trade the rum for slaves, and then sell these at the
Sandwich Islands, through that Chinese scoundrel Wong
Lee !" His wearied head fell, and he slept. Suddenly,
a thrilling vision of the night, the spirit of Constance Lee
roused him from the purposeless dream. It was as if she
pressed her dainty hands upon his brows, with magic impulse of loving earnestness, and whispered, " Rouse yourself! For life ! Death haunts your sleep !" and as he
struggled to his feet, May could hear a long-drawn wail of
tender appeal, " Philip ! Philip !" There is an unnamed
sense which makes the very heart's blood tingle in nature's
protest at the hour of deadly peril ! It is the soul's self-
protective appeal against creeping murder ! May peered
out into the night ! For the yacht's deck was silent, and

the watch with averted faces were gazing out from bowsprit and stern! The dark forms of the deck guard were huddled on the cabin-house.

" They are bringing some more cargo," sleepily muttered May, as a dozen light boats swept swiftly out of the murky fog, making for the yacht's quarter. With one spring to his guard's side, May yelled :

"Turn out all hands! Pirates!" Nature had thrown off her lethargy, and Philip was yet thrilled by the warning voice of Constance Lee, thousands of miles away, as he snatched the astounded guard's Winchester, and springing to the rail, opened a telling fire on the boats, thick with struggling forms. Beside him, before a single half-naked wretch, knife in teeth, had leaped the rail, his sentinel companion was emptying, at deadly range, his heavy revolver. A wild chorus of screams and savage yells broke upon the night air. With handspike and harpoon, the sailors of the watch on deck, rushed on the boarders, while the squad at the stern, grasping their weapons, raked the boats, now under the quarter. Borne across the deck by the rush of the yellow devils, Philip May, with clubbed rifle, cleared a circle around him. The stern voice of Obed Lake was heard as the cabin hatch gave out a band of hastily armed men, from whose repeating rifles quick flashes of spitting red fire were answered by the yells of the dying Chinese pirates. The first defenders of the deck had been rushed across and were facing the rail, where the pirates' boats were entangled under the vessel's side, their swarming occupants vainly throwing out their dead and wounded to gain space to reach the deck. Philip May was in a wild craze of fierce mental joy. He had caught up a harpoon from a dying sailor, and from behind the long boat lanced the cringing wretches who were pushed on by the crowding pirates behind.

A yell of triumph rose as Jorgensen, shouting in his Berserker rage, sprang out of the forecastle hatch, followed by the hastily armed coolies upon whose bravery Hop Wo had so confidently counted. Half the men were armed with heavy revolvers. With an instant appreciation of the situation, Philip cried, "Into the rigging ! Shoot them in the boats !" And Jorgensen laughed a grim laugh to think of the prisoner leading his captors in the defence of the stolen boat. Springing like tigers into the shrouds, Hop Wo's tried followers clung with one hand, while they emptied their revolvers into the boats which had stolen up to drift on the vessel's low rail with the tide. There was an awful hand-to-hand struggle of a few minutes. The pirates of the night fought behind their dead and dying, but from the stem and stern of the Halcyon a squad of riflemen were decimating the boats which could not reach the vessel's side. Crowded with yelling devils, mainly armed with knives, spears and cutlasses, the boats began to sheer off behind the parted fog-wreaths. At May's side, a tiger in ferocity, burly Kee urged on his men, a stout boat cutlass in his hand. The wild cry of Goodloe, startled in his sleep, had reached Philip May's ears. He too well knew that the Black Band's mercy was a cruel death. The sharks now swarming and tearing in the water crimsoned with blood would show more kindness.

Deserted by the boats which had fled, the pirates under the vessel's quarter, with the grim desperation of the Chinese in their final rage, strove to gain the deck and sweep the defenders overboard. But Obed Lake saw before him a rope dangling from the Lancaster's yardarm. He saw the failure of his hopes, old age, poverty, disgrace, perhaps assassination if he lost that mysterious cargo.

"Throw them overboard! Clear the deck!" yelled the mutineer, as he gathered his men at the stern, and came sweeping down to where Jorgensen, May, and the blood-thirsty Kee were pressing the band of screaming scoundrels into a compact mass between the masts. From below, the men who had not reached the deck were passing up loaded Winchesters, and with a wail of rage and baffled ferocity, the divided band's survivors sprang towards their boats.

Several of these had drifted away, and the riflemen of the Halcyon, from bow and stern, fired at every man holding a paddle. May, as the wretches turned, sprang to the front, a cutlass in his hand, caught up as a man fell at his side ; with a quick thrust, he ran the heavy blade through a wretch who had pinioned stout Jorgensen's neck in a death-grasp. The first "Hurrah!" raised by the Halcyon's maddened crew rang in his ears, as he pitched forward and fell on the deck. A singing confused sound of struggle, the snapping of shots, and sudden violent screams mingled in his ears.

It was an hour later when he opened his eyes. He felt the rush of unaccustomed cool air. Over him was bending Obed Lake and Jorgensen, grim giant, his head bandaged with a bloody rag. The gray dawn was stealing over the rippling waters. Philip May at once realised the vessel was in motion.

"Lie still, for God's sake, Captain," roughly pleaded Lake, as he forced a draught of cognac into May's parched mouth. "Now, wash it down. That will bring you all round. You had a bad rip from a spent ball. If these fellows' powder were not so poor, they would have blown a hole clean through you. But your ribs are tough."

Philip twisted his wearied head around. A squad of men were swinging a broad hammock to a set of boat davits.

"I'll have a shade for you, by Jove! You saved us!"

May was regarding the deck from his mattress, laid on the forward hatch. It was still cumbered with the dead and dying pirates. The good Halcyon sprang along under a freshening breeze. Kee and his followers were turning over the dead and dying pirates.

"What are they doing?" murmured Philip, the sharp pain in his side reminding him of his wound.

"Looting the rascals who wanted to steal our cargo, and then feeding the sharks," said Lake, as May turned his head away.

A sickening plunge attested this, and the wounded man knew no more.

"Jorgensen, I'll quiet that other fellow and tell him a part of the truth. Treat this man well, and call all hands to grog—coolies and all," cried Lake heartily. "Shape your straight course for Nagasaki light."

Three weeks later Obed Lake led Philip May, pale and

exhausted, on deck, as the saucy Halcyon ran past Tchusima, bound homewards towards America.

"May," said he, "you're a brick. You shall see the little widow again. You've saved your life and my fortune, but you must not tell them all this story."

CHAPTER XIX.

THE sheeted rain of a chilly December storm was driving against the walls of Mrs. Lee's mansion, throned on the peak of San Francisco aristocracy.

By the great window, framing the superb north bay view, a pale woman clad in black gazed on the darkening clouds hanging over distant Tamalpais. When the gusts drove away the falling torrents in broken spray, far glimpses could be caught of a green, white-capped waste of waters surging around the gloomy fortress of Alcatraces.

Distant point and headland were veiled in clinging fog-wreaths, and a tossing schooner driving home for shelter, with here and there a labouring harbour tug, alone was daring the storm.

"Five long months! Five weary months!" Constance murmured, as, clasping her hands, she looked out on the day of winter darkness. Her steadfast eyes were never turned until the light-house on the island fortress sent a pale yellow gleam across the blackened waters.

The watcher turned away. "'Could you come back to me, Douglas, Douglas!'" she quoted, as she faced the portrait of Philip May, the reminder of a haunting mystery.

"Well, Justine?" she wearily said, as a maid entered.

"Mrs. Delmar wishes to speak to you, madam. She has just returned."

"Ask her kindly to come to me," faltered the watcher. The girl went out. "Alas, all hope has fled. The same old story of months, I know." She buried her face in her hands.

Pauline Delmar's noble face was shaded with sadness when their eyes met.

"Nothing yet, dear Constance. But Captain Warner gives me ground for hope. He says the Bureau does not give up a vessel for six months. It is the rule of the underwriters. I know not why, but the old yacht-builder's faith buoys my hopes up anew. He says the vessel could not sink. There has been no reported collision. The Pacific has no iceberg drift; and the crew were picked for experience and knowledge. If cast on one of the thousand reefs or islands of the Pacific, they are perhaps now safe ashore with friendly natives. Think of it! four navigators, and a peerless vessel. You must not sorrow so: it will kill us all. It was in our cause they ventured their precious lives. Anita's burden is as heavy as yours, poor child."

"How are they?" Mrs. Lee asked.

"Dolores and Anita are hopeful yet. Harry telegraphs that Marquez has been released by the Yaquis who captured him, for they have just heard under the flag of truce of Pesquiera's amnesty and the quashing of the proceedings against him."

"And the Governor?" said Constance, with some show of interest.

"He will be here as soon as Vargas can return from the city of Mexico and meet him at San Diego. In ten days the Captain can reach San Diego from El Paso. Governor Pesquiera writes that he will send Vargas on a tour of every Pacific port, with *carte blanche* to visit the South Sea Islands. As every Lloyd's agency has the inquiry and the yacht's description, we could hear at once by cable to Captain Warner."

"And does Pesquiera go to Mexico?"

"He will take Anita to join her husband. With Pesquiera as governor, and Bligh and Hackmuller to control the mines, all the interests can be guarded and the Yaqui compact kept inviolate. This is all the victorious Indians ask. Anita and Dolores will come to us at breakfast to-morrow, for Governor Pesquiera will leave on the first steamer."

"Ah me!" cried Constance, "what is money when sorrow rends the heart! My wealth I would pour out on the man who would bring me tidings that the Halcyon is safe."

Sunshine was gilding the green hills of the land-locked bay when Mrs. Lee greeted her fellow-sufferer next day. Anita Delmar, pale and steadfast, whispered words of cheer. Dolores added the tender glances of her dark eyes. "I am so happy to leave Anita with you. Dear Constance, I know you will have good news soon! I feel it in my heart of hearts! Why, Harry writes me vessels have been gone longer by months and all have returned safe."

The sad eyes of the lady of the mansion roved around the room where May and Goodloe had sat on the day of her strangely gained triumph over Battles's intended robbery. "It is all over," she said. "There is no hope for me."

The butler entering whispered a word to Madame Pauline Delmar. "A gentleman would speak to you instantly. 'Say nothing,' he says, 'but come at once.'"

Gliding to the reception-room with a wildly beating heart. the steadfast comforter was suddenly grasped by the mighty clutch of Captain Warner.

"By the Lord Harry," cried the shipbuilder, "they're safe!" He had tightly closed the door of the reception-room. "Look here." He waved a yellow slip before Pauline Delmar's eyes.

"PORT ANGELES, WASHINGTON TERRITORY, Dec. 8.

"Halcyon here. Cargo safe. Both coming next steamer. Notify all. See Mrs. Delmar. Further to-morrow.

"MAY and GOODLOE."

Pauline Delmar reeled. "Careful! Careful!" she stammered. "It might kill Constance. Can it be true? Explain."

"Dead true, my beauty," answered the bluff old sailor. "It's a saw-mill town. I run ships up there. I telegraphed

my agents. Here's their answer. I got it this morning from the firm here. I was afraid of a hoax. This is regular."
He handed her a telegram signed Fosdick, Miller & Co. Its words left no room for doubt :

" Have personally examined yacht.   Both gentlemen answer your description.   No mistake.   May known to brokers here.   Will send yacht down under crew furnished by us.   Business confidential.   Both in good health."

" Now, you can go your last dollar on it ! Alick Fosdick never lied in his life."

" Stay here," said Mrs. Delmar, her bosom heaving with joy.   " Wait for me."

The excited bearer of good tidings opened the door.   A telegraph boy was standing in the main hall-way.

" Give that to me," she whispered, as the butler held up a telegraph envelope addressed to Mrs. Lee.   " Keep the boy."

Tearing it open, the words dispelled all doubt :

" Home Saturday, fourteenth.   Goodloe well.   All safe. Notify friends.   Steamer Idaho.   Keep our return quiet. Important.   Answer to Fosdick, Miller & Co.

" PHILIP MAY."

A blooming vision of mature beauty was Pauline Delmar as she flashed the document before the old mariner's eyes. "Silence !" she murmured, with a finger on her lip.

As the gentle messenger entered the room where her hostess sat in wonder, Anita Delmar caught the glance of her mother's happy eyes.   The intuition of love told the story more quickly than the words trembling on Mrs. Delmar's lips.

"You have good news, mother!" cried Anita. Dolores started towards Constance, who sat gazing with eager wonder at the girl, who clasped her mother in her arms.

"Both safe, and will be here in four days!" was the answer which brought Mrs. Lee's head drooping on Dolores Wainwright's shoulder.

A shout of happy confirmation aroused the lady of the Halcyon, for in the doorway Captain Abel Warner was executing a nautical war-dance of joyous frenzy.

"Let me read it. Give them all to me," said the Halcyon's owner. "Can it be true, Captain?"

"Lady-bird, every word's gospel truth. I told you there was some mischance."

In the bower on the hill where Constance Lee waited the return of her wandering knight, there was not a gilded clock whose frozen hands did not seem to crawl on the afternoon of December fourteenth.

The Princess of the Sierra Morena mine was alone in her boudoir. Only Dolores Wainwright kept guard below. Four long hours before, the signal station at the Heads had reported the Idaho. With a strange smile, Constance handed the glass to Dolores when the fleet ocean steamer swept across the blue north bay and passed behind Telegraph Hill. "It is the Idaho," said she; for Captain Warner had carefully instructed her as to the signal-flags.

She did not know that a fleet tug was bearing him with Madame Delmar and her daughter to anticipate the rounding of the Point and the delay of docking.

" It must be an hour and a half yet," the waiting woman mused, "and then also a long drive from the Brannan Street wharf."

With a feeling that she would like to meet her lover on the spot where for months her eyes had sought for the silver sails of the Flying Halcyon, she paced her chosen eyrie alone. The face on the mantel seemed to move its eyes, but the clock was malignant in its obstinate inertia.

" How shall I greet him? I must think. I cannot tell him of these lonely months of sorrow, and all my agony that another's quest should bear him away from my life forever. A weary hour yet!"

While the dark-robed woman gazed lovingly at the silent face upon the onyx slab, a quick footstep sounded on the stair.

She was leaning on one rounded arm resting lightly on the mantel. She turned in quick surprise, and Philip's arms were clasping her to his heart before the ceremonial speech of welcome returned to her.

She led him to the window and showed him the sunlit bay covered with fleeting barks.

" I have watched here for you day and night, Philip," she faltered, as her happy eyes met her lover's. " Tell me all; tell me now," she cried, when her lover's kisses had sealed a silence sweeter than silver speech.

"My own darling," May answered, "Goodloe and the others are coming, self-invited, to dine with you. You shall all hear the story together. Let us go down, for I hear them even now below."

"It is simple enough," said May an hour later, pressing fondly a slender hand stealing into his own. "Lake and Jorgensen believed that we had unlawfully smuggled Pesquiera out of Mexico. Undoubtedly, Wong Lee told them of the Governor's great treasure. It seems that Wong is a member of a secret organization engaged in smuggling opium into the Pacific ports. Lake and Jorgensen had made these desperate voyages before. When we were seized, we were simply confined apart and permitted to be led on deck alone under guard for exercise. A resolute silence was maintained by all the crew. I saw that we were sailing west. It was two months after we left Honolulu when I heard the clatter of Japanese junks around us. Ah Sam, the Chinese cook, who was faithful to the last, managed to whisper 'Nagasaki.' I could only learn from him that Goodloe was well. I must say we were not abused. I tried in vain to effect communication with Basil. I had a forecastle cabin, prepared for the sailing-master, and Jorgensen took charge of me. Lake was similarly hospitable to Goodloe in the stern cabin.

"From sheer weariness I ceased to rail, and policy also counselled patience. I easily divined that our Yaqui treasure was safe so far in its leaden casing. A stay of fifteen days at Nagasaki was devoted to loading the yacht to the hatches with tons of opium cased in fish-barrels of innocent appearance. It seems that American packed fish come in free of customs duty and inspection.

"At last we set sail from Nagasaki. I was none the wiser as to our destination. My sailor's eye told me it was toward the American coast of the North Pacific we sped. The prevailing fog and wild storms showed us to be in the northern edge of the Japanese current, sweeping homeward over the Behring Sea. We were baffled, driven around, and even the grinning mutineer Lake lost his temper. We were driven back a thousand miles. Strange to say, the crew acted in superb discipline. It was evident to me they had some common interest. I did not even suspect the character of our cargo until weeks later, and Ah Sam was kept in ignorance also. I gnashed my teeth as I saw several sealing-vessels within hail. I was hustled below at the cry, 'Sail ho!' These are a duplicate of Goodloe's experiences." Basil nodded, as May resumed :

"It was impossible to divine our whereabouts until two weeks ago. We were both kept below, and Ah Sam only managed to whisper, 'Pretty soon come on shore.' He was watched by a sentinel always when serving me. At last the sound of a tug alongside proved that we had made the coast. I expected some dramatic dénouement. Lake and Jorgensen would never speak to me. I waited in vain. Finally down rattled the anchor. I was doomed to fret my soul into madness for two long days while our cargo was discharged. Then the easy gliding motion of the boat and the snorting of a tug proved that our location was being changed. The strange voyage continued for hours. The mooring of the yacht in still water indicated that the voyage was ended. It was on the third day of silent rocking on a river current, that Ah Sam jubilantly threw open my cabin hatch, hitherto bolted and guarded save when he brought my meals. 'All right. Can come now. Bad men all gone,' he cried. I sprang on deck. A dense pine-clad forest swept along a half-mile inland. As the fresh incense of the trees was blown from the shores, I knew the Oregon coast. A sailor approached, followed by two boat-keepers. Touching his hat, he said, 'Captain May, I am directed by your "partner" to turn this boat over to you in good order.' Ah Sam was fumbling at the main cabin hatch. In a moment Goodloe was rushing down the deck to me. The unknown mate handed me a brief scrawl. I rubbed my eyes as I read it and handed it to Basil, whose face seemed strangely unfamiliar. His beard was alien to my memory. The words were laconic : 'Good-bye. Good luck. The yacht is neat as a pin. You made a good haul, so did we. Mum's the word. Shipmates.' Ah Sam now whispered the nature of the smuggled cargo. By common impulse we rushed to the after cabin. There in the lazaretto hold, and beneath, in the cabin hold, lay Hackmuller's dingy leaden bars.

" ' What can we do for you, Captain ? ' said the stranger. ' What's that place ? ' I asked, pointing to a settlement three miles below, where the smoke of steam factories rose high in air. ' Port Angeles saw-mills, Washington Territory,' answered the stranger. I sprang to the bow. We were moored to a floating buoy. ' Can you take her in there ? '

I inquired. 'If you'll all lend me a hand to make sail,' he cheerily replied. In an hour we ran up to the mill wharf. Leaving Goodloe in charge, I found Fosdick to be a man of a thousand, and he knew Captain Warner. After Warner's telegraphic replies, I found, in confidential chat with the merchant, that Obed Lake was well known as the 'Opium King.' The evasion of the customs by this daring raid was supposed to have netted enough to buy several Halcyons. He told me, 'I have known an opium run neatly done, but ten dollars a pound never tempted such a dashing band to dodge our old six-knot revenue cutter here before. Why, your boat has been flitting over the Sound like a white phantom for two weeks. I dare not even whisper the word "Opium ring" here. A rifle-ball will easily cut a pane of glass,' said Fosdick. 'I would keep quiet if I were you.' 'And if the schooner had been chased?' I cried, as my mind caught the whole neat plot. 'Then Lieutenant Goodloe and yourself would have each gone down with a kedge anchor strapped to your heels, and Lake would have run the stuff in near Bolinas, or below Monterey. Let me advise : take the steamer to San Francisco. You are innocent. Say nothing. You will be watched. You know not how far the feelers of the opium-smuggling octopus may reach. I'll send your schooner safely down. I have a Sound steamer to bring up from Benicia.'"

"And the treasure?" Mrs. Delmar eagerly inquired.

"Was sent aboard the Idaho and brought down as base bullion. It is in the hands of Wells, Fargo & Co. Anita's dowry is safe, thank God!"

"Those fearful men! shall they not be punished?" cried Mrs. Lee, appealing to Goodloe.

He laughed. "Madam, I am about to be married, and 'somebody' is anxious to see Graystone Manor. I will leave my share of the punishment to be doled out by Mrs. Delmar, who is about to go into the general Mexican mining business with the new firm of Pesquiera, Wainwright & Co. I believe she and Anita are the Company. You can never punish the smugglers."

"Ah, you are going East." Mrs. Lee dropped her eyes before the burning gaze of the Captain without a yacht. "When do you think of leaving?"

"As soon as Governor Pesquiera arrives. He telegraphs that he is on his way now. The marriage will not delay us long," said Goodloe. It was Anita's turn to show the varied rose shades of a maiden's blushing cheek. Wreathed smiles adorned the merry circle.

"Is this true?" queried the lady of the Halcyon.

"I suppose so. If Basil says it is, I must agree," faltered Anita. "And you, dear Mrs. Lee, what will you do, when mother and Dolores go back to Guaymas?"

"I have made no definite plans," said Constance, rising and walking to the north front of the splendid hall. "I am tired of the city. I think I will travel." She was gazing out at the sparkling bay.

"Graystone Manor is your home if you will come to us," cried Goodloe. Anita's smiles seconded the invitation.

"I am anxious to take a run along the coast at least as far as Santa Barbara, on my fly-away yacht," said Constance. ' But—I have no Captain."

"Will I do?" quietly asked Phil May, as he took her hand.

"The very man I would have chosen," the hostess said. "I believe you are a good sailor. Others say so."

He raised her hand to his lips, and remarked, with an impressive earnestness, "Then I ship for Life."

THE END.

BRADBURY, AGNEW, & CO. LD., PRINTERS, WHITEFRIARS.

MY OFFICIAL WIFE.

BY

RICHARD HENRY SAVAGE,

Author of "The Little Lady of Lagunitas," &c., &c.

For Sale Everywhere !   Shortly to be Dramatised !

The American Success of the Season !

THE VOICE OF THE PRESS.

"A vivid and stirring story."—*New York Tribune*, August 2, 1891.

"Abundance of action.   Very cleverly written."—*San Francisco Chronicle*, June 21, 1891.

"Something thoroughly stirring."—*Omaha Bee*, June 27th, 1891.

"The denouement is intensely dramatic."—*Boston Advertiser*, July 3rd, 1891.

"A striking story."—*Portland Oregonian*, May 31st, 1891.

"Something extraordinary.   Worth reading."—*Louisville Commercial*, July 6th, 1891.

"Full of life and go and very entertaining."—*Chicago Times*, June 20th, 1891.

"Events and situations increasing in excitement.   The reader will dash through with wild eagerness."—*New York Herald*, June 21st, 1891.

"A very exciting web of complications."—*New Orleans Picayune*, July 12th, 1891.

"A story of absorbing interest."—*Cleveland Plaindealer*, June 14th, 1891.

"Occupies the close attention of the reader."—*San Francisco Call*, June 21st, 1891.

"Amusing and exciting."—*Town Topics*, Nov. 12th, 1891.

"Overflowing with human interest and intensely dramatic."—*New York Home Journal*, Dec. 16th, 1891.

"Decidedly original.   The making of a very effective play.   Ingenious and daring in conception."—*New York World*, August 2nd, 1891.

"The story is racy and will be a favourite at the clubs."—*San Francisco Evening Post*, June 27th, 1891.

"Abundance of action.   Extremely interesting."—*San Francisco Newsdealer*, August 1st, 1891.

"The novel is of unusual interest."—*New York Journal*, June 28th, 1891.

"A story of great power and originality."—*Minneapolis Commercial Bulletin*, Oct. 24th, 1891.

PRINCE SCHAMYL'S WOOING

A Story of the Russo-Turkish War,

By RICHARD HENRY SAVAGE.

EUROPEAN OPINIONS.

" Colonel Richard Henry Savage wields a pen of power."—*Saturday Review*, Nov. 5, 1892.

" Really good pictures of life in St. Petersburg and Constantinople —a good example of the modern picturesque school."—*Literary Review* (London), Nov. 1892.

"But there are *better* things than probability in a novel ; and in ' Prince Schamyl's Wooing ' Colonel Savage has provided substitutes that will satisfy the most exacting."—*The Scotsman*, Oct. 17, 1892.

" The novel reader who likes a change of scenery and character cannot do better than secure this vigorously told story."—*Yorkshire Post*, Dec. 7, 1892.

"Likely to be as popular as the author's well-known *powerful* novel of Russian life—' My Official Wife.' "

" We must leave the reader to find for himself in this absorbing narrative."—*Morning Post*, Jan. 12, 1892.

"An eventful and thrilling story, where diplomatic intrigue, mountaineering, campaigning, moonlight raids, oriental wiles, and love-making, are deftly interwoven by a practised hand. An eventful and thrilling story."—*Broad Arrow*, Jan. 7, 1893.

"The story is one of considerable power and originality."—*News-dealer's Circular*, London, Oct. 29, 1892.

" An exciting tale full of incident and spirit. All who are interested in Russian affairs will find both instruction and interest in ' Prince Schamyl's Wooing', and when he *next* doth ride abroad may I be there to see."—*Manchester Courier*, Oct. 29, 1892.

" Wonderfully true observation and descriptions—a keen knowledge of human affairs—and *we* (the Germans) would do well to closely study what the author says of our *war-seeking* neighbour (Russia). How clearly he expresses *our* mistake in underestimating the secret causes which produce *national* bitterness."—*Berlin Post* (Germany), Oct. 11, 1892.

EIGHT EDITIONS IN EUROPE.

" Extremely interesting . . . highly instructive ! . . . Plot well woven and all-absorbing—the graphic detail and dramatic scenes fascinate the reader from the beginning." . . . *Eastern and Western Review*, Nov., 1892.

PRINCE SCHAMYL'S WOOING

A Story of the Russo-Turkish War,

By RICHARD HENRY SAVAGE.

AMERICAN CRITICISM.

"A very exciting romance. . . . Whoever reads the first page is sure to read to the end."—*Town Topics*, Sept. 15, 1892.

"As nervous and direct as the masterpieces of Maupassant and Zola."—*Buffalo Enquirer*, Oct. 28, 1892.

"Throbbing with a passion of love."—*New Orleans Picayune*, Nov. 2, 1892.

"A thrilling story!"—*Rocky Mountain News*, Denver, Nov. 2, 1892.

"Creatures worthy of heroic times. An ingenious and fascinating story."—*New Orleans States*, Nov. 2, 1892.

"It possesses a value to well-read people, apart from the human interest of the tale."—*St. Paul Despatch*, Minnesota, Nov. 8, 1892.

"Vigorous and exciting."—*Morning Journal*, New York, Oct. 9, 1892.

"A stirring tale of Russia's intrigues."—*Evening Telegram*, New York, Oct. 17th, 1892.

"A lively series of incidents."—*San Francisco Argonaut*, Oct. 26, 1892.

"The best work Colonel Savage has yet done."—*San Francisco Chronicle*, Sept. 18, 1892.

"Embellished with the exciting periods he handles so easily."—*Rochester Herald*, Oct. 1, 1892.

"A dashing, rattling story."—*San Francisco Post*, Sept. 24, 1892.

"The book is intensely exciting."—*Philadelphia Bulletin*, Sept. 20, 1892.

"A tale of crackling brilliancy."—*Detroit Sunday News*, Sept. 29, 1892.

"A charming story of the Russo-Turkish war. To give a mere synopsis is to break the spell."—*San Francisco Call*, Sept. 25, 1892.

"He rises to the height of his peculiar talent."—*Baltimore News*, Sept. 28, 1892.

"Interesting, and at times thrilling."—*Columbus Despatch*, Ohio, Sept. 22, 1892.

"To look into the book haphazard is to be seized with a desire to read the whole story—and, it is worth reading."—*New York World*, Sept. 24, 1892.

"Original and vivacious in the highest degree."—*Boston Times*, Sept. 21, 1892.

"Full of action and adventure."—*Syracuse Herald*, Sept. 18, 1892.

"Of thrilling interest."—*Denver Times*, Oct. 30, 1892.

"Crammed with incidents—read with enthusiasm."—*Independent*, New York, Nov. 3, 1892.

"Told with delightful spirit."—*Toledo Blade*, Nov. 19, 1892.

ROUTLEDGE'S
FLORIN NOVELS.

251 VOLUMES.

Crown 8vo, Cloth, 2s. each.

AINSWORTH, W. H.

The Tower of London.
Old St. Paul's.
Windsor Castle.
Miser's Daughter.
Star Chamber.
Rookwood.
St. James'.
Flitch of Bacon.
Guy Fawkes.
Lancashire Witches.
Crichton.
Jack Sheppard.
Spendthrift.
Boscobel.
Ovingdean Grange.
Mervyn Clitheroe.
Auriol.
Preston Fight.
Stanley Brereton.
Beau Nash.

AUSTEN, Jane.

Pride and Prejudice.
Sense and Sensibility.
Mansfield Park.
Emma.
Northanger Abbey, and Persuasion.

COCKTON, Henry.

Valentine Vox.
Sylvester Sound

COOPER, Fenimore.

The Deerslayer.
The Pathfinder.
The Last of the Mohicans.
The Pioneers.
The Prairie.
The Red Rover.
The Pilot.
The Two Admirals.
The Waterwitch.
The Spy.
The Sea Lions.
Miles Wallingford.
Lionel Lincoln.
The Headsman.
Homeward Bound.
The Crater; or, Vulcan's Peak.
Wing and Wing.
Jack Tier.
Satanstoe.
The Chainbearer.
The Red Skins.
The Heidenmauer.
Precaution.
The Monikins.
The Wept of Wish-ton-Wish.
The Ways of the Hour.
Mercedes of Castile.
Afloat and Ashore.
Wyandotte.
Home as Found.
Oak Openings.
The Bravo.

FLORIN NOVELS. Cloth—*continued.*

DICKENS, *Charles.*

Sketches by "Boz."
Nicholas Nickleby.
Oliver Twist.
Barnaby Rudge.
Old Curiosity Shop.
Dombey and Son.
Grimaldi the Clown, with CRUIKSHANK's Illustrations.
Martin Chuzzlewit.
Pickwick Papers.
David Copperfield. (Copyright.)
Pictures from Italy and American Notes.

DUMAS, *Alexandre.*

The Three Musketeers.
Twenty Years After.
Monte Cristo.
Marguerite de Valois.
Chicot, the Jester.
Forty-five Guardsmen.
Taking the Bastile.
The Queen's Necklace.
The Conspirators.
The Regent's Daughter.
Memoirs of a Physician.
The Countess de Charny.
The Vicomte de Bragelonne, Vol. 1.
——————————————— Vol. 2.

FERRIER, *Miss.*

Marriage.
The Inheritance.
Destiny.

FIELDING, *Henry.*

Tom Jones.
Joseph Andrews.
Amelia.

GRANT, *James.*

The Romance of War.
The Aide de Camp.
The Scottish Cavalier.
Bothwell.
Philip Rollo.
Legends of the Black Watch.
Jane Seton.
The Yellow Frigate.

LAWRENCE, *George.*

Guy Livingstone.
Sword and Gown.
Barren Honour.

LEVER, *Charles.*

Harry Lorrequer.
Charles O'Malley.
Jack Hinton.
Arthur O'Leary.
Con Cregan.
Horace Templeton.

LOVER, *Samuel.*

Handy Andy.
Rory O'More.

LYTTON, *Lord.*

Author's Copyright Revised Editions containing Prefaces to be found in no other Edition.

Pelham.
Paul Clifford.
Eugene Aram.
Last Days of Pompeii.
Rienzi.
Ernest Maltravers.
Alice; or, The Mysteries.
Night and Morning.
Disowned.
Devereux.
Godolphin.
Last of the Barons.

iine

FLORIN NOVELS, Cloth—*continued.*

LYTTON, Lord—*continued.*

Falkland Zicci.
Zanoni.
The Caxtons.
Harold.
Lucretia.
The Coming Race.
A Strange Story.
Kenelm Chillingly.
Pausanias: and The Haunted
    and the Haunters.
My Novel, Vol. 1.
———— Vol. 2.
What will He Do with It? Vol. 1
———————————Vol. 2.
The Parisians, Vol. 1.
———— Vol. 2.

MARRYAT, Captain.

Frank Mildmay.
Midshipman Easy.
Phantom Ship.
Peter Simple.
The King's Own.
Newton Forster.
Jacob Faithful.
The Pacha of Many Tales.
Japhet in Search of a Father.
Dog Fiend.   .
Poacher.
Percival Keene.
Monsieur Violet.
Rattlin, the Reefer.
Valerie.
Pirate; Three Cutters.
Poor Jack.
Masterman Ready.
Olla Podrida.
Settlers in Canada.
The Mission; or, Scenes in
    Africa.
The Privateersman.
Children of the New Forest.
The Little Savage.

NEALE, W. J. N.

PORTER, Jane.

The Scottish Chiefs.
The Pastor's Fireside.

RADCLIFFE, Mrs.

The Romance of the Forest.
The Mysteries of Udolpho.

REID, Captain Mayne.

The Scalp Hunters.
The Rifle Rangers.
The War Trail.
The White Chief.
The Quadroon.
The White Gauntlet.
Lost Lenore.
The Hunter's Feast.
The Boy Slaves.
The Cliff Climbers.
The Giraffe Hunters.
The Ocean Waifs.
The Half Blood.
The Wild Huntress.
The Tiger Hunter.
The White Squaw.
The Headless Horseman.
The Guerilla Chief.
The Maroon.
Wood Rangers.
The Desert Home.
The Bush Boys.
The Plant Hunters.
The Boy Hunters.

RICHARDSON, Samuel.

Clarissa Harlowe
Pamela.
Sir Charles Grandison.

SCOTT, Michael.

Tom Cringle's Log.
The Cruise of the "Midge."

SCOTT, *Sir Walter.*

With Steel Frontispiece to each Volume.
Waverley.
Guy Mannering.
Old Mortality.
Heart of Midlothian.
Rob Roy.
Ivanhoe.
The Antiquary.
Bride of Lammermoor.
Black Dwarf, and Legend of
    Montrose.
The Monastery.
The Abbot.
Kenilworth.
The Pirate.
Fortunes of Nigel.
Peveril of the Peak.
Quentin Durward.
St. Ronan's Well.
Redgauntlet.
Betrothed, and Highland
    Widow.
The Talisman, and Two
    Drovers.
Woodstock.
The Fair Maid of Perth.
Anne of Geierstein.
Count Robert of Paris.
The Surgeon's Daughter.

SMOLLETT.
Roderick Random.
Humphry Clinker.
Peregrine Pickle.

SUE, *Eugene.*
Wandering Jew.
Mysteries of Paris.

THACKERAY, W. M.
Vanity Fair.

WARREN, *Samuel.*
Ten Thousand a Year.
The Diary of a late Physician

YATES, *Edmund.*
Nobody's Fortune.
Black Sheep.
Kissing the Rod.

BY VARIOUS AUTHORS.
Gideon Giles the Roper.
        THOMAS MILLER.
The Clockmaker.
        HALIBURTON.
Scottish Chiefs. JANE PORTER.
The Prairie Bird.
        Hon. C. A. MURRAY.
Humorous American Gems.
Arthur Bonnicastle.
        J. G. HOLLAND.
Marjorie Daw. T. B. ALDRICH.
Nick of the Woods.
Salathiel.   Dr. CROLY.
Jane Eyre.
        CHARLOTTE BRONTË.
Land and Sea Tales.
        "THE OLD SAILOR."
The Green Hand. G. CUPPLES.
Elsie Venner. O. W. HOLMES.
Shirley. CHARLOTTE BRONTË.
The Greatest Plague of Life.
        HENRY MAYHEW.
The Night Side of Nature.
        Mrs. CROWE.
Wuthering Heights, and Agnes
    Grey.   E. & A. BRONTË.
Alton Locke.
        CHARLES KINGSLEY.
Whitefriars.
The Family Feud.
        THOMAS COOPER.

ROUTLEDGE'S RAILWAY LIBRARY,

Price *TWO SHILLINGS* each, Picture Covers.

ALPHONSE DAUDET.
WITH ILLUSTRATIONS.

Tartarin on the Alps.

Tartarin of Tarascon.

Jack.

Kings in Exile.

Thirty Years of Paris.

Recollections of a Literary Man.

Artists' Wives.

Robert Helmont.

Afloat (by *De Maupassant*).

Sister Philomène (by *De Goncourt*).

Madame Chrysanthème (by *Pierre Loti*).

ROUTLEDGE'S SPORTING NOVELS.

With New Sporting Covers, drawn by JOHN STURGES, and others.

Crown 8vo, boards, 2s. each.

Jockey Jack. *Nat Gould.*

Running it Off. *Nat Gould.*

The Best Season on Record. *Captain Pennell Elmhirst.*

A Pink Wedding. *R. Mounteney-Jephson.*

Blair Athol. *Blinkhoolie.*

Beaten on the Post. *J. P. Wheeldon.*

The Tale of a Horse. *Blinkhoolie.*

Jorrocks' Jaunts and Jollities.

Life of John Mytton. *Nimrod*, with a Memoir of the Author.

The Tommiebeg Shootings; or, A Moor in Scotland. *Jeans.*

The Double Event. A Tale of the Melbourne Cup. *Nat Gould.*

Too Fast to Last. *John Mills.*

Won in a Canter. *Old Calabar.*

Nimrod's Northern Tour.

Frank Maitland's Luck. *Finch Mason.*

Horses and Hounds *Scrutator.*

Reminiscences of a 19th Century Gladiator. With Portraits.
J. L. Sullivan.

Euthanasia; or Turf, Tent, and Tomb.

The Young Squire. *"Borderer."*

Soapey Sponge's Sporting Tour.

Very Long Odds. *Campbell Rae-Brown.*

Banker and Broker. *Nat Gould.*

Harry Dale's Jockey. *Nat Gould.*

Thrown Away. *Nat Gould.*

ROUTLEDGE'S RAILWAY LIBRARY,

Price TWO SHILLINGS each, Picture Covers.

ARCHIBALD C. GUNTER.

Mr. Potter of Texas.
That Frenchman.
Miss Nobody of Nowhere.
Mr. Barnes of New York.
Miss Dividends.
Baron Montez of Panama & Paris.
A Princess of Paris.
The King's Stockbroker.

COLONEL SAVAGE.

My Official Wife.
The Little Lady of Lagunitas.
Prince Schamyl's Wooing.
The Masked Venus.
Delilah of Harlem.
For Life and Love.
The Anarchist.
The Princess of Alaska.

VARIOUS AUTHORS.

Moondyne : A Story from the Under-World. *John Boyle O'Reilly.*
Jane Eyre. *Charlotte Brontë.*
Can Such Things Be ? *Keith Fleming.*
Stories from Scotland Yard. *C. Rideal, F.R.S.L.*
Secrets of a Private Enquiry Office. *Mrs. Geo. Corbett.*
Vanity Fair. *W. M. Thackeray.*
At the Eleventh Hour. *Keith Fleming.*
Guilty Bonds. *Wm. Le Queux.*
A Fair Free-Lance. *Sir Gilbert Campbell.*
Mrs. Arthur. *Mrs. Oliphant.*
The Romance of an *Alter Ego. Lloyd Bryce.*
The Prodigal Daughter. *Mark Hope.*
David Copperfield. *Charles Dickens.*
Pictures from Italy, and American Notes. *Charles Dickens.*
Through the Mist. *Mrs. Adams-Acton.*
A Matter of Millions. *Anna Katharine Green.*
The Forsaken Inn. *Anna Katharine Green.*
A Diplomat's Diary. *Julien Gordon.*
Shirley. *Charlotte Brontë.*
Gleanings from "On and Off the Stage," *Mrs. Bancroft.*
Funny Stories. *P. T. Barnum.*
Toole's Reminiscences. Edited by *Joseph Hatton.* With Portrait and 36 Illustrations.
Foggerty's Fairy. *W. S. Gilbert.*
The Family Feud. *Thomas Cooper.*
Wuthering Heights and Agnes Grey. *Emily and Anne Brontë.*
Loyal.
Alton Locke. *Charles Kingsley.*

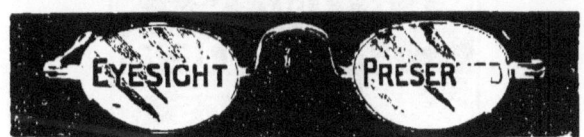

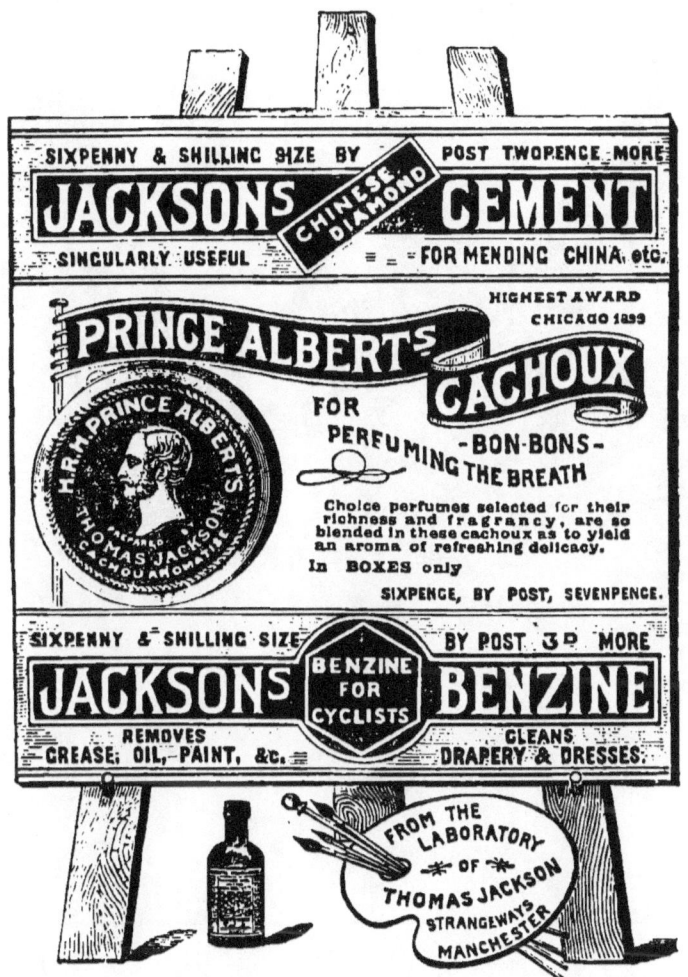

Brooke's Soap – Monkey Brand.

FOR SCRUBBING KITCHEN TABLES AND FLOORS.

The World's most marvellous Cleanser and Polisher. Makes Tin like Silver, Copper like Gold, Paint like New. Brass Ware like Mirrors, Spotless Earthenware, Crockery like Marble, Marble White.

SOLD BY GROCERS, IRONMONGERS AND CHEMISTS.

AND EVANS, ENGRAVER AND PRINTER, RACQUET COURT, FLEET STREET, LONDON, E.C.